For the Love of Armine

Արմինեի սիրո համար
Ради любви к Армине

Other books by
ABIE ALEXANDER

AN AMERICAN IN SEARCH OF GOD
CHASING THE WIND
SOMETIMES WHEN WE MEET
MEMORIES AND MIRAGES
THE MIGRANT AND THE MAVERICK
OF MINGLED YARN

For the Love of Armine

Abie Alexander

Translated into Armenian
and Russian by
Anna Ayvazyan

Արմինեի սիրո համար
Ради любви к Армине

AA
BOOKS

Copyright © 2014 Abie Alexander

First published 2014 Infinity Publishing, PA, USA

AA Books ISBNs

Print	978-1-946593-40-5
EPUB	978-1-946593-16-0
AZW3	978-1-946593-17-7
MOBI	978-1-946593-18-4
PDF	978-1-946593-19-1

Published in the United States of America

Cover Design: Artur Hakobyan
Armenian Editing: Lusine Sargsyan

AA
BOOKS

7919 Mandan Road #103
Greenbelt, Maryland. USA 20770-2828
+1 (301) 335-5632
aa-books@outlook.com
www.abiealexander.com

To

Э

Even if I were presumptuous enough to suggest that this work proves your hypothesis about the correlation between unrequited love and creative inspiration, you still have the wherewithal to disprove it.

Ah, but a man's reach should exceed his grasp,
Or what's heaven or?

Robert Browning: *Andrea del Sarto*

The Principal Characters

Armine Hovhannisyan	Armine
Kuriakose Mathew	Kuriakose [Kirakos]
Mikael Hovhannisyan	Hayrik [Armine's father]
Mayrik [Gayane]	Armine's mother
Appachen [Abraham Easo]	Kuriakose's grandfather
Ammachi [Annamma]	Kuriakose's grandmother
Ter Samvel Hovhannisyan	The Priest
Tikin Karine	Wife of Ter Samvel
Andranik, Varazdat, and Varduhi	Children of Ter Samvel and Tikin Karine
Armen Poghosyan	Armine's fiancé
Vilen Poghosyan	Armen's brother
Geevarghese Tharakan	Classmate of Kuriakose
Radhakrishnan Nair [RK]	Classmate of Kuriakose
Stepan [Horeghbayr]	Armine's Uncle

Contents

Part One

Thirty Years Earlier:

Twelve Months in 1975

A faithful friend is the elixir of life.

Ecclesiasticus 6:16a

Chapter 1: The Beautiful Apparition

He stared open-mouthed at the apparition on the opposite bank of the creek. Time stood still. He could hear the stream gurgling softly as it flowed in the shallow gorge between the two elevated banks.

'A *white* woman in this equatorial grove? And that too on a *horse*, an animal never seen in these parts?' his mind raced incredulously.

'Is this a dream?' he wondered.

There she sat, in silhouette, ramrod straight on the brown steed, staring regally into the distance. The late afternoon sun caught her auburn hair in a golden halo and gave her fair skin a burnished, gilded tinge. The aquiline nose and the diaphanous gossamer white dress completed the fairy-tale, ethereal look.

The only white women he had seen in real life were the wives of missionaries who had come for the annual convention of Orthodox Christians. The famed gathering was held on the dry sandy bed of the Pamba River before the onset of the southwest monsoon that flooded the entire area and made it a sea of churning water that stretched as far as the eye could see.

'This must be a Greek or Roman goddess come back to life. Or Guinevere,' he thought.

He wondered if his mind was playing tricks on him. Had English literature come alive? Was he dreaming? It was as if the ballad of Keats that he had been reading before he fell asleep under the jackfruit tree had preternaturally come to life and *La Belle Dame Sans Merci* was on the pacing steed sans her knight-at-arms.

Without taking his eyes off the surreal damsel on the horse, he moved his hand around to pick up his textbook, *The Six Ages of English Poetry*, that had slipped from his chest. He had dozed off lying on his back on the ground in his sleeveless vest and sarong-like *lungi,* with the rolled-up checked *madras* shirt over the exposed roots of the jackfruit tree serving as a makeshift pillow.

'This is not a dream. This is real,' he told himself. 'She must be a statue!'

Almost immediately he realized how foolish that thought was. He could not have napped for more than fifteen minutes. In that short time, who could have noiselessly carried a heavy, life-sized statue of a golden princess - *and* her even heavier horse - and placed it on the banks of this small rivulet of a stream in this remote southern Indian village? And to what purpose? It was too preposterous.

Just then the horse snickered, shifting its front feet restlessly and the light breeze gently tousled the lady's reddish-brown hair while billowing out her flowing white dress.

'No, definitely not a statue,' he concluded.

At that moment, she turned sideways to look in his direction and he instinctively pressed himself lower against the earth.

'I hope the clump of amaranth blocks her view and she does not see me,' he wished.

Then, as he watched, she turned and whispered softly to the horse. He realized with relief that she had not seen him. A gentle tug of the reins and the horse turned, and after a few steps, began to amble down the slope into the stream that separated them. The steepness of the slope and the broken ground caused the rider to sway vigorously from side to side as they descended into the small ravine, but she did not, for a moment, lose her royal poise. The feet first, and then the legs of the horse, slowly disappeared from view where the edge of the bank on his side cut off his field of vision. He hastily dragged himself upright to watch the princess, for that is what she seemed to be to him, with delicate firmness guide the steed towards the water.

'Oh, my goodness! She is going to come up this way!' he thought in panic.

There really was nowhere else for the horse and rider to go.

If she turned to her left the stream went under the only macadamized road of the village. The low culvert was a dead end. To her right the creek flowed where no man dared to go—into the dreaded cave of death, at the foot of the towering piles of rocks that stretched far in both directions. Unlike the lush green equatorial vegetation of the region (the consequence of the plenteous monsoonal rain and the rich alluvial soil that the rivers washed down from the hills of the Western Ghats mountain range during the annual summer floods) this stretch of black volcanic rocks piled about sixty meters (two hundred feet) high was devoid of any trees or green plant life. The steepness of these large rocks made climbing them a foolhardy proposition, with the result that this rocky ridge served as nature's own barrier and fortification to humans and as a natural dam to the flood waters which wreaked havoc during the summer monsoon every year.

There was just one way left for the princess. He was sure the princess and her horse would head up the embankment on his side of the stream. This filled him with trepidation. The horse stood still midstream as it drank from the clear water while the princess gazed up towards the mango and coconut trees on his side and the tall bamboo thickets on both banks that canopied the sky over the stream.

He saw her prod the flanks of the horse with her feet and, to his surprise, instead of heading up the bank in his direction, the horse turned to the right and headed towards the feared cave in the hillside that lay beyond the bend.

The initial alarm of confronting a beautiful, alien woman suddenly changed to chilling fear. Anyone going into that cave, especially a woman, had to be supernatural. The hair on the nape of his neck tingled and goose bumps formed on his arms.

As he watched, the horse walked slowly down the middle of the shallow creek, the water coming up barely to its knees. He could see the clear water muddying as the horse lifted its feet at each step. Soon the horse and rider disappeared behind the bend, which was a cul-de-sac except for the dreaded cave of no return.

He stood motionless for a long minute staring in the direction of the cave hidden behind the bend before stooping down to pick up his *madras* checked shirt and the college textbook of English poems. Then in disbelief mixed with fear he turned to go home.

All of a sudden, reflexively he made the sign of the cross. He was so surprised by his own involuntary action that he chided himself. Ever since he had left the Orthodox Church two years ago, much to the sorrow and shame of his grandparents, he had eschewed everything remotely Orthodox, even making the sign of the cross. He was now not merely a Protestant but a far-right charismatic Pentecostal.

Sheepishly he turned to go back home to his grandparents' house. He loped effortlessly through the grove of coconut, areca nut, coffee, mango, *sapota*, cacao, and jackfruit trees lovingly tended by his grandfather. At the edge of the grove there lay a small lush green paddy field. He did not have to watch his step even if his mind was on the apparition he had just seen. He could have sped along the narrow mud ridges in his sleep without a misstep that would have caused him to fall into the stagnant muddy water in which the paddy grew. But half way through he paused.

'Was it a dream? Perhaps an illusion? Or was it real?' he asked himself.

A thought struck him. There was one sure way to find out. Doubling up the *lungi* so the bottom edge came to knee level and thus freed his lower legs, he turned around and raced back along the thin ridges of the paddy field all the way to the grove, dodged the trees there, and then scampered sideways down the steep slope of the path that led down to the stream. He looked to his left in the direction the princess and her steed had gone. The limpid water was clear once again and he could see tadpoles and small fish darting below the surface. He paused only for a moment before frenziedly wading through the knee-deep water to the path leading up the steep embankment on the opposite bank. He bent down to inspect the ground near the water closely. One look was enough. There in the mud were the clear impressions of horse's hooves.

It was not a dream. The horse and the princess were real!

Inexplicably, anticipation now replaced the earlier fear. As if on air, he raced all the way home.

The first thing his grandmother said was, "Child, why is your book wet? If you want to play in the water can't you leave your book on the shore?"

"It is all right, *Ammachi* (grandmother)," he said. "Books have to get wet sometimes."

The grandmother gaped at him in astonishment. She knew how he worshiped books and took the greatest care of them.

Chapter 2: The Premonition

Being close to the equator, the southern Indian State of Kerala has no seasons, except for the deluge of the southwest monsoon every year, when floods inundate large swathes of the low-lying areas. The temperatures do not fluctuate much all year. This was a warm February afternoon.

He lay in a trance bare-chested on his bed, a rush mat laid over a cot strung with coir ropes, staring at the thatched roof. His eyes might as well have been shut. All he could see, eyes open or closed, was the fair damsel on her horse, her chestnut colored hair gently wafting in the breeze.

The German-made vintage Telefunken radio was tuned to *Top of the Pops* from the BBC. But he was oblivious of the music as he wracked his mind searching for a rational explanation. 'Was she the daughter of a visiting missionary family staying at a house nearby?' That had never happened before. Missionaries always stayed at the vicarage or the newly constructed guesthouse of the Orthodox Church, both of which were five kilometers (three miles) away. And they definitely would not have brought a horse along with them from America or England. That was ludicrous.

He again wondered if all this was a figment of his imagination. He cringed when he recalled Kafka's *Metamorphosis*. 'Would his mind turn delusional?' If the worst came to the worst, he told himself, she would turn out to be *La Belle Dame Sans Merci*.

The young man that he was, without ever having had a friend of the opposite gender, he hoped the beautiful young maiden on the horse was not only real but also not unkind.

"Child, are you not hungry tonight? Won't you eat rice? What happened to you? Are you unwell?" *Ammachi* called from the kitchen.

"I'm OK. I'm coming, *Ammachi*," he answered, reluctantly raising himself up from the bed.

"There's something wrong with that child. He did not read anything at all today. He has been lying on his bed ever since he came from college," he heard *Ammachi* say to his grandfather as he walked towards the kitchen.

Appachen (grandfather) was his usual taciturn self and merely grunted, not looking up from his plate of rice, beef curry, and the yellow broth of buttermilk cooked with turmeric called *moru*. *Appachen* was a devout Orthodox Christian held in high esteem by all in the church and by Hindus and Muslims alike in the village. He was stern and strict, and people feared his temper. Ammachi, on the other hand, was soft and gentle; the perfect foil for her husband.

He remembered the morning many years earlier when, in a fit of anger, *Appachen* had hurled to the ground his umbrella and the lunch box Ammachi had prepared for him. Ammachi had wordlessly collected the spilled food, not saying a word in protest or in anger. That incident was forever etched in his mind.

The only time *Appachen* had not exploded in anger was the time Kuriakose had most expected him to—when he had announced to his grandparents that he had left the Orthodox Church. It was a Sunday evening two years ago. The blistering heat of the day had ebbed somewhat. *Appachen* was resting in his quaint easy chair, the wooden chair with the slung canvas seat and long arms on which he stretched his arthritic legs. Standing at church and teaching at Sunday School had exhausted him. The brewing thunderstorm, as it always did, had exacerbated the arthritic ache in his legs. Ammachi was standing alongside and massaging his legs with coconut oil.

"Where were you the whole day?" *Appachen* had asked in his usual blunt manner without any preamble.

"Appacha," he had replied with a calmness that surprised himself, "I have joined the Ceylon Pentecostal Church. I was baptized today in the Pamba River."

He waited for the thunder to roll.

Instead there was only the gasp of surprise from Ammachi who covered her mouth in shock and dismay.

Appachen did not say a word. He motioned to Ammachi to stop the massage, lowered his feet to the floor and wiped his bare chest with the thin towel that was always on his shoulder. His face grave and impassive, he stood up slowly and walked out to the field in the fading dusk.

"What have you done, my child?" wailed Ammachi tearfully.

All the dogmatic arguments against icons, confession, child baptism, and all the rituals of the church stayed within him. There was no argument or debate.

His grandfather never mentioned the subject again.

It was a week later that he met the parish priest on the road.

"Why didn't you kill him, you traitor?" the priest had screamed at him. "You brought shame upon him and the family. For years of faithfulness to the Church is this the reward you gave your grandfather? It was better you had eloped with a woman of easy virtue!"

Before he could reply, the priest had spat on the ground and walked on.

Beef was his favorite meat and Ammachi had cooked it the way he liked best, small pieces, dry roasted with herbs and chopped coconut. But he only pecked at the food today. His mind was on the ethereal being he had seen by the stream.

Before he slept, he updated the current affairs journal he maintained every day. He noted down the major events and the names of presidents, prime ministers, and other important people making the news. He was ambitious about getting through the government's civil services examination or, better still, qualifying as a probationary officer in a bank. News and current affairs were key ingredients of all competitive tests.

He reviewed the journal entries for January. The Watergate conspirators Mitchell, Haldeman, and

Ehrlichman were convicted. In Cambodia, the *Khmer Rouge* commenced their offensive on Phnom Penh. Sheikh Mujibur Rahman, the liberator of Bangladesh, and leader of the *Awami League* party declared an emergency and banned all opposition parties. Closer at home in India, the Union Minister for Railways, LN Mishra, was assassinated at a public meeting by a bomb placed under the podium.

***

The next day at college, he walked around in a daze like a zombie. Feelings of secret elation alternated with confusion and doubt. Then at lunchtime, as he opened the banana-leaf-wrapped rice, lentils, and *pappadam* Ammachi had packed for him, a notion settled on him with near certainty.

'The beautiful lady would come again today.'

His reverie was interrupted by Radhakrishnan Nair, who everyone called by the shortened nickname, RK. Although a devout Hindu (he had the three parallel ash stripes of piety on his forehead every morning), he was the only one who did not mock him when he had become a Pentecostal.

"Why are you so quiet today? You look like you have seen a ghost," RK said.

He smiled wanly at the irony of how accurate RK's jibe was. The other classmates were less kind. In the period after lunch, the rudest bully had sarcastically asked in a loud voice if he had lost his virginity the previous night.

He really did not care what his friends or classmates thought. He just wanted to get to the grove at any cost. He decided to confide in his friend Geevarghese who had converted him to the Pentecostal church.

"I had a strange experience yesterday. I need to go home."

Geevarghese wanted to know more but Kuriakose balked at saying anything more. When Geevarghese realized that he would have to wait till later for the full story, he merely said, "Be careful of the devil. He will tempt you and defeat you when you least expect it."

He sat through Professor Ann Thomas' class on Tennyson's *Morte D'Arthur*. The next session was that of Professor Iyer, the expert on Shakespeare. He had never missed any of Professor Iyer's lectures but today he was going to skip the first act of *The Tempest*. Professor Iyer's theory was that this play of Shakespeare had as its backdrop the English slave trade to the West Indies. He knew how important the lecture was but nonetheless he hurried home to the witching hour. Somehow, he had got it into his head that the lady would appear again today at the very same hour she had yesterday.

The distance from the college at Kozhencherry to his home in the next village of Maramon was covered in a trice. He crossed the bridge without even a glance at the Pamba River below. He loved Pamba so much, he would, often, on his way to and from college, stand at the center span looking down at the turgid, swirling waters below. The Pamba River reminded him of Sholokhov's *And Quiet Flows the Don*. Although it was placid now, when the monsoon came the river would be transformed into a swift-flowing, muddy sea, with jetsam and flotsam of every kind in its vortex, including massive trees.

On reaching home he decided not to change from the formal white shirt and linen *mundu* (a plain white sarong) to the casual checked *lungi* that he usually wore at home. He reasoned it was necessary to be appropriately dressed for meeting royalty and this was the best clothes he had, one of only two sets that he wore to college and church.

The humid heat required him to change his clothes daily. Ammachi washed one set while he wore the other. The Hawaiian rubber slippers he wore like everybody else as footwear caused mud to splatter on the back of his clothes during the monsoon. For the aging grandmother getting the mud stains off the white clothes was almost as difficult as getting them dry again in the middle of the torrential rains. On those days, he ironed the wet clothes dry at night with the heavy antique iron filled with burning charcoal.

He gulped the hot coffee but declined uncharacteristically the crisp *vada* (fried lentil patty) that he loved so much. His grandmother shook her head in puzzlement as he bolted for the outdoors in his Sunday best. He had a premonition he was going to meet the phantom white maiden again.

'What has got into this child?' she muttered aloud. 'It will take all my strength to get the mud off those white clothes if he wears them to the fields.'

Chapter 3: "Barev," She Said

Neither the horse nor the rider was to be seen. He was acutely disappointed. He kept staring at the bend in the creek expecting his equestrian goddess to materialize miraculously out of thin air. For once his intuition appeared to have failed him. After about ten minutes of waiting, he turned around dejected to go home. He had brought a book of poetry, but he did not wish to make laundry more difficult for his grandmother by sullying his white clothes sitting down on the ground. Shoulders drooping, he was about to turn around to head back home when he heard the sound—a steady *klop, klop, klop.* That was a completely unfamiliar sound, but he knew instinctively what it was. He whirled around to see the beautiful brown horse at a canter with the princess, her reddish-brown hair streaming, come up from the hollow on the culvert side. He froze at the mesmerizing sight as the princess slowed the horse to a trot. Joy and fear gripped him simultaneously. Joy and elation that his intuition had not failed him and that the princess had returned. Fear and trepidation at the thought of actually meeting the beautiful lady face to face and being tongue-tied.

The notion of making a quick dash back to the security of the grove crossed his mind. But it was too late.

The beautiful apparition had spotted him.

She reined the horse to a complete halt. There they were, on opposite embankments separated by the chasm of the small stream. Their eyes met. Each seemed as surprised as the other as they stared at each other. His tongue clung to the roof of his mouth. Her face was impassive except for a faint smile as she turned the horse in his direction. In a reflex action, he raised his right hand in the universal gesture of greeting.

"Barev!" she said moving the reins to her left hand as she returned the greeting with her right.

He did not understand what he heard.

"What?" he croaked hoarsely in English and then, *"Ningal enthuva paranjathu?* (What did you say?)" in *Malayalam*, the language of Kerala.

"Barev!" she repeated raising her voice.

Seeing the puzzled look on his face she added, "That means hello or *namaskaram.*"

The wind and the creek carried half her words away. He wanted to say something in reply but could only stare open-mouthed, smiling confusedly and still waving his hand.

She nudged the horse nearer to the edge, closing the distance between them. He stood rooted to the ground. Except for the motion of the hand, he could have been the 'statue man' at the local fair.

She looked at him levelly. "Is this your land?" she asked in slightly accented *Malayalam.*

In spite of being closer than before the gurgling of the stream from the chasm between them drowned her words. He had a sudden idea and inexplicably his courage returned.

Signaling with the raised open hand to wait he raced to the steep descending path that went down to the water. He stopped for a moment at the edge of the water to hitch up his *mundu* and then splashed across to the other side and ran up the incline of the opposite bank. He had to brake suddenly when he reached the top to stop from running into the horse. The princess had brought the horse closer to the path.

He looked up into her face, framed against the clear blue sky and the sunlight that caught her auburn hair in angelic halo. Her beauty took his breath away.

Again, it was she who said the first words.

"*Barev*," she said repeating what she had said the first time.

"*Namaskaram!*" he replied recalling what he had half-heard from across the stream and bringing his palms together in the traditional Indian gesture. "Parev is in which language?" he found the courage to ask.

"It is ba – barev and it is Armenian. It means hello," she replied with a faint smile.

"Armenian?" he asked in surprise. "I did not know there were Armenians here anymore. I thought all Armenians had emigrated to Australia or America."

"No, there are many of us still here," she replied. Then noticing that he had to twist his head up to talk to her, she dismounted in one swift motion.

"Actually, we are a whole village," she added matter-of-factly, smoothening her crumpled dress and straightening up to look him in the eye.

They were of nearly the same height. She was slim and he was wiry and thin. Other than that, they were a study in contrasts. Her hair was reddish brown and his was jet black. In complexion, she was as fair as a Caucasian and he a dark coffee-brown. They were both physically attractive, she like a Grecian goddess and he a Dravidian nobleman.

Even on level ground, without the elevation of the horse, she had a royal demeanor about her. He had forgotten that he had doubled up the *mundu* for crossing the stream. His legs below the knee were exposed. Quickly he undid the second hitch so that the *mundu* covered the lower half of his body up to his feet.

"What is your name?" she asked transferring the reins to her left hand and holding out her right hand.

He blushed crimson as he took her hand. This was the first time he had touched a woman outside the family. Her hand was soft and cool even in the burning afternoon heat.

"My name is Kuriakose," he replied his throat catching.

"*Kirakos!*" she repeated, bursting into a happy laugh that surprised him.

Seeing the look on his face she continued. "I was not making fun of you. Kirakos is an Armenian name."

"Really? I never knew. I thought it was a pure *Malayali* name."

"It is a long story. I will tell you about it another time," she said resuming her serious demeanor.

He rejoiced instantly at the implication. 'That means we will meet again!' he said to himself. His heart raced wildly at the possibilities of friendship with this beautiful young Armenian princess. He who had never had the courage to say more than a few words to the female classmates at college now had miraculously found a female friend, and that too a *madamma* (a white woman), in the most astounding manner.

"By the way, your bushy eyebrows look quite Armenian," she said with a smile.

Since she was the first Armenian he had met and her eyebrows were quite unlike his, Kuriakose did not understand what Armine meant.

"Is this your land?" she asked. "That's the question that I asked when you were on the other side."

"I could not hear you. That's why I came running over to your side," he said smiling. "This land belongs to my grandfather. I live with my grandparents in our ancestral home behind the trees and the paddy field," he said pointing towards his favorite haunt, the grove.

"At least I won't be arrested for trespassing!" she said with a wry smile and a twinkle in her eye. "Where are your parents? Are they working in some big city?"

"No. They are dead," he said bluntly.

Her eyes widened and she turned pale. For the first time, she looked emotional, vulnerable.

"I ... I ..." she faltered.

"It's all right. Don't worry. It happened eight years ago," he said forgivingly. Nevertheless, the mere mention of his beloved parents stirred up memories of their tragic death causing his voice to break. Changing the subject, he said, "You haven't told me your name."

"You did not ask!" came her immediate retort which discomfited him. She had resumed her normal poise.

"Sorry ..." he began apologetically but she cut him short.

"My name is Armine. AR – MI – NE"

Before he could respond she added, "I have to go."

His heart sank. "When will I see you again?" he asked desperately.

"What makes you think we will meet again?" she asked. After a brief pause, she added, "I don't know. Time will show. It is not easy for me to come here."

He was crestfallen. He could not find any words to say. The hopes that had been raised just a short while ago came crashing down.

Seeing the dejection writ large on his face she softened.

"I may come again—if you don't tell anyone of our meeting today."

He brightened visibly. "No, I will not tell anyone. You can trust me," he promised. "Not even Appachen and Ammachi."

"Who?"

"Grandfather and grandmother. That's what everybody calls their grandparents in *Malayalam*."

"I don't have grandparents and we speak Armenian at home. I call father Hayrik and mother Mayrik, although others use the modern papa and mama."

Armine turned, placed her left foot in the stirrup and in one swift move mounted the horse again.

"What is the book in your hands?" she asked.

"It is Peacock's *English Verse*, volume four. Romantic poetry. It is my college textbook."

"I like poetry, especially Keats and Shelley." Then to the horse, "Let's go!"

Armine's gentle prod set the horse ambling. Kuriakose walked alongside till they reached the incline to the stream where it was too narrow to walk side by side. He scrambled behind the horse that hastened to the water. Once in the stream, Armine stopped and turned back to look at him while the thirsty horse lapped up the clear water.

Without thinking, he asked the question that had been bothering him the day before.

"How do you go through the cave?"

She smiled at him. "You mean the 'Cave of Death'?" she asked teasingly.

"Yes. You even know the name!"

"If you come on Saturday morning by ten o'clock, I will show you," she said with a twinkle in her eye.

Appachen had sternly warned him never to go anywhere near the cave. His father had told him the same thing years ago, when they had visited the ancestral home during the school holidays. The cave had always been taboo. But he was willing to risk anything for meeting this bewitching damsel again.

"I will be here at ten," he said with a sense of intense excitement at the prospect of meeting her again. He was barely able to hide his secret exultation.

An idea struck him. He wanted to make sure she would come back. He took two steps forward and held up the book of poetry. "Here, you can bring it back on Saturday."

She appeared to hesitate for a brief instant but then leaned down to accept the book. "If possible, bring me another book of poetry – the Metaphysical poets or the Brownings – on Saturday."

He felt joyful. This chance first encounter was not going to be the last. They would meet again!

But their first meeting had come to an end. With a wave of the hand, the rider and the horse went quickly past the bend at a fast trot.

For the first time since his parents' death, he felt palpably lonely. He trudged up the bank unhappy that the meeting had ended so abruptly. When he reached the grove, he sat down on the protruding roots of the jackfruit tree, careful not to dirty his white *mundu,* to ponder over the strange encounter with Armine the Armenian damsel.

The more he thought about his rare good fortune, the less miserable he felt. In a short while the expectation of the next meeting in three days and the joy of having a beautiful female friend eclipsed the sadness.

'If only my classmates could see me and Armine together, they would forever be silent! They would not make fun of my shyness around girls.' He smiled at the thought as he rose up to go home.

Appachen had gone to the vicarage for a meeting. Kuriakose had supper alone, with Ammachi fussing over him and plying him with extra helpings of *moilee*, pomfret cooked in delicious coconut milk.

"The fisherwoman had more of the costly pomfrets than mackerels today," Ammachi said.

But Kuriakose's thoughts were not on the price of fish.

Chapter 4: A Day in the Life

Geevarghese was the first to accost him at college the next day.

"I want to know about yesterday. What spiritual experience did you have?" he asked coming straight to the point.

"Please forget about it. It was not a religious experience. It was nothing," hedged Kuriakose.

"As fellow believers, we have to support each other. Something did happen, didn't it?" persisted Geevarghese.

Kuriakose did not want to lie. But he was not ready to tell his remarkable story either.

"There is nothing to share now," he said evasively.

But Geevarghese was not one to give up so easily.

"Is your grandfather forcing you to rejoin the Orthodox Church?"

"I told you before. My grandfather has never discussed this issue. He has not mentioned our Pentecostal group even once since my baptism in the Pamba River. Maybe he is in denial."

"Don't be too sure. We have seen too many backsliders returning to their original churches like dogs going back to their vomit. I am quoting the Bible," said Geevarghese.

"I have no plans to go back to the Orthodox Church," replied Kuriakose with a smile. "Not even if I could understand the Syriac and Greek portions of their liturgy."

With that, he slowly moved away to his first class. It was Professor Ann Thomas lecturing on Chaucer's *Canterbury Tales*. Chaucer fascinated Kuriakose, especially *The Miller's Tale* and *The Wife of Bath's Tale*. He found his usual spot next to his friend RK.

"The class is full—as usual," said Radhakrishnan with a wink. He was referring to Professor Ann, who though in her early forties, still maintained a trim and attractive body.

But lascivious thoughts could not invade Kuriakose's mind today. His mind was filled with Armine and Armine only.

Professor Ann lectured as usual with her Oxonian intonation completely oblivious of the lewd stares of the male students. It was *The Reeve's Tale* today. Instead of taking the notes the professor dictated, his pen drew doodles in his notebook.

"Why are you drawing a horse?" asked RK. "Who is the woman? Lady Godiva?" he asked with a mischievous smile.

"No, no," replied Kuriakose hastily defacing the picture he had been drawing.

"Why are you blushing so much? Your Godiva has her clothes on!"

The second session was on linguistics, a subject that he had liked instantly from the first lecture.

During the lunch break, he went to the college library and borrowed *The Oxford Book of English Verse* and *Sonnets from the Portuguese* for Armine.

The afternoon sessions on Hardy's *Far from the Madding Crowd* and post-modern poetry went by in a flash.

He rushed home after classes as quickly as he could and hastily drank the hot coffee, blowing into the steel tumbler to cool the scalding beverage, and wolfed down the thin rice pancake *dosa* Ammachi had prepared for him.

As usual, Ammachi did not sit down to eat with him but only waited on him.

"How were the classes today? Did you learn anything?" asked Ammachi.

"Yes, Ammachi," he replied respectfully. "There is much to learn in the last four months. We are two months behind because of the student strikes of last year."

"Don't get involved in politics. Study well and get a first class," said Ammachi making the sign of the cross. "Your parents in heaven would be proud."

Although he knew Armine would not be coming, he nonetheless went to the grove with Hardy's novel and the Oxford poetry book he had borrowed for Armine.

Her absence caused a deep sense of emptiness, but he consoled himself that she had not promised to come today. After a short while, the sadness dissipated, and he began to read *Far from the Madding Crowd* marveling at the skill of Hardy. The story of Bathsheba Everdene, Sergeant Troy, William Boldwood, and Gabriel Oak was riveting.

Unmindful of the surroundings he continued reading till the sun went behind the coconut trees and the light began to fail. The cawing of crows looking for a place to roost for the night and the mooing of cattle filled the air as he walked home unhurriedly.

When he reached the pebble-strewn courtyard of the house he remembered that he had forgotten to feed the cattle on his return from college. Laying the books on the edge of the *verandah* he went to the cone shaped haystack, as tall as a tree, and pulled down clumps of hay which he carried over to the cowshed by the edge of the courtyard. Although it was over eight years since he had moved to the village from the city, he still found the stench of cow dung and urine overpowering. Quickly he spread the hay in front of the three cows. The buckets still contained enough of the oil-cake fodder that Ammachi had fed the cows in the afternoon. As he stepped out of the cowshed he reached up and playfully drummed the side of the black canoe hanging from the eaves.

He walked over to the well and tugging on the coir rope drew up a bucket of water to rid his hands and feet of the odor of the cowshed. He then drew more water from the well to carry in a plastic bucket to the outhouse of a bathroom behind the house. There, stooping down to scoop up mug after mug of cool water he sloshed them over his body. He dried himself with the thin, porous cotton towel, remembering the advice from his childhood—first the back, then the head and only then the face.

He then went into the house and studied in the light of a naked sixty-watt bulb at the dining table.

He turned on the enormous Telefunken radio and tuned into the BBC. The *John Peel Show* played in the background as he studied. When the program ended, he switched to the Voice of America and listened to Willis Conover's *Music USA Standards*. When his grandfather came home, he respectfully stood up.

Deferentially he greeted his grandfather by calling out "Appacha!"

Appachen nodded his head and said, "Studying, eh? Well, study hard."

He resumed his reading till his grandfather returned after a bath.

During supper, Appachen announced: "The anarchist Edakiruku has released another book on atheism. He calls religion the opium of the masses."

"It was Marx who said that," said Kuriakose.

"Who?" asked Appachen testily.

"Karl Marx."

"Are you trying to teach me?" asked Appachen.

"No, Appacha, I was ..." began Kuriakose in embarrassment.

Appachen cut him off. "Our state was the first in the world – the whole world – to vote Communists to power in the 1957 general elections. All the rest of India voted for the democratic Congress party. Now we are paying the price. They will impose atheism here like they brainwashed the school children in Russia."

"But early Christianity was also a version of Communism," suggested Kuriakose completely forgetting that he was speaking to his grandfather.

The silence was unnerving. Appachen glared at Kuriakose, his face livid.

"Never mention Christianity and Communism in the same breath," Appachen thundered. "One is the gospel of love and sacrifice; the other is the creation of the devil for power and repression over fellow human beings."

That ended any further conversation which, in any case, was not unusual because meals were silent rituals in this society.

As he finished his supper of rice, lentils and fried mackerels brushed with pepper, Kuriakose wondered within himself, 'Isn't the village cooperative bank where Appachen is the sole employee also a by-product of Communism?' But he dared not articulate his thought.

After the meal, Kuriakose resumed his reading of the emotional travails of Bathsheba Everdene. But it was now the turn of Appachen to listen to the radio. Kuriakose tuned the dial to FEBA Radio from the Seychelles transmitting a fifteen-minute gospel program in *Malayalam*.

Even as the evangelist on the radio declaimed about fire and brimstone Kuriakose's mind was at peace contemplating his angelic friend Armine. In two days, he would meet her again. He counted the hours and then multiplied them by sixty to get the number of minutes to their next rendezvous.

The pyramid of mental arithmetic he was building was leveled to the ground by a call from his grandfather.

"Son, come and massage my legs. They are breaking."

Putting the books away Kuriakose went over to the *verandah* where Appachen reclined in the easy chair with his legs on the chair's long arms that jutted far out to the front.

"Today coconut oil will not do. Use the *Ayurvedic* oil. The shins feel as if they are being twisted and split open. If this is so painful how much more terrible will be hell that the evangelist was preaching about!"

Kuriakose poured the pungent oil into his hand and began to firmly, but lovingly, massage the throbbing arthritic varicose veins of the spindly legs of his grandfather.

Before going to bed he entered the day's headlines into his current affairs journal. For the month of February, he had the following entries, among others. Turkey annexed half of Cyprus with Rauf Denktash declaring the Turkish State of Cyprus. Bulganin, the former Premier of the Soviet Union died. In neighboring Nepal, the coronation of King Birendra took place in Kathmandu at an auspicious moment after a wait of three years. Paralleling the strong female leadership of Indira Gandhi in India, their former colonial rulers chose the Iron Lady, Margaret Thatcher, as the leader of the Conservative Party and the first woman leader of the opposition in the House of Commons.

Chapter 5: The Cave of Death

When Saturday morning came, Kuriakose was beside himself with excitement. He milked the cows early and mixed the oil cake and rice bran feed for them. He shaved twice to remove the last stubble and carefully trimmed his mustache and sideburns. After the bath, he spent a long time before the mirror rubbing coconut oil into his hair and shaping it into a pompadour. He carefully ironed the shirt and the white sarong *mundu* with the charcoal heated iron. At last, he was ready for the rendezvous with the angelic princess.

He was at his favorite spot in the fruit grove almost a full hour before the scheduled time. He had brought with him a thin cloth towel to sit on lest he dirty the crisp, clean clothes. He tried to read Orwell's *1984* but almost every other minute he would look up expectantly towards the bend in the stream to see if Armine was coming. After about ten minutes he gave up the battle and put the book away. Instead, he marveled at the beauty of the surroundings with new eyes, as if he were seeing them for the very first time. The blue and green kingfisher skimming the water and the yellow and green parrot on the tree seemed new and resplendent. The cawing of crows sounded more raucous than usual. The cool breeze reminded

Kuriakose of Armine's auburn hair waving in the wind. The first week of March was slightly warmer than February. It would keep getting hotter until June, when the monsoon would sweep up from the Indian Ocean in the south bringing with it a deluge of water accompanied by frightening thunder and lighting.

Then, at long last, it was ten o'clock. There was no sign of Armine. Another minute passed. There was still no sign of the horse and its rider. He held his watch up to his ear to see if it was ticking. At five minutes past the hour, he rose and walked over to the edge of the embankment to get a clearer view of the bend in the stream behind which lay the cave. After ten more minutes the anticipation turned to worry. Kuriakose began to doubt if Armine would keep her word.

'Maybe it was all a figment of my overheated imagination,' he thought. 'Or maybe she is real but as fickle as the women I've read about in books.'

He sat down again with a feeling of despondency. The heightened perceptions of his surroundings only a short while ago had nosedived into sullen familiarity.

'To stay or to go?' he asked himself.

He decided to stay and read.

So engrossing was the story of Winston Smith and his love affair with Julia and their arrest by the Thought Police that he became oblivious to his surroundings.

He literally jumped to his feet, rearranging his *mundu* in confusion, when "Barev!" broke through his consciousness.

His mouth fell open as he saw Armine barely two arm lengths away. She wore an electric blue blouse and a white fluffy skirt that came down just below her knees. On her feet, she had shiny black leather shoes. But what he noticed most was her eyes. They were a deep blue.

"How did you ... how did you ... get here?" he spluttered.

Subconsciously he thought again that she was an ethereal being to have just appeared out thin air.

"With my feet like everyone else," she responded in an irritated tone. "I don't have wings to fly."

He was nonplussed.

Sensing his hurt she added placatingly, "You were so absorbed in your book you wouldn't have noticed even if a real angel had dropped from the sky!"

He wanted to say that that was just what had happened but thought that would be too forward. She craned her neck to look at the book he was holding.

"That is a favorite book of my father's," she said. "He thinks Communism destroyed religion in Russia. You haven't said a word. At least say 'barev'."

"Barev," he said self-consciously. Then he added, "This is a powerful book. Sheer genius. Did you know Orwell was born in India?"

"No, I thought he was born in Burma."

"No, he lived in Burma for some years as an adult and carried the guilt of the racial divide for the rest of his life. But he was born in a town called Motihari in Bihar, of all places! Wretched, squalid, boorish Bihar!" He could not hide his bewilderment.

Armine's demeanor changed and she smiled. "It is clear that you love books and literature. Father does too." Then suddenly remembering she added, "Did you bring any books for me?"

"Yes, I did." Kuriakose stopped down to pick up the books wrapped in an old issue of the newspaper *Malayala Deepika* "Here," he said stepping forward and holding out the books.

Armine opened the wrapping carefully to reveal *The Oxford Book of English Verse* and *Sonnets from the Portuguese.*

"Elizabeth Barrett Browning!" exulted Armine. He had never seen her so animated before.

"I thought you would like them both since you said you like Romantic poetry."

She was quick to retort, "I never said that. I said I like Keats and Shelley."

He was taken aback. "Sorry. You are right. You will make a good lawyer." He then added, "You also wanted metaphysical poets. There are several poems of Donne in the Oxford book."

She ignored that. "Don't you want to see the cave? Your book is in a bag on the horse."

"The horse?" Where is the horse?" The moment the words were out of his mouth, he knew it was stupid.

She seized upon it instantly. "You think I walked here all the way on foot?"

This trait of her of asking a counter question instead of giving a simple straightforward answer he interpreted as unfriendliness and was to cause him much anguish in the future.

As Armine turned and walked towards the sloping path to the water, he realized that she had not thanked him for the books. But the sheer joy of walking beside her eclipsed all such thoughts and the embarrassment that her responses had caused him. Armine's steps were shorter than Kuriakose's strides, but her briskness resulted in their walking together at the same pace.

When they reached the edge of the slope, he saw the horse standing placidly in the water. 'Why couldn't she just tell me the horse was here?' he wondered.

Before reaching the muddy ground, she took her shoes off to hold them in her hand.

"Qurkik-Jalali! Qurkik-Jalali!" Armine crooned and the steed whinnied.

She put the books and her black shoes in the bag hanging by the side of the horse. Without another word, she took the reins in her hand and led the way towards the cave.

After a few steps, she began to recite:

> *I come from haunts of coot and hern,*
> *I make a sudden sally*
> *And sparkle out among the fern,*
> *To bicker down a valley.*

"*The Brook*?" asked Kuriakose.

But she did not seem to notice. She continued reciting the whole poem melodiously.

When she reached the last stanza, he joined in to complete the poem.

For men may come and men may go,
But I go on for ever.

"Do you like Tennyson?" she asked.

"Yes, he was a great poet. Modernists accuse him of being too shallow, but I think he is one of the greatest English poets."

They had reached the bend in the stream. He had never gone past this point. It was expressly forbidden. But for Armine's sake, he was willing to throw caution to the winds.

"Ready to enter the Cave of Death?" she asked teasingly.

"I feel like Cortez," he said excited by the rush of adrenalin.

"Who?"

"The Cortez from Keats." With that, he recited the stanza.

Or like stout Cortez, when with eagle eyes
He stared at the Pacific – and all his men
Look'd at each other with a wild surmise –
Silent, upon a peak in Darien.

"Good!" she said and for the first time, he detected a trace of appreciation.

"Come, let us go. We don't have much time to lose," she said.

"What did you call the horse a little earlier?" asked Kuriakose.

"I named the horse Qurkik-Jalali after the famous horse of the epic hero Sasuntsi David, or David of Sasun in plain English."

> *The folk hero Sasuntsi David, though born of human parents, had supernatural powers. He drew his strength from the waters of Katnaghbyur (Spring of Milk) and from the butter and honey of Sasun. He loved freedom and independence and could not stand the oppression of foreign rule. While still a young man he challenged Msrah Melik to a duel and killed him and released his people from the tyrant's power. Qurkik-Jalali was this brave man's horse.*

Kuriakose followed behind the Qurkik-Jalali as Armine went around the bend.

What he saw made him stand still in his tracks. The cave looked dark and foreboding.

"Scared?" she asked with a wicked smile.

"No. If you can do this, I can too."

But deep inside him he somehow felt that this decisive step of disobeying family orders would forever change his life.

Thankfully Armine was businesslike again.

"It will get completely dark in the cave like the night. The stream makes a left turn and then it curves to the right in a wide arc. Then it makes a left turn before the exit. It is shaped like the Greek letter omega. The bends at both ends shut out the light. Just follow after Qurkik-Jalali."

The stream did not get deeper. The horse had to lean forward to lower its head to enter the cave. It turned out to be exactly as Armine said. Soon after they turned left it became pitch black. The bend behind had cut off the light from the mouth of the cave and there was no light coming in from the other end. Kuriakose followed Armine and the horse. After a few minutes, his eyes adjusted to the darkness. He saw to his surprise that the ceiling was higher inside and the horse could walk upright without stooping down. The cave had also widened to several times the width of the entrance. Kuriakose realized that this was a large underground cavern. Water dripped from the ceiling on the bed of soft white sand.

As he followed on behind, he noticed that the stream curved to the right in a wide arc as Armine had said. He looked to his left and froze. At the apex of the curve, below the stone ceiling of the left bank, lay piles and piles of bones and skeletons. His stomach churned and he got goose bumps but taking control of himself he followed on behind Armine.

Just when he thought the darkness would never end, he saw that it was lighter to the left up ahead and sure enough there was a bend to the left and after about twenty more steps they were out of the cave and in broad daylight again.

Armine had turned around to watch him emerge squinting into the bright sunlight.

"Are you all right?" she asked.

"I am fine," he replied. "But you didn't tell me about the bones and skeletons inside."

"If I had told you, you may not have come," she said matter-of-factly.

Then, seeing the questioning look on his face she added, "My theory is that during the floods the stream carries down carcasses from upriver. These get stuck at the top of the curve where the fast-flowing stream curves to the right."

"There might be human skeletons too?" wondered Kuriakose.

"Who knows? There might be. Maybe those killed during flash floods whose bodies were never found. How bad are the floods for you?" asked Armine.

"Every year during monsoon the floods come. We get chest-high water for two or three weeks. We have to use boats then to get around. Every house has at least one small canoe."

Kuriakose looked back at the towering black volcanic rocks that dotted the steep hillside. He could not see anything of the other side from where they had come.

"I know what you are thinking. This is a secluded valley. If you are not tired, we can walk a bit more."

Armine swung atop the horse and Kuriakose followed on behind. He could hear the unseen stream rushing noisily downhill to the right. The brush was not thick because of the stony ground. The several trips Armine had made to the cave had created something of a noticeable path.

After some time, Armine stopped and waited for Kuriakose to catch up.

"Do you want to see my village?" she asked.

He nodded. When they had gone around the biggest rock of them all he stood speechless in his tracks.

There below them lay a beautiful hamlet, the like of which he had seen only in books.

"That's Nor Garni, my Armenian village," said Armine.

As they watched, a beautiful rainbow materialized, arcing over the hamlet.

"That's a sign," said Armine with reverence.

Chapter 6: An Impromptu Picnic

Kuriakose was dumbfounded.

He could not believe that he had been living for years this close to an Armenian village. He did not think the people of his village knew either. He had never heard any mention of Nor Garni or of the existence of an Armenian village.

"I know what you are thinking," said Armine with a knowing smile. "How did we stay hidden from the public eye?"

"Yes, that's exactly what I was thinking."

"You've already seen the natural barrier on this side. It's almost like a fortress. On the other side of our village stretching for about a hundred fifty kilometers (ninety miles) lies the Vandiperiyar reserve forest. That is government land. No encroachers can come from that direction."

"How do you travel to the nearest town?" asked Kuriakose still disbelieving.

"You see there is a government check-post on the edge of the reserve forest. Vehicles can come up to there. From there we reach home using cycles or horses."

"How did you build your houses?" persisted Kuriakose.

"I asked my father the same question. Building the houses was not easy. They were built before I was born. Cement, sand, and other material were brought by truck to the check-post. From there they were carried by horse carts and bullock carts up to the village."

"I still cannot believe it. This must be the best-kept secret in our State of Kerala!" exclaimed Kuriakose.

"We don't publicize our village. We live a secluded life. We grow our own vegetables and grain. The soil is very fertile."

"Since your land is so low you must have floods during the monsoon?" queried Kuriakose.

"No floods at all! That's the biggest surprise. The stream we came through carries the waters to a steep gorge on the right. There is another stream further down to the left of the village. These two streams drain the water away from the village into the Pamba River."

"That is unbelievable! No floods!" Kuriakose was amazed. "During the monsoon, we have to carry everything to a central attic. Tables and chairs float around inside the house. We have to store even drinking water. It is a difficult time."

"That must be terrible!"

"Hopefully this will be the last year of floods. When the new Pamba dam is completed, there will not be any floods anymore."

Armine looked at him silently. She was on the verge of saying something but changed her mind.

"What about education and schools?" Kuriakose asked.

"We teach our own children up to the primary school level. Then we send them to live with our relatives in Cochin or Trivandrum or Madras. I was enrolled in an expensive boarding school in faraway Nilgiri Hills. It was very cold up in the mountains. I came home only once a year for Christmas."

"And what did you do for college?"

"I attended the Mother Mary's College for Women at Kottayam. My father worked for the government and was posted at the government collectorate there at that time. I came on weekends with my father in his government jeep. He kept the vehicle locked at the check-post and we rode home on cycles."

"This is like a fairytale," Kuriakose said quietly.

"Are you hungry? Want to eat something?" asked Armine.

"What is there to eat here? I am more thirsty than hungry."

"That can be taken care of too," said Armine.

She lowered the bags that had been slung on either side of the horse. Next, she pulled down the *dhurrie*, a thick cotton rug, that was on the back of the horse and laid it on the ground. From the bag, she brought out three stainless steel vessels and a thermos flask. She also took out Peacock's *English Verse* and held it out to Kuriakose.

"Here, before I forget," she said.

Kuriakose looked at the book. Armine had taken good care of it and she had not forgotten to bring it back as promised. 'Both hallmarks of true book lovers,' he noted mentally.

He noticed that she did not thank him explicitly but that did not rankle him. Being with Armine was the experience of a lifetime.

"Come, sit down. We can have a small snack and some coffee and go our separate ways before it is dark," offered Armine.

Kuriakose did not need a second invitation. He sat down with his feet tucked under him, yoga style. Armine delicately knelt down and then leaned back to sit on her haunches. Kuriakose was fascinated by her reddish-brown hair and blue eyes as he watched her apportion the contents of the three vessels into two and handed one to him.

"There's *lavash* and *khorovats*. There's chicken, beef, pork, and vegetables on each skewer. I hope you eat pork?"

"I have eaten pork while living in the city with my parents. I like it. I eat everything. The food looks delicious."

"It has to be. Mayrik cooked it."

"Who?"

"Mayrik. Mother. I already told you at the first meeting. Mayr is the word for mother in Hayeren. Mayrik is the affectionate form."

"Hayeren?" asked Kuriakose puzzled.

"That is the name of our language. It comes from what we call our nation—Hayastan. For others, it is Armenia and Armenian."

"I never knew! It is like Hindustan, the Hindu name for India, and Hindi the language."

Armine crossed herself and waited for Kuriakose to start.

"This is the most delicious food I have ever had," said Kuriakose. "There are herbs in this, but it is not spicy hot like our food."

"You put too much *masala* and hot *chillies* into food. The natural flavor of the food is lost."

"What is the name for this again?" asked Kuriakose holding up a skewer.

"*Khorovats*. The same as barbecue."

"This is the first time for me to have barbecued food. Then the flatbread must be called *lavash*?"

"Yes, you are right! *Lavash* is the Armenian national food. Distinctly Armenian."

"I love it! It is so thin! It is so much better than *chapati* or *paratha*. It is like the *rumali roti* we get in Mughlai restaurants. The name literally means 'handkerchief bread' because it is thin and folds like a cloth."

"It sounds very similar to *lavash*," said Armine.

"It is similar in appearance but tastes different. *Lavash* is much better! Tell me Armine, how did Hayastan get its name?" asked Kuriakose.

> *Hayk, after whom all Armenians and their nation Hayastan is named, lived three centuries before the Patriarch Abraham. Hayk was the son of Togarmah, who was the son of Japheth, the eldest son of Noah. Hayk was strong and handsome and was one of the builders of the Tower of Babel in the plains of Shinar. Fiercely independent, Hayk left the kingdom of Bel and brought his family to the land below Mount Ararat where his great-*

grandfather Noah's Ark had rested. He conquered all the people living there and established the nation of Hayastan. Bel came after him and his people to subjugate them, but Hayk defeated him in battle and slew him. Hayk was an outstanding archer.

"Do you think Haig is Armenian?" asked Kuriakose with a smile.

"Who?" asked Armine, her forehead creasing in thought.

"Alexander Haig."

"I don't know who that is," said Armine.

"Nixon's Chief of Staff at the White House! His name was in the papers every day during the Watergate affair," Kuriakose said with a sly smile.

Armine was not amused.

"That's not funny. You are making fun of the ancestor of all Armenians," she said sternly.

"No, no, no!" Kuriakose protested. But Armine ignored him and did not respond.

"Now I know the origin of Hayastan but how did the name Armenia come about?"

Aram was the sixth descendant of Hayk, the founder of Hayastan. Aram expanded the boundaries of Armenia as far as Asia Minor by conquering the Phrygians, the Cappadocians, the Medes, and other nations. He imposed the Armenian language on the people he conquered with an iron fist and mercilessly crushed insurrections. His fame was so great that the nation he led came to be also called

> *Aramia, from which evolved the present name of Armenia.*

When they had finished eating, she poured coffee into the two caps of the thermos flask that also served as cups.

"This is the strongest and thickest coffee I have ever tasted!" exclaimed Kuriakose.

"This is how we make our coffee. Not like *Kerala coffee* where you mix milk and sugar and make it a sweet watery apology for coffee," derided Armine.

Kuriakose was stung by her deprecating words. "People from all over the world like our coffee," he said defensively.

"But that does not make it real coffee," said Armine with finality.

This put an end to the conversation for some minutes. Kuriakose did not know how to restart their dialogue. It was Armine who broke the silence.

"There was also Ara the Beautiful," she said.

> *Ara the Beautiful was the son of Aram. Queen Semiramis the wife of King Ninus (Nimrod) of Assyria was bewitched by this handsome King of Armenia. But Ara spurned the gifts and presents that she sent him. He rejected all her overtures for a rendezvous. Infuriated by the rejection, Semiramis led her army to Armenia to capture him and fulfill her desires. Although Semiramis gave orders to her generals to capture Ara alive, he was slain in battle. Queen Semiramis was devastated. She mourned his death and even attempted to bring Ara back to life through witchcraft. To pacify the Armenians, she had one of her*

soldiers impersonate Ara. Later she installed Ara's twelve-year-old son as the King of Armenia and named him Ara. The city of Van, so dear to Armenians, but now in present day Turkey, was built by Semiramis. Armenians call it Shamiramakert, meaning built by Semiramis. Van stands on the banks of Shameramasu, the river of Semiramis.

"Remember my telling you that your name was Armenian?" asked Armine.

"Yes. You called me Kirikos or Kirokos or something."

"I called you Kirakos. That is a very famous name amongst *Hayers*. The first Bishop who bore the title Catholicos of all Armenians was Bishop Kirakos."

"Is that the Armenian church?" asked Kuriakose.

"Yes, our church is the Armenian Apostolic Church. Bishop Kirakos moved the Catholicate back to Ejmiadzin in Eastern Armenia from Sis the capital of Cilicia after it fell to the Muslim Mamluks of Egypt. Cilicia was also called Armenia Minor or Little Armenia."

"Where is Ejmiadzin?" asked Kuriakose.

"It is just outside Yerevan, the capital of the Armenian Socialist Republic."

"Is Armenia a part of the USSR?"

"Yes, Armenia became a republic of the Soviet Union in 1920. We can have the history class later. Now back to your name."

"There is more?" Kuriakose asked.

He was thrilled to sit this close to Armine. Her blue eyes transfixed him. All the eyes he had ever seen were black or dark brown. The blue eyes, the fair skin, the reddish-brown hair, the red lips that moved rapidly as she talked, the aquiline nose, and her quiet assurance all gave her an angelic look.

"The other famous Kirakos was Kirakos Gandzaketsi," said Armine.

> *Kirakos Gandzaketsi is remembered as a renowned travel writer. He was a member of the entourage of Haithon, the King of Little Armenia, who traveled all the way to Karakoram in Mongolia seeking an alliance with the Mongols against the marauding Muslims. It took many months to get there. The journey was not easy. As they journeyed through the Turkish states in Asia Minor, they disguised themselves to avoid detection by their Muslim enemies. An alliance was struck with the Mongols but that did not prevent the plunder of Armenia.*

"That trip must have a taken a long time," remarked Kuriakose.

"Yes, I think it took two years. Anyway, they had to disguise themselves while traveling through Muslim nations to avoid attacks from the Muslims who have been our enemies for centuries."

"There are many Muslims here in Kerala, but they live in harmony with the Hindus and the Christians," said Kuriakose.

"That may be, but the Turks killed two million Armenians in the first genocide of modern times."

"Two *million*?" Kuriakose was so aghast that he almost shouted out his question. "That is twenty *lakhs*!"

"You have not heard of the Armenian Genocide?" it was Armine's turn to be surprised.

"No, it was not part of the history we were taught in schools. I had heard the term Armenian but hardly know anything more than that."

"If you know so little, how much less would the others, with less education, know," said Armine dejectedly. But collecting herself she continued, "There is also the beautiful Fortress of Kirakos in Cilicia."

"I did not know I was so famous!" Kuriakose laughed.

"We have variations of your name as a surname too—Kirakosian."

"Now do you want to know what your name means in my language, *Malayalam*?" asked Kuriakose with a mischievous smile.

"No, tell me. I'm all ears."

"Armine is a nice name. It sounds nice. In *Malayalam* *'ar'* means river, like Pamba Ar for Pamba River. And *'meen'* means fish. Therefore, Armine means river fish!"

"What an insult!" Armine said in mock outrage. "In Hayeren my name has nothing to do with rivers or fish. It is a very popular name for Armenian daughters that is very close to our nation's name, Armenia. For sons, the equivalent is Armen."

When she mentioned the name Armen she blushed and averted her eyes. 'Was it just an accident or was there more to it?' he wondered.

"What is your full name?" he asked.

"Our family name is Hovhannisyan. What is yours?"

"You want to know my full name?" he asked laughing. "My name is Thazhakandathil Kuriakose Mathew."

"That is a long name! Is your name Kuriakose or Matthew? And what is that first long name?" asked Armine.

"To start from the end Mathew with one 't' is my father's name. It is like the Russian patronymic middle name. The middle name Kuriakose is my own name. The first is our clan name. All who are born in our clan will have that in their name. Thazhakandathil literally means the lower paddy field."

"So, your clan was born in a paddy field! Interesting!"

Kuriakose started to explain how clan names are derived but then decided against it.

Armine changed the topic quickly. "There is something I must tell you lest you be disappointed later. There can be no romance between us. Don't even think about it. You don't have the standard. Have no hope."

Kuriakose was taken back. He did not understand why Armine was telling him this.

"And now it is time to go," said Armine getting back to her feet.

The end was again too abrupt for Kuriakose. He was lost in the joy of being in Armine's proximity. Sadness enveloped his heart as he thought of the imminent parting. Armine was objective and detached.

"Can you go back on your own?" she asked.

"I think I can," said Kuriakose not very convincingly. His mind still on what Armine had just told him.

"I will come around and watch you from the rock till you go into the cave. From there you can find your way home."

"OK. Thanks for the meal."

She twisted her mouth to indicate it was nothing and held out her hand. He blushed this time, just as he had done the first time, when she had offered her hand. This time, though, it was only the tips of her fingers which she withdrew very quickly.

"When will I see you again?" he asked unable to bear the thought of not seeing her again.

"Next Saturday at the same time?" she suggested.

He was happy again.

As he looked at her, Wordsworth's Lucy came to mind.

> *She dwelt among the untrodden ways*
> *Beside the springs of Dove,*
> *A Maid whom there were none to praise*
> *And very few to love:*

Hitching up his *mundu* he began to run back up the path towards the cave. When he was half-way through, he turned back to look. She was still there on horseback beside the rock. He waved and resumed running, with Peacock's *English Verse* in his right hand. When he reached the mouth of the cave he stopped and waved several times. She waved once before turning around and disappearing behind the huge rock.

Hitching his *mundu* up even higher, he sloshed through the cave in claustrophobic haste, avoiding even a glance at the skeletons and bones, now to his right.

When he came out at the other end it was almost as if he was reborn. He had not only conquered the cave of death, but had also discovered a mysterious village, and had had an impromptu picnic with an angel.

***

Unbeknownst to her Armine was being watched. Her brother-in-law to be, the illiterate cowherd Vilen, had been following her movements at a distance. She had disappeared on earlier days to reappear alone but today he had seen her, from a far distance, with a man. Rage and jealousy consumed him. He spurred his horse to Armine's house to inform her father and mother.

***

Her father was waiting for her when she got back. Without any preface, he thundered at her.

"Who is the man you met secretly? How many times have I told you not to be friendly with outsiders, with *otarner*, especially men? We marry only our own people. Hayks—not *otar*. Why do you think we sent you to a women's college? Have you forgotten you are promised to Armen?"

"Hayrik, I have not done anything wrong. He is an MA student. A book lover who reads English poetry in the fields. We talk only about books and literature. He lent me these poetry books to read," she said taking out the books from her bag. "His name is Kuriakose. He is a Christian."

"Why didn't you tell us? Why are you keeping it a secret?"

"Hayrik jan, Mayrik jan. I have never kept anything secret from you in my life. You both are my whole world. You know there is no one educated left in our village."

That seemed to soften her father's anger. Her mother did not say a word but kept wringing her hands.

"I was riding around on Qurkik-Jalali when I saw him reading English poetry. I was planning to bring him to meet both of you," added Armine.

"Riding around? I told you many times not to go to the check-post without telling us," her father's anger returned.

"I didn't go to the check-post, Hayrik jan. I went to the other side of the mountain."

"What! How did you do that? That is almost like a fortress?"

Armine hesitated. "Hayrik jan, please don't be angry with me. I went through the cave of death to the other side."

The father was thunderstruck. He stood rooted to the spot. Then he said in a softer tone, "You have always been a daring one. I remember how you jumped into the river on a college excursion to save a drowning classmate when no one else dared to. But don't take too many risks. You are lucky we don't live in North India. You would have been kidnapped by strangers. Don't be reckless."

"No, Hayrik jan, I won't. Kirakos is well behaved. He is a book worm, an MA student."

"His name is Kuriakose or Kirakos?"

"It is actually Kuriakose, but I think of him as Kirakos. He is a gentleman. He will not harm me. I told him at the start not to have any hopes even of friendship."

That appeared to reassure Hayrik.

"Nevertheless, I want to meet him. What are the books you brought?"

Chapter 7: Returning the Favor

Kuriakose walked on air till Wednesday. He had just read *The Secret of Life of Walter Mitty* by Thurber and thought he was Mitty come alive. The country songs he had heard on Voice of the America's *Breakfast Show* presented by Phil Irwin and the songs by the Beatles he had heard on the BBC acquired a new meaning as he daydreamed about Armine. His classmates noticed the marked change, but he clung to his secret. How could he tell them? His story was so far-fetched that they would have considered him mad.

The closest he came to divulging the fantastic story, was to his friend Radhakrishnan.

"Do you know any Armenians personally, RK?" Kuriakose asked him.

"No. There were many thousands in Kerala at one time. They engaged in the spice trade and were also astute in managing money. They increased their wealth at a much faster rate than other communities. This made them envied and disliked by those who had less success in business. After Independence, most of the Armenians emigrated to Australia, Europe, and America. They kept mostly to themselves and rarely married outside their race," RK said.

This was nothing new. Kuriakose knew all of this already. RK did not seem to know about the religious side of the Armenians but that that was not a surprise since he was a Hindu.

"Why are you asking so many questions about Armenians?" RK asked suddenly.

Kuriakose fumbled for an answer. He came very close to revealing the story. But quick thinking saved the day.

"Now that I have changed my denomination, I am trying to find out more about the history of Christianity in Kerala," hedged Kuriakose.

He knew that would not interest RK and he was right.

On Wednesday, their world almost fell apart. The news arrived during the lunch break. Kuriakose, RK, and Geevarghese were sitting under the casuarina trees that lined the driveway, away from the smokers, when the news reached them.

In tears, Mercy, one of their classmates, told them, "Jessy died."

It took a few moments for the news to sink in.

"Which Jessy? *Our* Jessy?" asked Geevarghese incredulously.

"Yes, our Jessy. She had a fever since Saturday and this morning she died suddenly."

"Died from a fever?" RK said in disbelief.

"That's the news we got."

Geevarghese interrupted. "What time is the funeral? We must go."

"They already buried her," said Mercy.

Geevarghese was livid. "I know we don't keep dead bodies overnight. Whether Hindu, Muslim, or Christian we bury the dead the same day. At least they should have waited till evening so we could pay our respects."

Kuriakose, as was his wont, had not participated in the conversation but only listened passively. But inside of him, he was in turmoil. He remembered Jessy as the always-smiling daughter of the local postmaster. They were not very rich, and she almost always wore the same light pastel pink sari. It was difficult to accept that her life had ended even before her adult life had begun.

He did not stay for the afternoon classes. He went home to his secret grove while his mind wrestled with the religious ideas he had learned recently of salvation, everlasting life, eternal damnation, and predestination. Would Jessy's soul be saved, or would she forever be lost? He realized that he could not know the answer but that did not reduce his sorrow.

Kuriakose fed the cows and cleaned the cowshed floor, sweeping the dung and the urine to the gutter that led to the pit outside. He then bathed himself thoroughly and lay on his cot staring at the thatched coconut-leaf ceiling. The beauty of Armine and the attraction he felt for her contrasted with the sudden death of his classmate Jessy and the transitoriness of life.

Appachen had not come back from the cooperative bank. He took the opportunity to ask his grandmother about the cave of death.

"Ammachi what can you tell me about the cave of death?"

"Son, we don't talk about that in our house."

"Why is that Ammachi? Why is the cave of death unmentionable in our house?" he asked.

"Shush!" she said in a low whisper. "The cave swallowed Appachen's youngest brother. He was not even twenty. Don't ever mention Satan's cave in this house again," she admonished him.

"Sorry. I did not know, Ammachi," he was contrite.

His sleep that night was filled with terrifying dreams; of Jessy lying dead; of the bones in the cave of death coming back eerily to life as in the book of Jeremiah; of Appachen's younger brother drowning in the cave. Most of all he dreamed about two million hapless Christian Armenians slaughtered by the merciless Muslim Turks.

> *The Kurds stole our young women and sold them to the rich Turks who owned estates along the Bosphorus. The strong ones were forced to work as slaves in the fields. The beautiful and pretty were destined for the harems. Our copious tears were more than the waters of the Bosphorus.*

> *The Ottomans took our men and women, and even children, to the middle of the Bosphorus and drowned them for sport. Beneath the beautiful, blue waters the Bosphorus hides a deadly, cruel secret.*

> *Our dead bodies floated down the Kara River, a branch of the Euphrates, the river that flowed beside Paradise. We drowned in our tears, we submerged in our sorrow, as they killed our children.*

He woke up earlier than usual, finished all the morning chores in the cowshed and had a bath. As he walked back from the outhouse, he passed Appachen sitting on the pebbles of the courtyard on his haunches, despite his age, interweaving the leaves of the coconut tree into thatch for the roof. He marveled at his grandfather's skill in crisscrossing the leaves so tightly as to make them watertight to resist the heaviest monsoons.

"Appacha, the milk is reducing day by day," Kuriakose said.

Appachen grunted. "I will call the veterinary fellow to come."

College was a somber affair for the next two days. The sudden death of Jessy, even though she was an introvert who had kept to herself, had cast a pall on everyone. The saving grace was Professor Iyer's masterful lectures on *The Tempest*. He wished he had not missed the opening class.

The notes in his journal for the month of March were significant. King Faisal of Saudi Arabia was shot and killed by his own nephew. The Viet Cong army of North Vietnam made inroads into American-controlled South Vietnam, inching closer to Saigon. Fratricidal massacres were taking place in Ethiopia and Cambodia.

***

When Friday dawned, the thoughts of his meeting Armine the next day pulled him out of the melancholic mire he had been in since Jessy's sudden death on Wednesday. Kuriakose decided to return the favor.

"Ammachi, I'm meeting a friend tomorrow morning. Can you cook lunch for me and my friend?" asked Kuriakose.

"What time will he come?" asked Ammachi.

"Actually, we are going to sit by some paddy field and study together. Lunch packets would be better."

Kuriakose felt guilty about lying but he did not know how to tell his grandmother about meeting a young woman, that too almost a foreigner. According to the custom, all marriages were arranged. Go-betweens connected the two families, and the boy and the girl met each other for the first time only the day of formal betrothal. That was when the dowry that the girl's family had to pay was also negotiated. For a young man to meet a young woman clandestinely without any chaperone was unheard of.

"What do you want me to cook?" asked Ammachi. "Fish or beef?"

"Beef. But please reduce the *masala*, Ammachi. My friend doesn't like it if the food is too spicy."

"Is he a *sayp* (white man)?" asked Ammachi in mock irritation but Kuriakose only smiled.

"Will it be ready by ten o'clock?"

"If you can get me the meat by seven o'clock, it will be."

Refrigerators were unheard of in those days. Only the very rich in the cities had them. The heat caused any food left unconsumed at the end of the day to turn stale and rancid by morning. He had to buy the meat in the morning.

Just after dawn on Saturday, he crossed the bridge over the Pamba River to go to the big market at Kozhencherry town. He chose the best cut of meat and hurried back to Ammachi. He was so excited at the prospect of meeting Armine that he could not do any reading. Instead, he busied himself by sweeping the leaves and chicken droppings off the pebbled front yard. Radio FEBC's *Morning Coffee* program played on the Telefunken radio as he worked. He then cleaned the cowshed and mixed the feed for the cows. As he worked, the aroma of Ammachi's cooking wafted out to him along with the smoke that seeped through the eaves of the house.

By the time he had bathed and dressed, the tall aluminum tiffin carrier was ready on the dining table.

"Rice is in the bottom two containers, beef and vegetables are in the one above that, and the top container has buttermilk," Ammachi explained.

Kuriakose beamed in gratitude.

Carrying the tiffin box gingerly in his right hand and two books in his left, Kuriakose left in the opposite direction towards the college and Kozhencherry. Once he was certain that Ammachi could not see him from the house, he took the narrow path between two adjacent cassava (locally called *kappa* in Malayalam and tapioca in Indian English) fields and swung back in an arc towards the stream behind. He set the books and the tiffin carrier in the grove before walking to the edge of the creek. He did not walk towards the cave of death but waited by the banks for Armine.

Chapter 8: The Orthodox and the Heretic

He did not have to wait long. Armine, astride Qurkik-Jalali, arrived earlier than scheduled. This time she wore a floral print dress with yellow and red roses.

"Barev!" she greeted solemnly.

"Barev!" he shouted back down into the gulch, less self-conscious than the last time.

"Aren't we going to the other side?" asked Armine.

"Can we sit here for some time?"

"Just once through the cave and you are scared of it!" remarked Armine sarcastically.

"No, it is not that. I have brought lunch."

"I am not hungry. I already had a big breakfast before leaving home," said Armine without dismounting.

Kuriakose was perplexed. He had hoped that she would enthusiastically accept his offer but, as he was to learn many times later, Armine was wary of displaying interest in any gifts or offers of help and was reluctant to express her gratitude as well.

"Ammachi cooked it," he said pleadingly.

"Did you tell her you were meeting me?" asked Armine bluntly, seizing the chance.

"No, I told her I was meeting a classmate to study together. She assumed it was a male friend because it is taboo to meet someone of the opposite gender alone."

"So, you lied," said Armine accusingly.

"Yes, I did." He added dejectedly, "But it does not seem to have done me any good."

Armine smiled as she dismounted from Qurkik-Jalali.

"For the sake of your grandmother, I will join you for the meal."

Kuriakose realized that he had forgotten to bring anything to sit on. With Armine's permission, he ran down to the stream to get the thick cotton *dhurrie* from the back of Qurkik-Jalali. He laid it over the roots of the jackfruit tree for Armine to sit on while he sat on the two books. He handed over one of the rice containers to Armine and spooned in the beef, fried ladies' fingers (okra), and the cooked yellow buttermilk over it. He then handed the spoon to Armine while he ate with his fingers.

"How do you like the food?" he asked hesitantly and immediately regretted it.

"The beef is too spicy and the okra too oily," she said. Then, seeing his disappointment, she added, "Your grandmother is a good cook. It is actually tasty."

As he walked down to the stream after the meal to wash his hands, he wished her praise had been more fulsome.

"What books did you bring for me today?" she asked.

"Actually, I did not bring any. A classmate died on Wednesday." He narrated the whole story of what had happened.

"What church do you belong to?" asked Armine out of the blue.

"I belonged to the Syrian Orthodox church but not anymore," answered Kuriakose.

"Are you a Communist?" asked Armine. "This State is full of Christians turned Communist-atheists."

"No, I am not! I am now a member of the Ceylon Pentecostal Church."

"*What!* You changed your church?" Armine almost exploded. Her normal composure was gone. He had not expected her to be this agitated.

"What's wrong with that? My new church is closer to the Bible than any other church," said Kuriakose defensively.

"You have no idea what you are talking about," stated Armine emphatically. "The Orthodox Church is the only true church."

"What about all the superstitions you believe in?" countered Kuriakose.

"Superstitions?" Armine was furious. "You Pentecostals believe in speaking in tongues, refusing medical treatment, and being bitten by snakes. That is not superstition?"

"What about rituals then?" asked Kuriakose.

"They are not rituals! They are traditions handed down from the beginning of Christianity," Armine said stoutly.

"Nonetheless they are man-made traditions."

"Your drum-beating during the worship service is a man-made tradition too! You use the powerful drum beats to intimidate people." Armine was clearly nettled by Kuriakose's derision. "The Orthodox traditions go back to apostolic times. They have been carefully preserved. If it was good for the apostles it is good for us too," she continued.

"Let me ask you something? What do you think of Martin Luther?" asked Kuriakose.

"He must be burning in hell for what he did. He caused dissension in the church."

"I am so shocked by what you just said. I don't know what to say. I don't want to argue ..." Kuriakose threw in the towel.

Armine was not done yet. "What about icons? Do you reverence icons?"

"No! No way!" Kuriakose objected vehemently.

Armine's response was just as forceful. "You know what you are? You are an iconoclast and a heretic!"

Kuriakose was too stunned to respond. He did not want to argue with Armine anymore and only stared at the ground. Armine realized also that she had pushed him too far. For some time, they sat quietly letting their emotions subside.

"What Orthodox Church do you belong to?" asked Kuriakose breaking the silence.

"The Armenian Church, of course! The Armenian Apostolic Church is the Orthodox national church of Armenia!" said Armine joyously.

Then she added. "Do you know that Armenia is the oldest Christian nation in the world?"

"Really? I did not know that," said Kuriakose skeptically.

> *King Trdat III was a pagan king who worshiped many gods and was against Christianity. Once, when he ordered a soldier to lay a wreath at the statue of the goddess Anahit, the soldier refused. That soldier was Gregory (Grigor) who later become Saint Gregory the Illuminator (Grigor Lusavorich).*
>
> *St. Gregory was tortured and cast into Khor Virap, a deep pit, in the Ararat plains near the historical city of Artashat. While he was in the pit the cruel King Trdat III had Rhipsime, a virgin nun who refused to marry him, and her thirty-four companion nuns tortured and killed. King Trdat III was then struck by a vile disease and he began behaving like a wild boar. The King's sister remembered St. Gregory in a dream, and he was brought out miraculously alive after thirteen years in Khor Virap. When St. Gregory healed him, King Trdat III accepted Christianity. The King issued a decree in 301 AD adopting Christianity as the state religion, making Armenia the first Christian nation in the world."*

"The whole nation embraced Christianity. All Armenians are Christians."

"*All?* The *whole* country?" asked Kuriakose in disbelief.

"Yes, the whole country. St. Gregory was the first bishop of the Armenian Apostolic Church."

"I never heard this story before. Did you know that Christianity came to Kerala even before that? St. Thomas himself brought the gospel to this part of the world. He was martyred near Madras in 53 AD."

"Yes, I learned that at Church. All the Orthodox Churches here claim they are directly descended from the first Church established by St. Thomas. When did your family become Christian?" asked Armine.

"We are not recent Hindu converts. My family traces our Christian lineage all the way back to the visit of Saint Thomas," said Kuriakose with some pride.

"And you still left the Orthodox Church," stated Armine contemptuously.

Kuriakose did not have an answer.

"Tell me. Why did you leave your father's church?" asked Armine in a softer tone.

"I left the Orthodox faith on Biblical principles. I could not understand portions of the liturgy which was in Greek and Syriac. In my first year at college, I had a Pentecostal friend. He told me about true Christianity. I also listened to gospel broadcasts on the radio by evangelists from America and England."

"True Christianity?" mocked Armine. "Don't make me laugh. All Protestants are heretics."

"Please let us not argue about religion anymore. Can we talk about something else?

"What did your grandparents say when you left the Orthodox Church?" asked Armine ignoring Kuriakose's request.

"They were very sad. Grandfather was heartbroken. He is a Sunday School teacher. He has a short temper but regarding my conversion, he was so devastated he did not even say a word."

"You should not have done it."

"What can I do? Religion is a personal thing and I must act according to my own convictions."

"Were your parents also Orthodox?"

"Yes," answered Kuriakose.

"Just imagine how happy they would be if you correct your mistake and go back to your own church?"

Although Kuriakose considered the suggestion absurd, he did not say a word. He found it curious that she spoke of his deceased parents as if they were still alive.

As if divining his thoughts, she said, "You must pray for their salvation every day."

This was contrary to the Protestant belief that after death there were no further chances for redemption, but he did not want to enter into another argument.

"Can I ask you a personal question?" Armine was uncharacteristically gentle.

"Yes, please go ahead. I'm an open book," replied Kuriakose.

"How did your parents die?"

The question was like a punch in the solar plexus. He could not answer her straightaway.

Nervously he stood up and paced around for a few minutes. Then making up his mind, he turned to face her.

"Do you remember the Vembanad rail accident eight years ago, when the Bangalore-Trivandrum Express went off the rails and plunged into the Vembanad Lake? They were on that train. They were coming to see me. Instead of meeting them at Appachen's home, I had to identify their bodies at the morgue of the government hospital from among the corpses of hundreds of passengers placed in rows on the floor and covered with white sheets."

Armine looked up at him wide-eyed from the ground where she sat. Her eyes brimmed with tears.

"I am so sorry," she whispered.

Neither of them spoke for many minutes.

They deported us from our own land. They exiled us from our own homes. In the scorching sun, they made us walk hundreds of kilometers (miles), from Erzerum, Arabkir, Sivas, Diyarbekir, Harpout, Tchemesh Gedzak, ... from Van. Even the weak, the infirm, and the old were not spared. Stragglers were mercilessly whipped and struck with rifle butts, and then killed or left to die. Mothers lost their minds when their children were snatched from their hands and dashed on the rocks in front of their very eyes. Girls and young women, stripped naked, walked in shame to be despoiled by the zaptiehs when fancy took hold of them. As we marched painfully in the burning heat towards the Syrian desert, we saw the bodies of our men – fathers, brothers, sons – whom they had led

> *out before us, lying in rows or clusters by the side of our path, executed in cold blood.*

Then she slowly stood up. "It's time for me to go," she said quietly. "Walk with me to Qurkik-Jalali. I will return your books."

Armine touched his bare arm lightly. Her touch was gentle, but it was electric.

"You must go back to your first church. That is the only true church – the Orthodox Church of your fathers."

It was then that Kuriakose lost his head. Just as she turned to mount Qurkik-Jalali, Kuriakose touched her left shoulder from behind and quickly turned her around. Before the surprised Armine could say a word, he had taken her in his arms in a passionate hug. He held her tight, his cheek pressed against hers, feeling the warmth of her body against his. Armine who had been tense and rigid at the start relaxed and for a few moments reciprocated his ardor. But just as abruptly she brought her hands to his chest and pushed him forcefully away.

She glared at him, her face livid.

"What did you just do? I will never see you again! I thought you were not like the others. You have spoiled it all! Why did you do this?"

"Armine, I'm sorry. I don't know what came over me. It just happened. I promise you it will never happen again."

"How can I trust you anymore?" asked Armine.

Kuriakose was contrite. "Armine, I value your friendship. The hug was a mistake. I did not do it deliberately. I am also human. Please forgive me as a Christian."

"Do you know, traditional Armenian women do not even shake hands with men? Our society here has adopted British customs. I broke our tradition when I shook hands with you."

"Sorry. I'm very sorry,"

Armine looked at him for a long time. The anger in her eyes slowly evaporated.

"All right, I will give you one more chance. There will not be another. This is the last chance. You make one more mistake and it will be the end. Remember what I told you. Have no hope of love. It cannot happen."

With that, Armine mounted Qurkik-Jalali and slowly trotted away.

Kuriakose looked at her retreating figure.

> *Full many a gem of purest ray serene,*
> *The dark unfathomed caves of ocean bear:*
> *Full many a flower is born to blush unseen,*
> *And waste its sweetness on the desert air.*

Kuriakose walked back to his home kicking himself for his indiscretion.

Chapter 9: An Alien in Nor Garni

The following Friday he cajoled Ammachi into making special dishes for him early in the morning on Saturday. He could not bring himself to tell the truth just yet. So, he told her he was going on a picnic with a few of his friends. Immediately after waking up, before he went to the cowshed, he slaughtered a chicken and dressed it for the table. By the time he was ready, the aluminum tiffin carrier was on the table with what Ammachi had prepared for the picnic.

After thanking Ammachi profusely he played the same charade again, pretending to go towards the college before sneaking back unobserved to the back of the property. This time he did not wait on his side of the cave. He hurried through the dark cave to the other side and continued walking towards the gigantic rock that hid Armine's village of Nor Garni.

Before he reached it, however, he spotted Armine and Qurkik-Jalali headed up his way. Armine saw him at almost the same time. She reined the horse and waited for him.

"Barev!" he called out tentatively when he was within hearing range, not sure how Armine would respond after the last unfortunate incident.

"Kirakos jan, barev!" was the happy response.

When he reached her, she graciously leaned down from the horse and offered him her hand, but only the tips of the fingers. He took it as a sign of forgiveness.

"You changed my name?" he asked.

"Yes, from now on I will call you Kirakos instead of Kuriakose. Kirakos is much nicer—and famous."

"What was the suffix you added?"

"Oh, that! I forgot to tell you. We Armenians add 'jan' after the name when addressing another as a sign of affection. So, you are Kirakos jan!'

"And you would be Armine jan?" Kuriakose asked doubtfully.

"Yes! That's correct! Jan is used for both men and women."

He set the tiffin carrier and his shoulder bag of books on the ground and fetched the *dhurrie* spread from Qurkik-Jalali to lay out on the ground.

"What have you brought today?" asked Armine.

"It is a surprise. This is a typical Christian breakfast for very special occasions. It is called *palappam*—literally milk pancake. Ground rice is mixed with milk into a thick paste which is then cooked like pancakes in a frying pan."

"For once the curry is not a fiery red," commented Armine.

"It is not spicy at all. There are no green or red *chillies*. It is chicken cut into small pieces and cooked in thickened coconut milk with light spices."

"Here try this," offered Kuriakose holding out the section of the lunch box with the curry. Armine

75

responded by extending her hand and Kuriakose poured some of the gravy onto her palm.

"You are right. It is not spicy. It is almost Armenian!" she laughed.

"Who knows! Maybe it is another of your peoples' contributions to our heritage," Kuriakose shot back.

When he had poured a small portion of the curry into the lid of the box for himself, he handed over the whole section of the tiffin box to Armine. He placed the tiffin box with the rice pancakes between them.

Armine made the sign of the cross before starting to eat.

"That is your prayer?" asked Kuriakose with a half-smile.

"You don't even do that," she shot back. "And never make fun of the cross. You have no idea how many Armenians died for the sake of the cross. Ten of thousands refused to lift their little finger signifying acceptance of Islam. Their fate was worse than death. They were tortured but they still would not convert to Islam."

> As we huddled under the minaret of the mosque, they went to call the khateeb to receive our conversions, to take the rek'ah, the oath to Mohammed. We only had to lift our little finger to save our families and ourselves. Many succumbed to the temptation and become apostates but even more held firm refusing to forsake the Cross and Christ. The vilest torture could not separate us from our deeply treasured faith. The Turks were not the first; there were the Saracens, the Mongols,

*the Tartars, the Kurds, the Aghja Daghis, the
Tchetchens, amongst others.*

She would have gone on if Kuriakose had not
made a pacifying gesture with his right arm.

"Please, Armine jan! Don't take everything I say
so seriously!" he pleaded.

"Don't ever joke about my faith," she answered
evenly. Then in a conciliatory tone, she added, "I
love the crisp fringes of these pancakes. The edges
look like white lace! A perfect complement to the soft
and thick center."

"The *palappams* are fried in coconut oil in a
concave frying pan to make them that way."

"Coconut oil!" laughed Armine. "You cook
everything in that oil, and you bathe in that too!"

"You are making fun of my culture now,"
Kuriakose replied in mock seriousness.

Kuriakose was secretly glad that she had not
criticized the food today.

After the meal, Kuriakose unwrapped the books
he had brought. This time it was the *Collected
Poems of Byron,* another anthology of poems, and
the novel *For Whom the Bell Tolls.*

"I like Byron's poems but don't subscribe to his
morals," said Armine.

"You seem to know a lot about English poetry,"
said Kuriakose in admiration.

"It is all due to my father. He loves books. His
collection of books is almost the size of a college
library."

"I'd love to see your father's library someday."

"How about today?" asked Armine with a big smile.

"Really? Today?" blurted out Kuriakose in surprise.

"Yes. If you have the time we can go today. But we will need to leave right away."

"How do we get to your house from here? Your village looks so far away."

"Since you obviously don't know how to ride a horse, I have arranged something else for you."

But plead as he might she would not reveal what the alternative was.

"You can leave the tiffin carrier and your bag here and pick it up on the way back. I have brought for you to take back the books you lent me the last time."

Armine mounted Qurkik-Jalali and started the downhill descent. Kuriakose followed on behind. The slope was not difficult to navigate but the randomly strewn rocks resulted in a zigzag trail.

"Are you all right?" called out Armine. "There's just a little more left."

Sure enough, after ten minutes they rounded the hill and to his surprise Kuriakose surveyed, not stones and forest brush, but cultivated, rolling land. There were plots of cassava (tapioca) and mango, cashew nut, *sapota*, and other fruit trees that Kuriakose did not immediately recognize.

Sensing his thoughts, Armine explained. "Apricots, pears, peaches, plums, and the most Armenian of all fruits— the pomegranate! We even grow grapes!"

"I feel as if I'm in a foreign land. I never knew those fruits could grow here. If Appachen knew he would have planted them."

"The saplings came all the way from Armenia by sea. But here is the bigger surprise for you," said Armine dismounting.

She then entered the fenced tapioca plot and brought out a bicycle.

"I'm sure you know how to ride a cycle. I will go ahead on Qurkik-Jalali and you follow me on the cycle."

This beaten path wound between fenced-in tapioca plots and open vegetable and corn lots bordered by fruit trees. He noticed right away that the ubiquitous coconut and the tall, pencil-like areca nut trees were conspicuous by their absence. What fascinated him most were the terraced paddy fields, which he had not even heard of before. After almost thirty minutes of navigating through a maze of vegetation, they were suddenly in the clear, on the very edge of the hamlet he had seen from a distance for the first time two weeks ago.

Armine stopped and dismounted. Kuriakose came up alongside and stood still straddling the bicycle but with his left foot planted on the ground.

"This is too beautiful for words," gushed Kuriakose.

"It is my heaven," Armine said quietly. But she let out a sigh that Kuriakose did not understand.

"What is that strange building in the center?" asked Kuriakose pointing.

"That's our Church. It is constructed in the traditional Armenian design."

Instead of walking through the center, they went towards the right on a path that circled the hamlet. Soon enough they reached Armine's house.

"Lean the cycle against the shoe-flower tree," said Armine. "Wait here while I take Qurkik-Jalali to her stable."

While Armine went around to the rear of the house, Kuriakose turned around to look at the route they had taken. It was a magnificent view of cultivated land slowly rising to the barren, rock-studded high wall with only the blue sky and white clouds above it.

Soon Armine was back. As they stepped into the house Kuriakose was amazed at how European the décor and the design were. The spacious sitting room he entered had a large sofa and two comfortable single-seaters. From the central room, three closed doors led out to the other rooms. He could hear Western classical music playing in one of the closed rooms.

"Mayrik jan, I have come!" called out Armine in Armenian.

"Armush jan!" came the reply from the directly opposite the front door.

Indicating to Kuriakose to be seated on the large sofa, Armine stepped into the back room. Kuriakose looked at the walls on which hung faded photographs of what appeared to be public figures. He also noticed a large, framed collage of photographs of dead bodies and realized immediately that these were of the genocide that Armine had told him about. Next to it was the painting of a towering, snow-capped mountain that rose straight from a flat plain into the azure blue sky to break through the white clouds above. Just as he was getting up to take a closer look the door opened, and Armine entered the room with a serene lady who Kuriakose immediately guessed from the similarity was Armine's mother. Armine's mother wore an ankle-length house dress the flowers of which had long since faded.

"Barev," said Kuriakose rising and folding his hands together in the traditional *namaste.*

"Barev," responded Armine's mother in a gentle, mellifluous tone. Her face was remarkably unlined and beautiful. Armine owed her beauty to her mother, Kuriakose reckoned.

"This is my mother. I call her affectionately Mayrik in Armenian. Mayrik doesn't speak English or Malayalam, but she can understand both languages to some extent."

Mayrik whispered something to Armine who shook her head in negation before walking over to the closed room from which emanated classical music.

"Who is the composer of that music?" asked Kuriakose.

"He is an Armenian composer by the name of Aram Khachaturian. The surname is written Khachaturian but pronounced Khachatryan. He is still alive and lives in Moscow," explained Armine.

> *Aram Ilyich Khachaturian, a son of the Armenian diaspora in neighboring Georgia, moved to Moscow, studied music and became one of the outstanding Soviet composers along with Prokofiev and Shostakovich. Beloved as the national treasure of Armenia he composed the Anthem of the Armenian SSR, Gayane,*

> *and Spartacus among other popular compositions.*

Knocking softly, she called out, "Hayrik jan! Hayrik jan! We have a visitor."

There was no immediate answer and Armine returned to her mother's side. The music stopped. After a few minutes the door opened and an irritated looking, white-haired man wearing linen pants and a long-sleeved, collarless linen *kurta* stepped out. Armine's father had bushy white eyebrows against which rested steel rimmed bifocals. He had long white sideburns and wavy white hair on the sides and back, but the top of the head was bald. He had the air of a man of learning, an intellectual, and also of one who did not tolerate laxity or laziness.

Kuriakose stood up again respectfully.

Glaring at Kuriakose he asked Armine in a stern tone, "Who is this?"

"Hayrik jan, this is Kuriakose. The English literature student I told you about."

Armine's father's face relaxed.

"Ah! I remember now. Which village are you from? Which family?"

"Maramon, near Kozhencherry town, Sir. The family name is Thazhakandathil. I live with my grandfather and grandmother. I'm a second year MA student."

"What is your grandfather's name?"

"Thazhakandathil Abraham Easo."

Hayrik shut his eyes and his forehead furrowed in thought.

"Is he the retired school teacher who manages the cooperative bank and teaches Sunday School in the Orthodox Church?"

"Yes, he is my grandfather."

"I met him when I was in the government. He was the chairman of the village council. He is well-respected in the community. How many brothers and sisters do you have?"

"I don't have any brothers or sisters. I am the only son. And I am an orphan," Kuriakose answered.

Armine's father's face softened into a look of kindness and sympathy.

"Sit down. Armine's Mayr will serve you coffee. You must get home before dark."

With that, he went back to his room and closed the door. The sound of Khachaturian's music wafted from behind the closed door.

"My father is at heart a very kind man," said Armine. "Let me give your books to father."

Chapter 10: Ter Samvel and Family

When Armine and her mother returned to the kitchen, Kuriakose got up to look at the photos on the wall. The grainy photographs of the corpses of women and children broke his heart. He was reminded of the corridor of the hospital morgue where the bodies of his father and mother and other victims of the train accident had lain in a long row.

'That was an accident. This is deliberate massacre—the inhumanity of man against man,' he told himself. 'How heartless are the Muslim Turks!'

"Here comes coffee!" announced Armine as she entered the room along with her mother carrying trays.

She set two cups down and poured thick coffee from a conical vessel with a long handle.

"This is how we make our coffee. This utensil is called a *jazzve*."

Mayrik set down two plates filled with sautéed eggplant, tomato, fried chicken morsels, olives, and slices of cheese.

"Eat. We don't have much time," said Armine.

Kuriakose liked everything except the cheese. "What is this?" he asked.

When Armine explained what it was, he replied, "This is the first time I have eaten cheese. I hope you don't mind, I cannot eat more."

"Our palates have been trained differently. I could not eat the spicy food of yours. So, we are even."

"That food wasn't spicy. If you thought that was spicy you should try our authentic fare."

"Looks like you don't like olives either," observed Armine dryly.

"That is another first for me. What oil do you use for cooking?"

"We prefer olive oil, but it is expensive and hard to get. If someone goes to Calcutta or Madras, they bring it. Otherwise, we use refined oil."

Kuriakose noted with happiness how much more polite and mild Armine was in her own home than when they met outdoors.

When he had finished, she said, "I don't want to push you out, but you have a long trek back. Say goodbye to Hayrik before you go."

Armine knocked on the door and again the music stopped and after a brief wait the door opened. Armine explained that Kuriakose was leaving. Standing at the door of the study Hayrik addressed Kuriakose.

"Armine told me of your love for books and that you want to see my library," said Armine's father.

With great eagerness, Kuriakose rushed over. What he saw amazed him beyond words. Floor-to-ceiling bookshelves covered the walls except for the double window on the outer wall. The books were labeled and neatly arranged.

He did not hear the door close behind him. Armine's father and he were alone in the room.

"Sir, you take good care of your books," said Kuriakose respectfully in awe.

The compliment was ignored.

"What are your intentions?" asked Armine's father bluntly.

The question took Kuriakose by surprise.

"Nothing, Sir. Nothing," he stammered.

"Your grandfather is a very godly man. I met him several times in the government office when I was working." After a pause, he added, "Since you are from a good family, I will let you meet my daughter— but only on one condition. You have to come to our house. I cannot allow her to come to your side. Is that clear?"

"Yes, Sir."

"She has no one in the village with her level of education and intellect. You are welcome in our house at any time. I want you to know that Armine is engaged to be married to a young man called Armen. The marriage will take place as soon as he comes on leave from Australia where he is working. So, do not even think of falling in love with my daughter."

For a moment, it seemed to Kuriakose that they were enacting the famous scene from *The Tempest* where Prospero tries to protect his daughter Miranda from the young man Ferdinand.

"I will not harm a hair on Armine's head. I will take care of Armine like my own sister," Kuriakose declared.

"As I said I'm letting you meet Armine only because all the educated youth have left for the big cities in search of white-collar jobs. You have to take good care of my daughter. Your friendship has to be completely platonic."

"Yes, sir.

Just then the door opened. "Hayrik jan, it is getting late for Kirakos," Armine said from the doorway.

"Remember what I said," said the father before turning back to his desk.

Mayrik had come out of the kitchen. Kuriakose thanked her profusely before leaving.

"Charzhe! Noren hametseq!" said the mother smiling.

"That means 'it's nothing' and 'you are always welcome' in Hayeren," explained Armine. "Another phrase used commonly is *'vochinche'* which literally means 'nothing'."

Armine walked with him to the shoe-flower tree on the border of their property. "You can ride back on the cycle and leave it at the same place. It will be there the next time you come," said Armine.

Kuriakose was about to share with her what her father had told him privately in his study, but just then an obnoxious looking man with a red cloth tied around his head like a bandana came riding by on a horse. Without a word of introduction, he questioned Armine in a sneering, angry tone.

"Who is this *otar*? What is he doing in our village? Is he the same one you have been meeting secretly?"

"How dare you talk to me like that? This is my house—not yours! Who are you to question our visitors? You have no right!" she shouted at him.

Kuriakose marveled at the fierceness of Armine's swift response.

The man glared at Kuriakose with ill-concealed venom before responding to Armine.

"I'll talk to your father about your activities. This is not the last you will hear about this," he replied angrily.

"You don't need to bother. We are coming from my house after meeting my father and mother."

"Who was that?" asked Kuriakose when the interloper had ridden away.

"He is Vilen—my future brother-in-law. He is Armen's older brother."

"His name is Villain?" asked Kuriaose incredulously.

"No, not villain," said Armine laughing. "V-I-L-E-N," she added spelling out the name.

"What a strange name!" mused Kuriakose.

"It is not that strange if you know how the name is derived. It is from Vladimir Ilyich Lenin. V. I. Lenin."

Kuriakose laughed.

Armine asked suddenly. "Have you thought about rejoining the Orthodox Church?" asked Armine.

"No, not really. First I need to really understand what the Orthodox Church is all about."

"Why don't I show you our church today? You can meet the Father the next time."

Armine led Kuriakose to the center of the village. Within a circular fringe of pine trees stood the most unique-looking building Kuriakose had ever seen.

"That is our church. *Yekeghetsi* in Armenian. The center of our village, the center of our life," said Armine reverentially.

Kuriakose surveyed the two structures, both constructed in gray granite. Above the main building was a short octagonal steeple atop which stood a cross. He noticed that unlike the churches he had seen before the transept and the nave were almost of equal length. The structure to the left did not have a door and the steeple above it had openings on all sides. The cross at the top was at the same height as that on the church.

"Is that the bell tower?" asked Kuriakose.

"Yes, it is. We call it *zangakatun* in Armenian. It also contains a cross-stone or *khatchkar*."

They walked to the church. The *khatchkar*, an upright slab of stone with an intricately carved cross, surrounded by motifs of rosettes and other patterns, was awe-inspiring. Armine lit a candle and stood before it in prayer with eyes closed. In the flickering light of the candles within the darkened interior, Armine was angelically beautiful. Powerful feelings of piety and love rose in Kuriakose's heart as he watched Armine pray.

Kuriakose was surprised to find the church door unlocked.

"Anyone can come and pray at any time," explained Armine.

"How often do you pray every day?" asked Kuriakose.

"Every Orthodox should pray in the morning on waking and before going to bed. There are morning and evening prayers."

"How long are these prayers? How much time do they take?"

"Who looks at the clock when praying? You are so strange. How can prayers ever be too long? I think half an hour in the morning and about the same in the evening."

That seemed very long for Kuriakose.

The beautiful icons on the walls captivated Kuriakose. Armine went around reverencing the icons before lighting candles in an alcove near the entrance of the church.

They were about to leave when the front door opened and a person in the unmistakable black vestment of a priest entered.

Armine hurried over to seek the priest's blessings.

"This is my friend Kirakos. This is Ter Samvel, our priest. Ter means a priest-father like Achen in your language," introduced Armine.

Ter Samvel smiled kindly and held out his hand.

"I am happy to welcome you to our church, the St. Gregory Armenian Apostolic Church of Nor Garni. Are you a member of the Kerala Orthodox Church?" he asked gently.

"No. I am not an Orthodox now."

Armine intervened. "He was an Orthodox before, but he is now a Pentecostal."

Kuriakose was grateful that the priest did not chide him for leaving the Orthodox Church.

"I wanted to be a true Christian. I wanted to follow the Bible. I didn't get answers to my questions in the Orthodox Church," said Kuriakose.

Kuriakose saw wisdom and kindness in the burly figure with the bearded rough-hewn face, the bushy eyebrows, and the long, windblown hair.

Instead of discussing theology the priest surprised him with, "Do you have a few minutes? I'd like you to meet my family."

Kuriakose looked at Armine. Armine nodded and said, "Yes, we have the time."

"You can call me Ter Samvel," said the priest as they stepped out of the church. "Everyone calls me Ter Samvel or Ter Hayr."

"My name actually is Kuriakose. Armine changed it to Kirakos."

Ter Samvel only smiled. As they walked up the winding path Kuriakose recognized the other distinctive feature of the village. Every house had an immaculately maintained flower garden. Roses of various hues, lilies, petunias, and a host of others that Kuriakose did not even recognize. When they reached the front of the vicarage two children came running out, screaming with happiness. The younger one, the girl, carried a cat in her arms and behind them came large dog of mixed breed.

"These are my youngest two children—Varazdat and Varduhi. The eldest, Andranik is studying at a boarding school in Trivandrum. And this is Tikin Karine, my wife," said Ter Samvel introducing his family. "And not forgetting Piso the cat and Chalo the dog."

Tikin Karine was a pleasant-faced, plumpish lady who looked a decade younger than Ter Samvel. She was ever-smiling and gregarious with a twinkle in her eye.

While they waited for the coffee to arrive, Ter Samvel gently queried Kuriakose about his family and his studies. The children Varazdat and Varduhi kept running in an out of the room chasing each other. On the prompting of their mother they came forward shyly to shake Kuriakose's hand giggling all the while.

"Armine is my niece," explained Ter Samvel. I am the younger brother of her father Mikael. If you like to talk about Christianity and the Bible you can come to me at any time. I may not have all the answers, but I will happily share with you all I know."

Along with coffee there was *alani*.

Noticing the unsure look on Kuriakose's face, Armine explained, "These are dried peaches pitted and filled with walnut bits and sugar."

After a very pleasant chat, Armine and Kuriakose took their leave. From the shoe-flower tree, Kuriakose fetched the cycle and rode it all the way to its last stop, the fenced tapioca field.

Chapter 11: Aryunashushan

So it was that the next Saturday instead of meeting outdoors, Kuriakose rode the bicycle to Armine's house. It was still an hour to noon and the day was just warming up. In the far distance, he could see the thick dark clouds of a thunderstorm in the making. He leaned the cycle against the shoe-flower tree before walking up to Armine's front door. On an impulse, he plucked a blood-red flower.

"You are early!" Armine said crossly.

Seeing his crestfallen face, she added, "Barev. It is only that I didn't expect you for another hour."

"Barev, Armine jan, I came early hoping to get a chance to talk to your father about books. It will also rain today. See the thunderclouds?"

"It is only the middle of April. The monsoon is still two and a half months away," she said dismissively. "What are you doing with the flower?"

"The flower is for you," Kuriakose said holding out the flower self-consciously.

Armine hesitated for a moment. She blushed as she accepted the flower. "Remember, it does not mean anything—anything at all. I'm accepting it because I don't want to embarrass you by refusing.

That's all." She stood aside for him to enter the house.

"I thought it is not the custom of Malayalis to give flowers?" Armine asked with a glint in her eye.

"No, it is not. The Hindus carry flowers in the morning to their temples for offering to the deities for *puja* rituals and for decking their idols at home," said Kuriakose.

"Yes, while I studied at Mother Mary's College, I remember seeing men, women, and children wandering about in the early morning plucking flowers from other people's gardens without their permission. As long as it was for their idols, they did not think stealing was a crime!" she laughed.

"That is a common thing. It is not considered stealing here."

"Taking what is not yours is stealing," Armine was adamant.

Kuriakose changed the subject slightly. "You know, women love placing jasmine flowers in their hair," Kuriakose said.

"Yes, I remember girls in college with wreaths of jasmine flowers in their hair. They smelt like a walking garden. Nobody wears perfume here. At least it is better than the artificial talcum powder which men and women seem to use in excess here."

The door to the study was closed. There was no music playing this morning. The house was deathly quiet.

As if reading his mind Armine said, "We cannot disturb Father today. He has been in his study since morning."

"Is he writing a book?" asked Kuriakose.

"I don't think so. He likes to study books on the history of the Armenian diaspora. He salvaged many rare, out-of-print books from Calcutta and Madras when there was an exodus of Armenians in the fifties. It is a long story. I will tell you later."

When he looked towards the door to the kitchen Armine added, "Mother is lying down. She gets acute stomach pain sometimes. We thought it was appendicitis, but it is not."

They stood around awkwardly in front of the pictures of the genocide. It was Armine who broke the uneasy silence.

"After you left the last time, Father told me about the conversation he had with you. I cannot come to your side anymore," Armine said impassively enough but Kuriakose detected a trace of regret.

"He has allowed me to come and meet you here. But today does not look like a good day." Kuriakose swung the shoulder bag to the front and began taking out the books he had brought.

"I have an idea. Let's go outside. That way we won't disturb Father and Mother," Armine suggested.

"Are you sure? Father wanted me to meet you only in the house in their presence."

"Don't worry. Being outside in my own village is all right. We are more like an extended family here. It is only that I can no longer come to your side."

Armine led the way through the kitchen to the back door. Kuriakose was stunned by the picture-perfect kitchen garden at the back of the house. He could see eggplants, tomatoes, ladies' fingers, onions, squash that hung from a wire-mesh overhang, and pumpkins that carpeted the ground. The flower garden was to the right. There was a variety of plants, some of them in cutaway tin cans.

"Mayrik loves gardening. Since we live so far from the nearest town we need to grow as much of our food as possible ourselves. Come, I will show you a very special flower. Have you seen that one before?" asked Armine pointing towards a red lily.

"No, this is the first time I've seen it. What is it called?"

"It has a beautiful sounding name— *aryunashushan*. Literally blood lily. It is from Armenia."

'It wouldn't be a hyperbole to say that you are rarer than that flower, Armine jan,' thought Kuriakose.

To the left of the vegetable garden, Kuriakose saw Qurkik-Jalali and another imposing black stallion in the stable.

"Sevuk or Black Horse is my father's," said Armine as if reading Kuriakose's mind. Qurkik-Jalali let out a high-pitched neigh when Armine stepped in to get the *dhurrie*.

Sounds of squealing and snorting greeted them as they walked further down the path.

"That's the pigsty and behind that is the cow pen."

The pen was empty. "You don't have any cows now?" asked Kuriakose.

"We don't keep our cows tied up like you do. We let them roam free."

"What about your crops and vegetables?" asked Kuriakose.

"We have pasture lands for grazing cows and there are cowherds who tend them. They bring them home in the evening. Vilen is a cowherd and a farmer. He studied only up to the primary level."

Armine stopped when they reached a small clearing. As she bent down to spread the *dhurrie* on the ground, her auburn hair fell forward around her face and the rays of golden sunlight streaming in through the leafy awning turned it into a shimmering halo. Kuriakose watched spellbound as Armine knelt down on the *dhurrie* to straighten the creases. Her svelte hips stirred the embers of desire in him. Her auburn hair fell around her face as she bent down exposing her fair sculptured neck.

"You are beautiful!" he blurted out spontaneously without thinking.

Armine's reaction was swift. She lithely jumped to her feet and faced him.

"Kirakos jan, don't start anything. Have you forgotten your promise so quickly? You are on your last chance. You also promised my father. I won't meet you again if you behave like this. Don't spoil this," she hissed at him angrily.

Kuriakose took a step backward in surprise.

"Sorry, Armine jan," he stammered. "I didn't mean ... anything ... It was a genuine compliment." His voice trailed off.

But in his head Marvell whispered:

> *The grave's a fine and private place*
> *But none, I think, do there embrace.*

Armine ignored the apology. "Sit down and show me the books," she said as if nothing had happened. They sat at the two corners of the *dhurrie*, Kuriakose with his legs folded under him in the yogic lotus-pose and Armine with her legs demurely tucked under her to the left. In the middle, between them, was Kuriakose's large cloth bag.

Kuriakose was grateful for the change of subject and hastily pulled out *Lyrical Ballads* and *Ulysses*.

Armine was quick to dismiss Joyce.

"I tried reading *Ulysses* a year ago. It gave me a headache. But I think I will enjoy the other book. Isn't this the one Wordsworth and Coleridge published together?

Kuriakose smiled in admiration. "You know so much about poetry!"

He knew that at least for the reason of their being kindred spirits who loved books and English literature he would never do anything to jeopardize her friendship. Anything more than that would be a gratuitous reward that he could only dream of, never expect.

"I brought something to eat," he said tentatively.

"You come to visit me and you bring food? You are my guest," Armine said annoyed.

"I cannot come empty handed. It is nothing," Kuriakose was apologetic. "It is something simple and typical of our cuisine. It is boiled *kappa* (tapioca) and fish curry, the staple diet of the poor people."

Kuriakose was delighted that Armine liked the simple food. As they ate, Kuriakose looked at Armine leaning forward over the tiffin box balanced in the palm of her left hand, her face flushed red from the curry, and he knew right away that he would always love her deeply even if that love would never be requited or come to fruition.

"I took out all the *chillies*," he said.

"It is still hot," was all Armine said though she seemed to like it.

"Did you see the National Bank of India's advertisement?" he asked.

"You know papers reach us a week late," she said reprovingly.

"Sorry, I keep forgetting this is Shangri-La," said Kuriakose in an attempt at levity.

Armine ignored the humor. "James Hilton wrote two of the most heartwarming English books— *Goodbye, Mr. Chips* and *Lost Horizon*. He was a great man."

"Did you know that he ended up writing screenplays for Hollywood and died in California?" asked Kuriakose.

"Don't spoil my image of him," said Armine. "He must have done that to earn a living."

"Talking about earning a living, will you apply for the probationary officer's job at the National Bank?"

"The advertisement you just mentioned?" asked Armine.

"Yes, there are two hundred vacancies. It is an all-India competition."

"There will be *lakhs* of applicants from all over the country. I don't think I am smart enough to be one of the few selected," Armine said without any enthusiasm.

"There is no harm trying. They have to select two hundred persons out of all the applicants. Who knows, it might be you," Kuriakose tried to encourage her.

"I know my limitations," Armine was adamant.

"English is one of the three tests. The others are logical reasoning and general knowledge. You are good at all three."

"The logical reasoning paper has arithmetic and I was never good at math."

"But you can beat everyone in the other two subjects!" Kuriakose was emphatic.

"Where is the exam center?" asked Armine.

"The nearest one is in Cochin."

"I will ask my father," said Armine and that was the end of the subject.

Overhead, a crow spotted the food on the ground and started cawing loudly. Other crows arrived in quick succession and soon there was a murder of them in full cacophony.

"We need to feed nature first when we eat outside. We forgot to do that," said Kuriakose throwing the pieces of hardened *kappa* that remained unconsumed as far away as he could. The crows descended in a swarm.

"Let us go home and have some coffee," suggested Armine getting up. Kuriakose was again struck by how graceful her movements were. But he bit his tongue and didn't say a word.

He gathered up the things and folded the *dhurrie*. As they walked back towards the house there was a pitter-patter in the leaves over their heads and raindrops began to fall. Armine began to run. Kuriakose followed but could not keep up with her pace. He marveled at how athletic she was even though she looked feminine and ladylike.

Mayrik was cooking in the kitchen when they came back. She smiled wanly at Kuriakose and he guessed that she was still in pain. The rain came down in right earnest, drumming a high crescendo on the corrugated iron roof.

"We just made it back in time," Kuriakose observed.

"You can't go in this rain. The cave of death will be full. I will go and make some coffee."

Kuriakose felt a twinge of anxiety about the cave of death but he remembered that a single rain did not raise the level of the creek for long.

Armine brought the *jazzve* and cups on a salver.

"What I wanted to tell you when we were outside, I could not because of the rain. It will have to wait till the next time."

"What is it Armine jan? Please tell me now." Kuriakose's curiosity was kindled.

"No, not today," Armine would not be moved.

Kuriakose waited a moment to see if she would change her mind but he knew by now that once she made up her mind, she never changed it. He burned with eagerness to know but had no option but to wait till Armine thought it fit to tell him. He decided to try a new tack.

"Armine jan while we wait for the rain to come down a little why don't you tell me about how Armenians came to this land of Kerala?"

Armine looked up abruptly. There was a light in her eyes.

"That I gladly will! It is a surprising story you need to know."

Vasco da Gama the Portuguese is credited with the discovering the sea route to India. He landed in Calicut on the Malabar Coast of Kerala on the 20th May 1498. But that honor actually belongs to Mar Thomas an Armenian who reached the same shore at Crangannore a full seven hundred and eighteen years earlier in 780 when a Shiv Raman was the ruler of that kingdom. Mar Thomas amassed a huge fortune trading in pepper, cinnamon, cardamom, and other spices. Armenians in Kerala flourished in their trade, but their inflow rose dramatically during the Mughal period in the 16th century. On one of his incognito tours within his realm, before his son Jehangir was born, Akbar the Great adopted the son of an Armenian merchant. This connection brought many Armenians to Agra. The birth of Jehangir is credited to the construction of the Armenian Apostolic Church in Agra. Their proximity to the Emperor and the favors he bestowed on them caused the Armenian traders to become wealthy and prosperous and, not surprisingly, as a result, stir jealousy in the hearts of the upper-class natives.

Chapter 12: A Catechism of Sorts

By then the rain had thinned out almost to a mild drizzle. Kuriakose decided not to take any books back with him because of the rain.

As they stood by the shoe-flower tree, Armine asked Kuriakose.

"When was the last time you cried, Kirakos jan?"

The question caught Kuriakose off-guard. He leaned the cycle back against the tree and turned to Armine.

"I know men are not supposed to cry but I cried like a child when my parents died," he said choking.

"That's understandable. The death of our loved ones makes children of us all," Armine replied.

"No, that's not it all. It was neither their death itself nor the identifying of their bodies in the long line of bodies at the morgue that did me in. It was the kindness of my grandfather," Kuriakose explained.

"I don't understand."

"You see when Appachen received word of the accident he sent a telegram at night to my school to send me home immediately. He didn't mention the accident—only that my father was taken ill and was at the hospital. The school authorities put me on the first train the next morning. I took a bus home from the station to Kozhencherry. From there I went on foot to my grandparents' house at Maramon. When I passed by the cooperative bank where Appachen worked, he was standing outside the locked front door waiting for me. I asked him how my father was, and he said everything was all right. He told me to go home and that he would come as soon as he finished some urgent work. I hurried home relieved that my father was all right but when I reached the house, I knew that something was seriously wrong. There was a taxi outside and there was a crowd of relatives I had not seen in a long time. When Ammachi started wailing and the others told me about the death of my parents, I ran into Appachen's bedroom, threw myself on the bed and bawled like a child."

"Appachen's deception must have hurt," said Armine quietly.

"That was my immediate thought. But I realized later how kind he was not to break the terrible news to me on the street."

"But he told you a lie."

"He did not lie. He said everything was all right. And indeed, it was. God's ways are perfect. There was nothing we could do. He said that as he consoled me. After a short while he, an uncle, and me, we got into the taxi and drove all the way to the morgue near the accident site. It took us almost two hours to get there."

"It must have been terrible," sympathized Armine.

"It was. But what was even more terrible was my selfishness. It took me almost two years to realize it was not just my father and mother who had died but also that my grandparents had lost their favorite son and beloved daughter-in-law. Appachen's grief must have been more than mine because he grieved for me and for himself and for my future as well."

"I'm sorry I raised this topic again."

"Don't worry about it, Armine jan. I had nobody to talk to about this. It is cathartic. I better go now."

He moved to get the cycle again but stopped suddenly. Turning to look Armine again he asked, "Armine jan, why did you ask me that question about crying?"

Armine looked at him with wide-open eyes.

"All right, I will tell you. My father has become an alcoholic," she stated matter-of-factly. "I cry myself to sleep every night."

Kuriakose was poleaxed. Words failed him. His face conveyed wordlessly the shock he felt.

"I shouldn't have told you. I don't know what came over me. You better go."

With that, she turned to the house and walked away, once more in control.

Kuriakose's first impulse was to run after Armine and console her but he knew she would not change her mind, she would not budge.

As he rode back towards the cave of death, he remembered the candy he had brought for Varazdat and Varduhi. Getting down from the cycle he turned it around and headed back to Ter Samvel's house.

The children were playing outside in the fresh puddles. Piso and Chalo sat on the *verandah* watching. On seeing him the children ran screaming into the house. It was neither Ter Samvel nor Tikin

Karine who came out to greet him, but their eldest son Andranik who had come home from the boarding school at Trivandrum.

Andranik was tall for his age and strongly built as his firm handshake showed.

"Barev! They told me about you. My name is Andranik. We don't get any visitors from outside. You are the first."

"Barev, nice to meet you! My name is Kuriakose. Is Ter Samvel at home?"

"He is at home. He will come out in a minute. You are a friend of my cousin Armine?" It was more a statement than a question.

"Yes. I brought some sweets for Varazdat and Varduhi," said Kuriakose taking out the candy from his bag. "I did not know you had holidays at this time. Armine did not tell me you are home."

"She doesn't know yet. We got holidays for a week because the seniors have their Senior Cambridge exams. They decided on the break very suddenly."

The children shrieked with delight when Kuriakose handed them the hard candy.

"Shnorhakalutyun!" they cried, laughing, and running around.

"You will spoil the children, Kuriakose jan!" It was Ter Samvel. "They like you. Do you want to talk today?"

"Ter Hayr, if you are free?"

"I will always have time for you. Have you thought further about what the Orthodox Church means to you?"

"I have been thinking, Ter Hayr. But I have many questions to ask. Too many."

"As I told you the last time, I cannot promise to have answers to all your questions. If I had all the answers, I would not be a human being," he said with a disarming laugh.

"I will value your wisdom and spiritual guidance, Ter Hayr." Then he added, "It was good to meet Andranik."

"He arrived here this morning unexpectedly. Since we don't have telephones here, my brother who lives in Kottayam is the point of contact. The school called him last night. He picked Andranik up from the Kottayam railway station and brought him here. Next month he is going to Delhi for a Scout's camp."

Just then Tikin Karine came wiping her hands on her apron. Clearly she had been washing clothes.

"Barev, Kirakos jan! We are happy to see you again, especially the children."

"I am more happy than all of you put together," said Kuriakose.

"Stay for some time. I will finish the washing first," Tikin Karine said before leaving.

Ter Samvel led Kuriakose into the study.

"The Orthodox faith is more a way of life than a church," said Ter Samvel. "Like every religion there are those Orthodox who take their faith seriously and those who take it lightly. But a true Orthodox is humble and modest, always striving to keep the high standards required of true Christians."

"Ter Hayr, that is one of the issues I have problems with. If salvation is by grace, why do we need to keep fasts and read set prayers? Isn't that work and not grace?"

"On the contrary. We pray and we fast because we are saved. As we live a life close to God, we observe these traditions. They strengthen our faith but do not save us."

"Ter Hayr, one of the reasons I left the Orthodox Church was that I did not understand the Syriac and Greek portions of the liturgy. Why can't liturgy be in the common man's language, in my case Malayalam?"

"Liturgy has been handed down to us from our forefathers and we believe they were divinely inspired. We trust in their wisdom and piety. Liturgy is a holy service and I see no harm in using a special language for this. We use a classical form of Armenian called *grabar* and the Russians use Church Slavonic. Both are used only in church. They are like Sanskrit which is not an everyday language."

"The main objection I have is to worshiping icons. Isn't that against the Bible?"

"First of all, we do not worship icons. Our liturgy states very clearly 'not unto idolatry'. When we reverence an icon, we are recalling the life and acts of the person represented by that icon and we often seek the intercession of that saint in prayer."

"But why have icons at all? Can't we just recall them in our minds?" asked Kuriakose.

"Icons are just like the photos of our loved ones we have on the walls of our home. We remember them more vividly when we look at their photos. If we can have photos or paintings of our family and friends why can we not have the same for our Lord,

Mother Mary, and the saints whom we love as much?"

"You have a point there. I never thought about icons in the same way as photos. I agree that they are not 'graven images' but I'm still a little hesitant to reverence them. The other element I'm confused about is confession. In the Pentecostal church where I worship as in other Protestant churches there is no confession to another human being."

"Confession is a very powerful element of the Orthodox faith. To actually articulate, to admit, to admit one's sins and shortcomings to God in the presence of another person is more difficult than praying about it in secret. And it is not just another human being that we are confessing to. We Orthodox believe in apostolic succession. That is our authority goes up the Apostles and to Jesus himself. So, you are actually confessing to God in the presence of a representative of God."

"I'm not sure I will be able to confess. It will not be easy. My sins are too personal. One last question for today. Why does the Orthodox Church use set prayers instead of praying spontaneously?"

"Good question! Have you looked at Orthodox prayers recently?"

"No, Ter Hayr. Not since I left the church. I never prayed even when I was in the church," admitted Kuriakose.

Ter Samvel rose to pick up a book from the shelf behind him.

"Here is a book of prayers by St. Grigor Narekatsi. He was a saint who lived in the 10th century. Take it home and read his prayers and then tell me if they are not the most beautiful prayers in the world."

"Thank you, Ter Hayr."

> *The son of a bishop, Gregory (Grigor) entered monastic life at a young age at the Narek Monastery at Narekavank where he lived all his life. (Hence the name Narekatsi.) He wrote his book of ninety-five prayers in the final years of his life at the end of the first millennium. The Book of Prayers is also called the Book of Lamentations because of the heartfelt nature of the prayers. But most Armenians refer to this beloved book simply as* Narek.

"You see," continued Ter Samvel, "the advantage of using a prayer book is that all the prayers in the book have been carefully crafted, each word carefully chosen. If you use the prayer book daily, you will realize what a big blessing it is. One can, of course, pray in the spirit wordlessly or in one's own words for specific requests in addition to the prayers in the book."

"Ter Hayr, there is something personal I want to share. That day when I entered the church with Armine something happened which I cannot explain. I suddenly felt a great sense of peace descend in my heart. Something clicked. I felt I was in the house of God."

Ter Samvel stroked his white and gray beard thoughtfully as he studied Kuriakose.

Then with a kind smile, he said, "It is not our intellect or our rational mind that brings us to God. True faith has nothing to do with logic. God will move your heart and open your eyes."

"Ter Hayr, you just made a very insightful statement. I left the Orthodox Church for rational reasons, but my current church is not based on logic and reason. I think no religion is."

"Yes, faith is faith and logic is logic. Come back whenever you want to talk more. My brother told me about you and Armine. Our family is grateful for the support you give her."

"It is probably the other way around. Thank you very much for answering my questions, Ter Hayr. With your blessings, I will go home now."

"I will pray for you, Kuriakose jan. May God show you the right way."

Kuriakose went to the kitchen to say goodbye to Tikin Karine and to the children before leaving.

As he sped on the cycle towards the cave of death, he wondered for a moment if he should stop by Armine's to inform her of meeting Andranik, but he decided against it and hurried home.

The rain started again before he got to the cave. He stopped under an overhang, but it did not afford him much protection. In no time at all, he was soaked to the skin. 'It was a good thing I decided not to carry any books back today,' he thought.

The notes in the current affairs journal for April included the fall of Saigon, the American withdrawal, and the raising of the Viet Cong flag over the Presidential Palace. The Socialist Mario Soares became the first democratically elected President of Portugal, the country that once ruled Goa, Daman, and Diu, twenty-eight ironical years after its colony India got its freedom. The *Khmer Rouge* captured Phnom Penh and the purge and massacres began, like the genocide in

Constantinople sixty years earlier. India's very first satellite, *Aryabhatta*, was launched into space from the Soviet Union.

Chapter 13: In Quest of a Job

In the morning as he ran around completing the chores Appachen sat on his haunches on the pebbled front yard weaving the strands of coconut tree leaves into thatch for the roof.

"Appachen, milk is very little today," said Kuriakose as he finished mixing pressed oil-cake feed for the cows.

"The veterinary assistant is coming today," said Appachen.

Ammachi called them in for the morning meal. As he absentmindedly mashed together with his fingers the steamed rice flour, coconut gratings, and ripe plantains, a combination he disliked, Appachen made one of his rare interventions.

"The family from Anjilavelil has come from the Gulf. Go and ask them for a job. Your final examinations will be over in a month. Who will give you a job with an MA English? Even engineers cannot find jobs these days. How long will you sit idle?"

For the first time, Kuriakose felt that his grandfather was seeing him as a burden. The sweet plantain and coconut turned bitter in his mouth.

Ammachi, the grandmother, leaning against the doorpost, ready to serve the men at the table, sensed his hurt.

"Son, Appachen means well. He wants you to get a good job. People who go to the Gulf come back millionaires. You won't get a job here in Kerala. It is not easy here. There are more job seekers than jobs and because of the Communist trade unions nobody wants to start industries or businesses in our State."

"Ammachi, I don't know anyone in that family! How can I simply go and beg them for a job? That too in a foreign country?" blurted out Kuriakose.

Appachen stopped eating to look up from his plate and gave Kuriakose a stern look.

"Obedience is the first step to prosperity. Read the Bible. They are not strangers. Our relationship with that family goes back several generations. Just mention my name and our family name. Try to learn from others who have been successful. He didn't go to college but now has a palace and a car."

Kuriakose did not say a word in response. He gobbled down the rest of the food on his plate and gulped down the coffee. He knew his grandfather meant well. The State of Kerala with the highest literacy rate in the country also had the highest unemployment rate in India. He longed to be independent; to earn his own living and live his own life. He wanted to go as far away from Kerala as possible, to the foreign countries whose radio stations he listened to every day. A sliver of self-pity stabbed his heart. 'If only my parents were alive, I would not have to hear these words.' But he quickly banished the thoughts and went to the well to draw water for a bath.

"Don't bathe immediately after food," Ammachi warned from the *verandah*.

"No, Ammachi, I will fill the water drums first."

He tugged furiously on the rope with a vengeance to draw water from the well; then ran with the filled bucket to fill the converted oil drums in the outhouse. The physical exertion gave his troubled soul respite. After he had filled both the storage drums in the outhouse, he bathed in the tingly cool water.

When he came out, he found the cow on the front lawn and a man retrieving a giant syringe from an icebox on the ground. For a moment, he did not understand what was happening. It was Appachen's visible discomfiture that gave him a clue of what was happening. Artificial insemination was in progress and his grandfather was not comfortable for him to be watching the procedure.

As he went indoors to change his clothes, he heard the veterinarian mention 'Jersey cow from England'.

***

When he reached the Anjilavelil house he realized what Appachen had meant. An imposing three meter (ten feet) high gate protected the two-story garishly painted concrete monstrosity. To its left stood the old thatched-roof house, decrepit but aesthetically beautiful. An elderly servant opened the front door and led him to the sitting room. The plush leather sofas, the mosaic flooring, the chandelier that seemed to have a hundred bulbs ... all stunned him. He had never seen opulence on this scale except in Hindi movies. What amazed him even more, was how cold it felt in the room. It took him a minute to realize that this was due to the air-conditioning. This was the first time he was in a house that was air-conditioned. So far, he had seen it only in expensive private wards at hospitals and at the morgue and in cinema halls. Kuriakose was fascinated by the Arabian rug that was draped on the wall. He could not bring himself to sit on the sofa or step on the carpet in the center of the room although he had taken off his rubber slippers outside the door. Instead, he sat on the folding chair by the door.

The wait was interminably long. The stillness of the house added to his unease. It was deathly quiet. When the door finally opened, he nearly fell out of his chair in surprise. Into the room walked not the elderly friend of his grandfather nor his non-resident son, but a frizzy haired, gum-chewing young girl in shorts and T-shirt. She had a Walkman in her hand and a headset over her ears. He guessed she must have been around sixteen years of age.

The girl stared at him disdainfully but did not say a word. In the land of chaste dressing, this girl was outrageously clothed. Instead of attraction, he felt a strong surge of revulsion. Kuriakose stood up but did not know what to say. Finally, he found his voice. He decided to speak in Malayalam.

"Is your father or grandfather here? My grandfather Abraham Easo of Thazhakandathil family sent me," he said.

"What do you want?" she asked in highly accented Malayalam.

"I ... I ..." he stammered in confusion. He could not bring himself to state the real purpose of his visit. His pride returned. He swore to himself that even if it was the last job on earth, he would not accept it from this family.

"No, it is nothing. I'm leaving," he said and walked out of the room.

As he walked back home, he wondered why his grandfather had sent him to the house by himself. 'Was it for them to see him as a possible matrimonial choice for their daughter?' he wondered.

He compared the impudent girl to the genteel and beautiful Armine and felt a strong sense of loathing.

When he reached home the cow was back in the shed, the veterinary assistant had left, and his grandfather was leaving for the cooperative bank.

"What happened? Did he give you some advice?"

"It won't work, Appacha," he replied, unable to hide his disgust. "Please don't send me to rich people asking for jobs. If it is God's will I will get a job without having to beg for it."

Appachen stared at him in anger but left without saying a word.

The morning's experience increased his determination to succeed in the National Bank recruitment.

***

On Saturday when he went to meet Armine, he carried with him the bank application form he had filled out during the week, the postal order he had purchased for the application fee, passport-sized photos, and the self-addressed envelope.

He was disappointed that Armine did not share his enthusiasm for applying for the job. She repeated the old argument of not being good enough to pass the written test.

"How will you know unless you try?" he asked raising his voice in frustration.

Armenian traders tactically aligned themselves with the colonial East India Company and worked their way into their good books. As a result, the Armenians were exempted from taxes on their trading in lieu of a nominal annual fee. The British also permitted the Armenians to construct churches wherever their population touched forty.

Khojah Gregory, the Armenian cloth merchant from Julfa, took on the native name of Gorgin Khan. He was ambitious and hardworking. He impressed the Nawab Mir Casim so much that he was entrusted with the responsibility of mobilizing and maintaining the Nawab's army. Gorgin did such an outstanding job that the Nawab's army came close to defeating the British in a skirmish. But instead of appreciation for a job well done, Gorgin's success stirred up jealousy in the Nawab's heart. He sent four of his soldiers to enter the tent of Gorgin and slay their Commander-in-Chief, the brave and enterprising Armenian Khojah Gregory, in treacherous cold blood. Khojah Gregory's hard work, spirit of enterprise, and success in an unfamiliar field continues to warm the hearts of diligent Armenians striving to earn a living in foreign lands not their own.

Just then Hayrik came out of his study. Kuriakose scrambled to his feet in respect.

Motioning to him to sit, Hayrik asked. "Is this for the probationary officer's job in the National Bank? When is the last date?"

"The 30ᵗʰ, Sir."

"Armine, apply for this job." It was an order. "Go to Pathanamthitta next week and get the certificates attested at the Sub-Divisional Office. They know me. You can also get the application form typed there."

He paused and then added in a resigned tone that surprised Kuriakose, "How long can we hope to stay here?"

The question puzzled Kuriakose. Before he could think further about it, Hayrik changed the subject.

"Do you know about Byron's connection to Armenia?"

"No," replied Kuriakose. "I know that he fought for the Greeks against Turkey and was a national hero in Greece."

"Don't mention the Turks in this house," said the father in anger. Then softening, he added, "Byron studied the Armenian language and even created exercises for learning Armenian. He could write and speak Armenian fluently. Byron considered Armenian the language given by God."

As he talked Kuriakose's thoughts went to Armine's comment about Hayrik being an alcoholic. He averted his eyes guiltily lest his thoughts be revealed.

"Byron also stayed at the Armenian monastery of the Mekhitarian Monks on the island of San Lazzaro in Venice. He studied Armenian grammar thoroughly while he was there. I don't think Byron believed in the Bible, but he was convinced that Paradise was indeed located in Armenia."

All this came as a surprise to Kuriakose. The Byron he knew was a decadent, dissolute, immoral rake. This facet of Byron he did not know.

"Byron's association with Armenia has not been mentioned in any of the books I read," Kuriakose began.

"If you read his biography, I'm sure you will find mention of his Armenian connection. Tell me, what are your hobbies? Numismatics? Philately?"

"I collected stamps when I was in school and I have a few old coins. But I don't think they are of any value," said Kuriakose.

"Someday I will show you my collection of the stamps of the Kingdoms of Travancore and Cochin which were merged to form the State of Kerala. You might be interested in the coins of these kingdoms and of Tipu Sultan, the King of Mysore."

"They must be very rare and valuable?"

"I think they must be, but I have no plans to sell them. So, the market value does not matter. Tell me, do you play chess?" asked Hayrik.

"I know the rules, Sir, but I am not good at it," replied Kuriakose.

"Tigran Petrosian the world champion is an Armenian," said Hayrik with some pride.

> *An orphan of World War II, he swept the streets of Tiflis to earn a living. Ashamed of his job he would wake up early to sweep while it was still dark and the streets empty. It was a kind aunt and the game of chess that saved his life. He became a Grand Master at eighteen and went on to become Soviet and World Champion.*

At this point, Mayrik entered with coffee and Hayrik withdrew to his study. Armine accompanied Mayrik back to the kitchen and returned with two steaming plates.

"This is the Armenian equivalent of *kappa* and fish. It is cracked wheat and chicken. We call it *harisa*," explained Armine. "But wait for one minute," she said running out of the room.

Armine came back with her well-worn prayer book.

"I'd like to read our prayer before meals," she said. "We need to stand," she reminded when Kuriakose bowed his head in prayer sitting down.

Kuriakose hastily scrambled to his feet. His heart melted as he listened to Armine reading the prayer. There was a divine beauty in the cadence and the intonation. 'Byron must have been right. Armenian must indeed be God's chosen language,' he thought.

Expectantly Kuriakose tasted the food when the prayer was over. It was as bland as bland could be. He tried to hide his disappointment, but he was never a good actor.

"You don't like it," stated Armine.

"No, I like it," Kuriakose said in embarrassment. "It is just that this is the first time."

With some difficulty, he managed to clear the plate. *Harisa* was that rare exception, the only Armenian food that he was not fond of on first taste.

While sipping coffee, he raised the topic of the bank examination again.

"When will you go to Pathanamthitta?" asked Kuriakose.

"Time will show," was Armine's noncommittal reply.

The deliberately indefinite and ambiguous response angered Kuriakose.

"Why do you have to be vague and secretive about everything?"

"And why do you have to be curious about everything I do?" countered Armine.

"This is due in two weeks' time. I was only trying to help," Kuriakose surrendered lamely.

There ended any further discussion. After they had eaten, Armine brought out the books for Kuriakose to take back. As they stepped outside the house Kuriakose expressed a desire to see the priest.

"Not today," was Armine's curt response.

Kuriakose was puzzled. He thought Armine would only be keen for him to meet Ter Samvel again. It frustrated him that Armine adduced no reasons for her decision.

"Will you tell me about your father?" asked Kuriakose. He knew immediately that he had made a mistake.

She gave him a withering look. "I told you too much already in a moment of weakness. I was not strong."

There was nothing more to be said.

They walked in silence to the shoe-flower tree. As he set the bicycle aright and clamped the bag on the rack behind the seat, Armine asked him.

"Do you want to stay for a few more minutes?"

The sudden about-turn surprised him even though he knew by now that Armine could be unpredictable.

All his anger vanished in a trice. He would give anything to be in Armine's company. He picked up the bag again and they walked to the spot behind Armine's house, past the pigsty and the cow pen, past the flower garden where bloomed the *aryunashushan*. Armine had not picked up the *dhurrie* from Qurkik-Jalali's stable this time. Kuriakose sat on the grass and Armine knelt and then leaned back to sit on her haunches as she had done before.

"You did not believe Hayrik when he said that Paradise was in Armenia, did you?" she asked.

"It is not that I doubted him. I don't think anyone knows where the Garden of Eden was. Some theologians think the story is only an allegory and hence there is no real place," Kuriakose hedged.

"But it is in the Bible," Armine said triumphantly.

"Yes, but at church, no one ever said Paradise was in Armenia."

"That is why you should attend the Armenian Apostolic church," said Armine with a seriousness that surprised Kuriakose.

"Tell me more about Paradise." Kuriakose's curiosity was kindled.

> *The Araks river (the Turks call it Aras and the Greeks Araxes) begins south of Erzurum, an ancient Armenian city that is now in the enemy territory of the Turks. The Araks River flows from there all the way to the Caspian Sea.*

One of its tributaries, Hrazdan, originates in the high-altitude Lake Sevan, the most beautiful of all lakes in the world. Along the shores of Lake Sevan are several Armenian churches and monasteries.

Armenia's ancient capital Artashat was built on the river Araks before the birth of Christ.

Even today the four rivers Euphrates, Jorokh, Tigirs, and Araks flow through this valley which is the site of the Garden of Eden.

Kuriakose listened with rapt attention. When Armine ended her story, they walked back to the shoe-flower tree where the cycle was. As he got ready to leave she surprised him again.

"I think I will go on Wednesday," she said.

"Where?" Kuriakose asked uncomprehendingly.

"To Pathanamthitta, where else!" she snapped in an annoyed tone.

Although she did not expressly request his help, he knew that this was her way of asking if he would go along with her. He could have taken a bus from his college and met her at Pathanamthitta, but he would sacrifice anything, even college lectures, to be with her.

"OK. I will come here early in the morning."

Kuriakose pedaled towards the cave of death in a cloud of happiness.

Chapter 14: The First Trip Together

Kuriakose left home at the crack of dawn. They had to get to the check-post before the only morning bus reached there around nine o'clock. Armine was ready and waiting when he arrived an hour later at their home. After goodbyes to her parents, they rode cycles from there to the check-post of the Vandiperiyar reserve forest. Kuriakose felt a great tenderness watching her sinuous body maneuver the ruts with ease. She was dressed in a half-sari in the manner of young girls fresh out of school. He especially liked the white translucent skirt with hieroglyphics that she wore over a white petticoat. The pale-yellow drape of the half-sari demurely covered her upper torso. They were just in time for the dilapidated bus which arrived honking its air horn. His hopes of sitting together with Armine were dashed when the bus pulled up. There was only standing room. Luckily Armine found a seat in the women's section in the front. Kuriakose had to stand jammed between sweaty villagers on the way to morning markets.

In spite of frequent stops to pick up more passengers, in half an hour they were at Pathanamthitta.

"Armine jan, shall we have a cup of coffee before we go to the office?"

"No, let us finish the work first."

They went to the nearest typing institute to have copies of the certificates prepared and to have the application typed. By the time this was done the government offices had opened.

The note Hayrik had given for the Sub-Divisional Officer cut through the red tape and avoided the need to grease the palms of government clerks. In a very short time, their work was all done.

Kuriakose tried again. "Shall we have coffee and snacks before we return?"

This time Armine agreed.

As they sat and sipped *Kerala coffee* Kuriakose was emboldened to ask, "What are the writings on your dress?"

"It is a skirt, not a dress. And they are not writings they are alphabets," corrected Armine not bothering to answer the question.

"Is it Armenian?" Kuriakose was not one to give in easily.

"No, it is Chinese. Invented by Mashtots," she said sarcastically.

Kuriakose was hurt by her mocking. The humor was lost on him.

"Of course, it is Hayeren!" continued Armine. "Why would I wear any other language?" she asked rhetorically.

"The alphabet and the dress are both beautiful," commented Kuriakose. "The script seems to be as complex as that of my language, Malayalam."

Saint Mesrop Mashtots invented the Armenian alphabet in 405 AD. The Vardapet (Archimandrite of the Armenian Apostolic Church) also translated the New Testament and portions of the Old Testament into Armenian. Saint Mesrop is revered by all Armenians because he devised more than the alphabet. He unified the nation and gave it its unique identity. Had it not been for Saint Mesrop's efforts, Armenia would most likely have been fragmented and assimilated by the neighboring nations of Persia, Syria, and others. Armenians owe the preservation of the language and literature of Armenia and the country itself to Saint Mesrop. His contribution to Armenia is much like what the Saints Cyril and Methodius did for Russia. After traveling all over the country setting up educational institutions, Saint Mesrop returned to Vagharshapat (Ejmiadzin).

"Will you teach me to read and write Armenian?" asked Kuriakose.

"Time will show." The same vague, evasive reply.

"Please," pleaded Kuriakose.

"It will depend on how well you behave."

"I will try very hard," said Kuriakose.

"Hayeren is not difficult to learn. It belongs to the Indo-European group of languages. There are many common words with Hindi and Sanskrit. *Hazar* is thousand in both. For ten *tas* and *das*. And *panir* is cheese in Hayeren and Hindi!"

Then changing topics, she asked him, "How well do you know the story of Noah and the flood?"

"I learned that in Sunday School," Kuriakose replied. "It is now almost the end of April. A little over a month before the monsoon arrives in the first week of June. Then even Noah will not stand a chance."

"Don't talk lightly of Noah. He is a saint," remonstrated Armine.

"Sorry, Armine jan. I did not mean to be disrespectful, but the monsoon rains are terrible. Thunder claps and lightning and incessant rain during the day and night. I don't like floods at all. I'm scared of the water and cannot swim. Many years ago, when I was a small boy I was visiting with my father and mother when we had to climb to the top of the roof. The water came up to the edge of the roof and we had to sit there for several hours before the water level came down."

"That must have been scary. Do you know in which country the first rainbow appeared?" asked Armine.

"In Israel?" answered Kuriakose hesitantly.

"You forgot what you learned in Sunday School."

"What is the right answer, Armine jan?"

"Think. If you know the story of Noah, you should know the answer." Armine was not one to give in so easily.

"I'm going to take a guess then. Since you told me that the Garden of Eden was in Armenia, I think the first rainbow also happened in Armenia."

"Your answer is correct," conceded Armine. "But it has nothing to do with the Garden of Eden. The first rainbow was a promise from God to Noah that there never would be a flood of that magnitude again. Since Noah alighted from the ark in Armenia, the first rainbow also should have been in Armenia."

"Noah in Armenia?" Kuriakose was doubtful.

"Why are you surprised? I already told you the story of Hayk. Yes, Armenia. Remember the Ark rested on Mount Ararat? Mount Ararat – we call it Masis – was in Armenia at that time. But it is now in Turkey."

"I never knew that!" exclaimed Kuriakose.

"It may be in Turkish hands now, but Masis will always belong to Armenia and be forever in the hearts of Armenians."

As they got up to leave, she said enigmatically, "What Nor Garni needs is a rainbow."

"But you said you have no floods?" Kuriakose was puzzled.

Armine did not respond.

The bus that went up to the check-post was only in the afternoon at four o'clock. Instead of waiting till then they decided to take the first bus to the nearest point on the main road and walk the five kilometers (three miles) to the check-post.

The umbrellas they carried were no solace for the blinding sun and the high humidity. It was while taking a break midway on a culvert, that Armine opened up without any warning.

"Do you know why I asked you about Noah and the flood, Kirakos jan?" addressing him by name which she rarely did.

Kuriakose surmised that she was going to say something significant.

"It has to do with the new dam being built across the Pamba River. Once it is ready your floods will stop. I still remember you telling me this year will be the last flood for you. Next year it will be the big flood for us. The first and the last." Armine was emotionally overcome.

"I don't understand," said Kuriakose.

Armine looked him full in the eyes. This was the first time he had seen her vulnerable, almost on the point of tears.

"The waters will cover our village. Nor Garni will vanish forever."

Kuriakose was dumbstruck. He had read in the newspapers that the reservoir of the new dam would submerge a portion of the forest reserve, but it had never crossed his mind that that included Armine's village, Nor Garni.

"Won't the government give you compensation and relocate you?" asked Kuriakose.

"You know how government compensation works. They call it gold price, but it is only a pittance. All the corruption and red tape! We cannot even buy a decent house with that money."

"What about relocation?"

"Some bureaucrat decreed that we are encroachers of the reserve forest and we are not entitled to any compensation. My father being a retired government servant, he and the others filed a case and won a reprieve. But they paid us only half of what we should have got."

"You already got the money?" asked Kuriakose.

"Yes, we did. They wanted us to go away. But that money has become a curse."

"How? Why?" Kuriakose was all worked up not only by the enormity of what was going to happen but also by the innate injustice of the whole project.

"It is the money that has made Hayrik an alcoholic. Earlier he drank only homemade wine that he fermented himself. But now he has taken to buying whiskey by the box. He is tired of moving. He had to relocate frequently while he was in the government job. Transfer orders came every two years. He says he is too old to move anymore. He says he will die here."

"We must do something," Kuriakose said.

"What can we do? He was so frugal with money when he worked. Now he is spending all the land compensation on whiskey. The wine he makes at home is not strong enough, he says."

For Kuriakose it was as if his world was ending. Armine, his miracle-friend of two months, and her family would soon be gone. The thought of the destruction of their idyllic life and the threat of destitution facing the people of the Nor Garni horrified him.

As if reading his mind Armine said, "That's why he is pushing me to appear for the bank exam. He wants me to get a job – any job – and get out of this place."

Kuriakose's thoughts went to Armen her fiancé who was in Australia.

Uncannily, this time again, she divined his thoughts.

"My fiancé is facing problems at work in Sydney. He may not come before we are forced to move from Nor Garni. That is why Hayrik wants me to work."

"If you get a job they can also come and live with you," said Kuriakose.

"No use talking about the future. What will happen, will happen. We cannot stop it. Let's go home."

They resumed their trek back to the check-post where they had parked their bicycles.

Kuriakose could not comprehend the imminent disappearance of Nor Garni. All the years of toil and loving nurture would disappear under water. It would be as if the village had never ever existed.

"Armine jan, I need to meet Ter Samvel today," said Kuriakose when they were nearing Nor Garni.

"If Ter Hayr is free, he will definitely have the time to meet you. Belonging to the right Church is more important than worrying about the future. God knows the future. When will you come back to the Orthodox Church?"

"It is not easy, Armine jan. I left the old church for reasons of conscience. I cannot do what I feel is not right."

"Why do you want to meet Ter Hayr then? Don't waste his time."

"Armine jan, I have questions. And if anyone can give me answers to those questions it is him."

"Kirakos jan, will you submit our applications from the post office near your college? It is much closer than Pathanamthitta," suggested Armine.

Kuriakose readily agreed, pleased that Armine appeared inclined to attempt the bank exam.

"Kirakos jan, tomorrow is a solemn day for us," said Armine.

"Tomorrow is Thursday," said Kuriakose.

"It is not the day but the date that is significant. Tomorrow is the 24th of April and we Armenians observe it as the Genocide Memorial Day. We remember the two million of our flesh and blood who perished in the genocide perpetrated by the Turks."

"I'm sorry, Armine jan."

"There will be processions in Yerevan tomorrow and a gathering of a large crowd of people at the Tsitsernakaberd Genocide Memorial. Almost everyone in the city and many, many more from every region will be there. I wish I could have been there."

Chapter 15: The Accident

It was not often that the postman came to the house. When Kuriakose saw him that May morning, his initial thought was that the postman had brought something for his grandfather relating to the cooperative bank. He soon found out to his surprise that the telegram was addressed to him and not to his grandfather.

The message was cryptic.

ANDRANIK HOSPITALIZED DELHI STOP ROAD ACCIDENT STOP COME IMMEDIATELY STOP

Kuriakose shared the telegram with Ammachi, hurriedly changed his clothes, and rushed to the cooperative bank to meet Appachen.

"Who is Andranik?" Appachen asked.

Kuriakose explained that he was the son of an Armenian family near the forest check-gate.

"Is he your classmate?"

"No, Appacha. I will explain all when I come back."

Appachen was sympathetic. "It must be serious. Otherwise, they would not have sent you a telegram. Take a taxi from Kozhencherry and go straight to their house," said Appachen handing over money from the till.

An hour later when he reached the check-post Kuriakose took the only cycle that was there and pedaled furiously to reach Armine's house. There was no one there.

Leaving the cycle there he ran to Ter Samvel's house. He saw from afar people on the *verandah*, including Armine's father.

It was Hayrik who broke the news.

"This morning my brother who lives in Kottayam town received a phone call from Andranik's school in Trivandrum. Andranik had an accident last night in Delhi. He was hit by a car. He is in the ICU at the Ram Manohar Joshi hospital."

Kuriakose was stunned. He had met Andranik only that one time when he had come home on an unexpected break last month. Now he was battling for his life in a big hospital in the nation's capital.

Of all the people he saw, the calmest appeared to be Ter Samvel, Andranik's father. It was almost as if the misfortune was not his own. He talked to everyone without the slightest trace of sadness or anxiety.

Kuriakose went up to Ter Samvel. He did not know what comforting words he could say to a priest.

"How did you get here so quickly?" asked Ter Samvel solicitously.

"My grandfather told me to take a taxi and come here straight away."

"He is a good man. Armine's father told me about him. Go to the kitchen and have something to eat," Ter Samvel said.

Just when Ter Samvel was about to move away to talk to someone else, Hayrik came over and whispered something in his ear. The two of them went indoors.

Armine came out to the *verandah*. She did not seem surprised that he had reached so quickly.

"Kirakos jan, did someone tell you already? Andranik has a head injury and is unconscious. His skull was fractured by a speeding sports car. There is no one from the family to take care of him," said Armine.

"It is very sad," was all Kuriakose could say.

Armine continued. "He does not speak Hindi. He will need help when he comes out of the coma. There are Hayers in Delhi, but we don't know any of them personally. A head injury is not a small accident." Kuriakose saw fear in her eyes.

The enormity of Andranik's plight struck Kuriakose. His initial anxiety turned to extreme dread. He wondered if they would see Andranik alive again. He could not believe that the strong, strapping lad was now lying senseless in the intensive care unit of a distant hospital.

Just then Armine's father called for Armine and she went back inside. A little later she returned.

"I was just talking to Hayrik and Ter Hayr. We have a problem. No one from our village can go to Delhi. Hayrik is the only one who could go but he cannot because of his health. Ter Hayr cannot go because we do not have another priest and he has not traveled anywhere far. Horeghbayr, that is my

Uncle Stepan from Kottayam, cannot go because there is no one else to take care of his business. Even if he or Ter Hayr could go neither of them can speak Hindi."

"But someone must go. Who will take care of Andranik? He is helpless," said Kuriakose.

"I told them you had been to Delhi several times and you know Hindi well enough to get by. Also, you would not stand out like an Armenian."

Kuriakose realized that Armine was asking, in her own usual way, for his help without explicitly requesting it. He was willing to do anything for Armine's sake.

"You want me to go to Delhi?" asked Kuriakose.

"Hayrik said we would cover all your expenses, including the plane fare."

"I will go," Kuriakose surprised himself by volunteering instantly.

Armine smiled. "I knew we could depend on you. Let me go and tell Hayrik and Ter Hayr."

Only after she had gone back into the house did he realize the implications of what he had just committed himself to. He had overlooked the fact that he was in the midst of his preparations for the final university examinations coming up in a month. He had also not sought the permission of Appachen, his grandfather, for the trip to distant Delhi.

Armine led him to the study where Ter Samvel, Hayrik, and the Horeghbayr Stepan from Kottayam were in deep discussion. On seeing him Ter Samvel smiled warmly and Hayrik gravely nodded.

"Kuriakose jan, we are very grateful that you have agreed to go on our behalf to Delhi. God will bless you for this," said Ter Samvel.

"Anything I can do to help, I will," answered Kuriakose.

"Thank you. After lunch is over, we will give you twenty thousand rupees in cash. Please go to Cochin and catch the first plane for Delhi."

***

So it was that, Kuriakose found himself several hours later on the evening train to Ernakulam, the nearest railway station to the airport at Cochin. To save time Uncle Stepan had driven him in his car to meet Appachen at the cooperative bank. After explaining all that had happened Uncle Stepan said, "Since Kuriakose can speak Hindi and since he has been to Delhi for the same Scouts' camp years ago, please allow him to go to Delhi and be with the injured boy, my nephew. Kuriakose will not have to spend a *paisa*."

"How long do you think he will have to stay in Delhi?" asked Appachen.

"We don't have a precise date. It depends on the boy's condition. We are praying that he will survive. It is a head injury. We know Kuriakose has examinations coming up in June. We will arrange for someone else to take Kuriakose's place if there is a delay."

"I am concerned only about his university examination. If he fails, he will lose one whole year. If his marks are low, it will affect his job prospects. But I am happy that he volunteered to help."

"Appacha, I will take some books with me so I can revise while waiting on Andranik," said Kuriakose.

"Use your time wisely, son." Then turning to Uncle Stepan he asked, "How much do you think all this will cost?"

"We have collected twenty thousand rupees which Kuriakose will take with him."

"That is a lot of money. I have known Hovhannisyan since many years ago, when he was a Sub-Divisional Officer at Pathanamthitta. I will permit Kuriakose to go. We need to help each other in time of need."

From the bank Kuriakose and the Uncle Stepan went to the house. While Ammachi prepared *Kerala coffee* for the guest, Kuriakose packed his clothes and books in a small airbag. Instead of the *Malayali* dress of *mundu* and rubber slippers which would have invited ridicule outside the state, Kuriakose packed the only two trousers he had and a pair of shoes. Soon they were on their way to Kottayam railway station. The evening train from Trivandrum was an hour late.

By the time he stepped down from the train in Ernakulam, it was nine o'clock at night. Kuriakose found a cheap hotel close to the railway station for the night. Early in the morning, he took a taxi to the airport. He managed to get a ticket for Delhi on the humanitarian quota when he showed the telegram even though Andranik was not immediate family.

The route to Delhi was not easy. He flew first to Madras on a noisy Avro turboprop aircraft with heavy turbulence on account of the pre-monsoon rains and from there to Delhi on a Boeing 707. By midafternoon he was enveloped in the sweltering heat of Delhi.

The Scouts' headquarters was glad to see a representative of the family. But as Kuriakose had expected, they evaded any responsibility for Andranik's accident.

"Instead of walking on the pedestrian sidewalk he kept running and playing on the roadway. It is a miracle he was not killed," stated Major Gulati the commanding officer.

"I still think it was the fault of the leader who failed to control all the scouts he had in his charge. What about compensation?" asked Kuriakose.

"There will not be any compensation from our organization. Where can we get the money from? But we have the name and address of the driver. If Andranik's family wants to pursue that we have no objection."

Kuriakose was furious. "You are trying wriggle out of your responsibility. The boy was under your care when the accident happened. We will file a case against you if you don't cover all the expenses."

The threat of litigation seemed to rattle the officer. He ordered tea for Kuriakose while he went into a meeting with some other officials.

"My driver will take you in my car to the Ram Manohar Joshi hospital. As for the expenses, I spoke to the other officers. You do not need to pay any hospital bills. That will be paid by us. We will give you forms to sign. You can also stay in the dormitory at the Scouts' hostel while you are attending on Andranik."

Chapter 16: The Abyss of a Hospital

When Kuriakose reached the hospital, he realized straight away why Major Gulati was not being generous. It was a government hospital. The actual conditions belied the fame the hospital had in the country.

Gopalan, a classmate of Andranik, who was keeping vigil in the hallway seemed lost. He did not know anything about Andranik's condition. He only had to wait outside till the next scout came to relieve him.

When Kuriakose saw Andranik his heart broke. The handsome face was puffed up to twice its normal size, the eyes swollen shut, and the head tightly bandaged. The upper torso was bare and intravenous tubes were attached to both arms.

Andranik was not alone. In a room meant for one patient, there were three. There were no curtains separating the three. The stench from the older man's corner was unbearable. The third patient, a construction laborer who fell from the third story of building, Kuriakose learned later, was almost entirely covered in bandages.

When the nurse came and Kuriakose inquired about Andranik's condition the answer was swift.

"Leave the room immediately! No outsider is allowed in the ICU. Only patients. Are we gods to predict the future? How many ICU patients survive? Go out and let me do my work!" the nurse shouted in Hindi.

Kuriakose stepped out of the room but watched from the door. When the nurse took out a large syringe and jabbed Andranik brutally in the crook of the elbow it was all he could do not to rush in to restrain the callous nurse.

But what stopped him was Andranik's reaction.

Kuriakose was stunned when Andranik responded to the jabbing involuntarily with, "De ... de ... de ..." in a loud voice.

'Andranik was not in a coma!' exulted Kuriakose.

He rushed to the office of the doctor on duty. The sight that greeted him shocked him. There were at least ten people in the room, all leaning over the dirty wooden desk, arguing with the doctor. The relatives of the patients seemed on the verge of violence. But the doctor was unmoved. He answered very little and, even when he deigned to answer, the replies were vague and noncommittal. Kuriakose joined the fray but could not make himself heard. Out of frustration he left the room.

Andranik was in the same motionless state as he was before the nurse's cruel injection. He waited patiently with Gopalan till the next scout, Sathyan, arrived to take Gopalan's place. He took the opportunity to buttonhole the troupe leader who brought Sathyan from the hostel.

"Which doctor can I talk to? Andranik is not getting the best treatment. He is not in a coma. He is conscious. I need to talk to a doctor now!" Kuriakose was emphatic.

"I will take you to the superintendent. Here politeness does not pay. One has to be aggressive. Standing in line does not work. Nobody respects the queue system. The strongest wins. It is the survival of the fittest."

The superintendent's office on the third floor was shielded from the public by a nurses' station. An oily man in the politician's garb of white *kurta* and a *Gandhi cap* was talking in a low voice with the doctor.

The doctor motioned them both to sit on the folding steel chairs against the wall.

"It is imperative that the death certificate is issued as instructed by the minister. There will be hell to pay otherwise. You will regret it for the rest of your life." The politician did not seem to care that there were others in the room.

"I cannot compel the examining doctor to write what you want," the superintendent protested.

"The boss does not care how you do it. You are the superintendent and you control your subordinates. Get it done. This is not a murder, for God's sake. All you need to say is that there is no evidence of anything non-consensual and that the woman was not a virgin. Is that too much to ask?"

After the man left Kuriakose was asked without any preliminaries what the problem was. Kuriakose described Andranik's reaction to the needle. "How can he be in a coma if he can feel pain and can respond verbally?" asked Kuriakose.

"Is the patient sitting up and talking? No! He lies unmoving for hours on end. Isn't that as good as a coma? We are not writing a scientific paper here. We are helping ordinary people understand complex medical situations. This is not a textbook."

Kuriakose had had enough. He went to the phone booth in the reception area on the ground floor and called Uncle Stepan in Kottayam.

"Please tell Ter Hayr, Armine, and Armine's parents that Andranik is not in a coma. He reacted verbally to a painful injection. He is definitely not in a coma."

Kuriakose decided to dispense with the scouts. He would wait on Andranik single-handedly.

The scoutmaster was secretly relieved. Now that Kuriakose had reached the hospital, he and the rest of the squad were now free to return to Kerala.

Kuriakose stood beside Andranik's bed. The blood on the bandage seemed to have spread further. Tenderly he took Andranik's hand and held it. When he gently squeezed it, he felt the pressure being returned. Andranik was conscious.

After a while, Kuriakose had an idea.

"Barev," he said softly.

"Barev," came the response from Andranik.

Hope began to rise in Kuriakose's heart. He prayed silently.

"Ov e vor?" (Who is that?) asked Andranik.

"I am Kuriakose," he replied with bated breath.

"Armine's friend? Kirakos jan?"

"Yes!" Kuriakose replied with joy at the discovery that Andranik's cognitive ability and memory were intact. He was even more thrilled to hear Armine's name spoken and the recognition of his friendship with her.

"Don't leave me, Kirakos jan!"

"I won't leave you till we leave this hospital together. I won't leave you ever!" said Kuriakose fervently.

"My head feels like a hundred tons. And everything seems to be moving even when my eyes are closed. It feels like I am on a heaving boat in a terrible storm."

"Try to sleep. God will heal you. We will leave this hospital and go back home together," Kuriakose said with conviction.

After a while, Andranik fell asleep. Kuriakose gently disengaged his hand and went to the door to bring the steel folding chair to the bedside. He pushed his airbag under the bed and laying his head on Andranik's mattress slept the sleep of death. The tiredness of the long journey, the stress of the turbulence on his first ever air travel, and most of all, the shock of the condition of Andranik, all got to him.

He woke up to a scratching sensation on his ankle. He jumped in horror when he saw a fat rat scurry away into the corner. He got up and went to the corner to see whether there was a hole in the wall behind the blue plastic bucket. The revulsion he felt after seeing the rat turned to nausea when he saw body parts in the plastic bucket. The realization that the contents of the bucket had remained there for several hours added to his distress and horror.

He swore that he would get Andranik out of this dump of a hospital as early as he could. But when he thought about all that needed to happen before Andranik was released, he realized how powerless and insignificant his own strength was.

He recalled the conversation he had had with Ter Hayr. Ter Hayr had stressed the humility of the Orthodox faith and how salvation by grace was the core of the Orthodox faith even though Protestants perceived it otherwise.

For the first time since his parents had died, he felt a sense of contrition and of complete surrender. He got up from the chair and prayed standing, in the Orthodox tradition. Peace and hope descended on him. Then he sat down and slept again.

He woke up when the night nurse came with the injection. This nurse was more gentle and understanding. Andranik whimpered only once. When Kuriakose told the nurse about the bucket in the corner, she was apologetic. A little later, a ward boy came to remove it, much to Kuriakose's relief.

Kuriakose rose before the arrival of dawn. After the morning ablutions, he stood by Andranik's bed and prayed from the heart. When he looked at Andranik he wondered if he was imagining things. The swelling of the face seemed to have lessened noticeably. Even as he watched Andranik opened his eyes and tried valiantly to smile.

Kuriakose's joy knew no bounds. He knew this was nothing less than a miracle.

"I can see now, Kirakos jan," said Andranik said in obvious relief. "My head does not feel as heavy as it did yesterday. The floating feeling is much less than before."

Before the team of doctors came on their morning visit, the old man in the corner died. When the wheezing turned to gasps, Kuriakose ran to the nurses' station. By the time the nurse arrived it was too late. The nurse pulled the bed sheet over the dead man's head and left. Two men who seemed in no particular hurry arrived with a gurney half an hour later to remove the body.

In less than ten minutes another patient was wheeled in. This time a thief who had been caught and thrashed within an inch of his life. A policeman chained the foot of the patient to the iron bedstead.

The doctors were impressed by the improvement in Andranik's condition.

"When can he be released?" asked Kuriakose.

"He will need to stay another week at least. But don't worry, since beds are at a premium, we won't keep him a minute longer than necessary."

When the nurses came to change the bed linen and clean the room Kuriakose went quickly to the cafeteria for a cup of coffee.

It was a different Andranik when Kuriakose returned. The nurses had winched up the headboard half of the bed. Instead of lying flat on his back Andranik sat with his upper torso raised against a pile of pillows. The blood-stained bandage on his head was gone. The new bandage looked more like a white turban. His face and body had been swabbed clean. The swelling of the face had subsided further. Kuriakose knew he was watching a miracle unfold.

"I feel ready to go home. I miss Papa jan and Mama jan, Varazdat and Varduhi," said Andranik. "I want to go running with Chalo in the fields."

"We will go back very soon. The moment the doctor releases you, we will leave."

Andranik was hungry. Instead of the saline and glucose fed intravenously, he was given soup and bread.

Kuriakose was getting to know how the hospital worked. By greasing the palms of the clerk in the superintendent's office he managed to secure a private ward room for Andranik.

In the new room, Andranik slept for long periods. Kuriakose did not know if it was because of the drugs or if it was on account of the injury to the brain. While Andranik slept Kuriakose left for the scout dormitory. He shaved, bathed, changed his clothes and washed the dirty clothes by hand. In the dry heat of Delhi, the clothes dried in no time. Before he returned, he phoned Uncle Stepan in Kottayam to convey the good news of Andranik's speed of recovery.

On the fourth day, Andranik walked with Kuriakose's help to the toilet. That was the end of the bedpan.

"Andranik, what can I get for you? What would you really like?" asked Kuriakose when Andranik was back in bed.

"I want an air gun!" Andranik replied with such eagerness that Kuriakose realized that what he craved for might speed up Andranik's recovery. He had been frugal with the money entrusted to him. No hotel room costs in Delhi, no expensive food, or anything else. The only big expense he had was the charge for Andranik's room in the pay ward and the bribe he had paid to get it. The government-subsidized cafeteria at the hotel was cheap.

He went to the city that afternoon while Andranik slept and bought him an imported air gun.

Since the hospital would not allow it in the room, he left it at the scouts' headquarters in safe custody.

Andranik was excited when Kuriakose told him of the purchase of the air gun. He wanted to desperately to see it, hold it in his hands, and test it out. As Kuriakose had guessed, the air gun proved to be the incentive that further hastened Andranik's recovery.

The very next day the doctors asked if Kuriakose wanted to take Andranik home.

"His recovery has been remarkable. But he needs to wear a hard hat to protect the fracture on his skull. We have placed a small metal plate there. We will remove it after the bone grows together."

Their joy knew no bounds. From a hopeless situation, just five days ago, Andranik had made a recovery that was so remarkable it was almost improbable. Kuriakose did not waste any time. He ran out and bought air tickets for travel the next day. He then informed Uncle Stepan of the travel arrangements.

He stood by the bedside while Andranik slept and prayed earnestly with tears streaming down his face. Kuriakose knew with certainty that this miracle that he experienced had changed his life. He thanked the Lord for leading him back to the Orthodox fold.

On the sixth day, they were in a taxi bound for the airport, with Andranik hugging the air gun case for dear life.

But he had to reluctantly part with it on the flight because the airline would not allow an air gun in the cabin. The air gun traveled in the luggage hold.

Chapter 17: Yellow Ribbon

When their flight landed at the naval airstrip that also doubled as the civil airport at Cochin, they were overjoyed to see Ter Samvel and Tikin Karine with Uncle Stepan from Kottayam. There were tears of joy as Andranik hugged his mother. Kuriakose had to caution them about the protective cap that Andranik wore. Kuriakose received heartfelt thanks from all three but Ter Samvel's words touched him most.

"You voluntarily played the Good Samaritan's role today. That is one of the most touching stories of the New Testament. We play both the roles in real life. Sometimes we are the victim, sometimes we are called upon to play the role of Good Samaritan. May all your kindnesses come back to you a thousand-fold!"

"Thank you, Ter Hayr. You are very kind."

"You know, we teach the Good Samaritan's attitude as a special Orthodox virtue. You were quite the Orthodox in this incident. We will always be grateful."

"Ter Hayr, please don't say that. It was nothing."

Andranik sat in the rear between Ter Samvel and Tikin Karine and Kuriakose sat in the passenger seat next to Uncle Stepan who drove the car. As soon as they left the town, Andranik fell asleep leaning against his mother. She put her arm lovingly around him and held him as the car sped through the narrow road.

On the way they stopped at a roadside shop for *Kerala coffee*. They stretched their legs while the shopkeeper poured the hot coffee from glass to glass to cool it.

Instead of dropping him home Kuriakose was driven to Nor Garni.

"You have been through this together with us. We cannot let you go just yet," said Uncle Stepan as he turned the car off the highway towards the check-post.

At the check-post, Armine and Vilen were among those waiting. To get Andranik home they had a horse cart ready with Qurkik-Jalali and another horse. All were delighted to see that Andranik could stand and even walk on his own. Their surprise was so great that Kuriakose guessed they had expected to see Andranik in a stretcher.

It was in a small procession that they wended their home in the late afternoon. Andranik sat cross-legged on a canvas blanket on the floor of the cart with the prized possession of the air gun resting in his lap.

The scene that greeted them when they neared the house amazed Kuriakose. There was music playing and smoke rising from an outdoor fire. For Kuriakose it was as if the song *Tie a Yellow Ribbon* by Tony Orlando and *Dawn* that he had often heard on Radio Ceylon, the radio station in Colombo, had suddenly come to life.

Kuriakose discovered that Armenians were great huggers, unlike the Malayalis who tried to avoid physical contact with another human being. He also noticed that they mostly hugged persons of their own gender. The only one who hugged Kuriakose was Ter Samvel. All the men, excepting Vilen, shook hands with him but none of the women did. Vilen merely scowled at him from afar. Armine was among the first to come and greet him, but she did not give him the slightest indication that a handshake could be hoped for. He would gladly have traded all the handshakes he got from the others for one, even perfunctory, from Armine.

Everybody seemed in high spirits and he soon found out why. Hayrik gave him a fumbling hug and then held out a glass of red wine. Kuriakose hesitated. He had never drunk alcohol in his life. Alcohol was taboo in his branch of Orthodox Christianity and even more so in the Pentecostal church. Only the poor and the depraved drank.

"It is all right. It is only wine. At the wedding at Cana too, there was wine. We are all happy today," said Hayrik tipsily.

Reluctantly he accepted the glass and took a sip. It smelled good, unlike the palm arrack that stank from the toddy shops that lined the roadside. He took a sip. It was pleasant to taste too.

"Drink up, drink up! There is plenty!" chortled Hayrik uncharacteristically.

Ter Samvel intervened. "Don't give Kuriakose more wine. Don't force him to drink," Ter Samvel said softly.

Kuriakose was grateful for the respite. The exhaustion of the long trip and the empty stomach combined to cause the wine to go straight to his head. He thought the whole world was spinning. He saw as if in a dream, Armine rush towards him in concern. The next thing he knew he was being carefully assisted to sit on the sofa. He sat there for some time till his head cleared. Armine brought him Armenian coffee and *khorovats*.

He got up to look for Andranik who was seated in a chair on the *verandah* watching the open-air cooking in the yard. The men were doing all the outdoors cooking while the women cooked indoors. Varazdat and Varduhi were having the time of their life running around. Piso and Chalo were nowhere to be seen.

At the opportune moment, Kuriakose returned the balance of the money with the detailed accounts to Hayrik, who was delighted that Kuriakose had not only been frugal but had also meticulously kept accounts.

Soon everybody assembled for Ter Samvel's blessing of the food.

Then the feast began. Kuriakose had not seen anything like this. Even joyous wedding feasts Kerala-style were quiet affairs with everyone sitting silently in neat rows. Here, there was unrestrained joy. Benches were placed haphazardly around the fire and everyone talked, moved around, and laughed.

Kuriakose learned something else about the Armenian way of life in the next few minutes. Uncle Stepan from Kottayam took upon himself the role of toastmaster and every few minutes one would stand up to say a toast. Some of the toasts must have been funny, guessed Kuriakose, because of the laughter they generated. Kuriakose did not drink any more wine and sipped only sweetened lemon juice instead.

Some of the toasts were for him and he wondered if he was expected to reciprocate but he did not know what to say or how.

Ter Samvel walked over to tell him, "You are the hero of the day—and well deserved too!"

The food was delicious. He had not had meat cooked in this manner, with very little spices, before. There were even grilled tomatoes and eggplant. The best part was the thin flat bread that was so large it was folded over in layers. Kuriakose had fallen in love with *lavash* the very first time he had tasted it in Armine's house. Tikin Karine and Mayrik kept piling food on his plate.

Armine came to sit on the bench by his side. For the first time, he saw admiration and gratitude in her eyes but, as usual, she did not articulate her feelings.

All she said was, "What can I give you? Which dish do you like best?"

Kuriakose looked over the tray she was holding and settled on *pastirma* and *lahmajun*. Armine took his plate and piled it high with food. Kuriakose had never felt so full in his life.

Armine began to sing a soulful, plaintive song that Kuriakose learned later was composed by Komitas.

> *Komitas was a priest of the Armenian Apostolic Church. He was also a musical genius. Had it not been for him much of Armenia's traditional folk music, especially of Western Armenia, would have been lost to posterity. Komitas also set the chants of the*

Divine Liturgy to music. His songs live in the heart of every Armenian. It is in their blood. Soghomon Soghomonyan (that was the real name of Komitas) was born in Turkey and was orphaned at an early age. He was monolingual in Turkish when he was chosen to study theology at Ejmiadzin. He became a priest and took on the name Komitas. He was later elevated to Archimandrite and was conferred the title Vardapet. He was arrested on April 24, 1915, the first day of the genocide of the Armenian at the hands of the Turks. The intervention of the US Ambassador saved his life, but the slaughter of his people caused him to lose his mind. He was moved from Constantinople in 1919 to a mental institution in Paris where he died sixteen years later in 1935.

Vilen nearly spoiled the evening when he came over to the bench and hissed something in Armenian to Armine. Kuriakose guessed that the offensive words related to him and Armine. She turned beet red in anger and jumped up to berate Vilen, who sauntered away with a wicked grin on his face.

Kuriakose realized it was getting late.

"Armine, it is time I went home. I haven't spoken to Appachen and Ammachi in a week."

"Horeghbayr will drop you home," Armine said.

Ter Samvel was also attentive to Kuriakose's needs. Before Armine could make the request, Ter Samvel and Uncle came over to their bench.

"We are not driving you away, but we don't want you to be too late getting home, Kuriakose jan," said

Ter Samvel in a kindly tone. "My brother Stepan will drop you home." Then turning to Armine, he said, "Armush pack some food for Kuriakose to take home for his grandparents."

In another ten minutes, they were off. They rode the pony cart with Kuriakose and Uncle Stepan facing each other, cross-legged on the canvas sheet. A young teenaged boy whom Kuriakose did not know by name drove the cart to the check-post.

When they reached Maramon, despite Kuriakose's protests, Uncle Stepan walked him to the house from the car and thanked Appachen and Ammachi profusely for allowing Kuriakose to travel to Delhi to take care of Andranik. Appachen, though obviously pleased, dismissed the gratitude with a wave of his hand. Ammachi asked about Andranik's condition. Uncle Stepan explained it as a miracle and the grandparents made the sign of the cross.

After Uncle Stepan had left Appachen asked Ammachi. "Where did you keep that letter that came for Kuriakose? Give it to him."

Kuriakose's heart leaped when he read the name of the sender. It was the National Bank of India. He tore open the envelope to find the hall-ticket for the written test.

He announced to Appachen and Ammachi. "The written test will be in two months' time in July."

Appachen's response was businesslike. "The time will go very fast. From now on you must concentrate on your studies. You have the bank test and the final MA examination in July. Both are equally important."

"Don't take the dirty clothes to your room. Leave them on the *verandah*. Who knows what diseases were there in that hospital," said Ammachi.

He did not think it necessary to carry the water to the outhouse. He bathed in the dark in the open, standing next to the well. The well-water was not cold, but he still shivered as he poured it over his head and scrubbed himself thoroughly.

Meanwhile, in Nor Garni the celebration continued. The children had all turned in for the night. When Ter Samvel retired, the drinking began in real earnest. Someone produced a bottle of cognac from Yerevan. The women initially moved out of earshot and then started drifting away to their homes. Armine found that her mother was with the Tikin Karine in the kitchen and her father was with the men drinking away to glory. In the absence of Ter Samvel, the restraints on story-telling vanished. The jokes and tales turned ribald eliciting raucous laughter.

Armine decided to go home and sleep. She went into the house to tell her mother and Tikin Karine before leaving. As soon as Armine left, Vilen surreptitiously slunk out and followed her. While Armine walked blithely unaware on the path that she knew like the back of her hand, Vilen followed, not on the path itself, but through the fields its edge, hidden from Armine and the eyes of anyone watching.

When they were a good distance from the house, Vilen's lust overcame him. He jumped out onto the path at a curve and sneaked up behind the unsuspecting Armine, grabbing her with his strong, calloused hands in a vicelike grip. Armine tried to scream in terror but Vilen clamped a hand over her mouth while he held her with the other.

"Don't shout. Nobody can hear you. They are all drunk and making too much noise," hissed Vilen.

He pulled her closer to him as he lifted her off the ground. The touch of her soft, sensuous body against him triggered his pent-up lust. Carrying her kicking and biting into the tall tapioca fields next to the path he possessed her with animal-like ferocity. It was all over in a matter of minutes. Armine lay in searing pain, stunned, violated.

"Don't you dare tell anyone!" panted Vilen holding both her hands pressed to the ground above her head.

No tears came for Armine.

When she found her voice, she asked, "Why did you commit this crime Vilen? You are Armen's brother. You will be my brother-in-law."

Vilen laughed a hollow laugh and said with venomous spite.

"You are concerned about my brother Armen? Who are you trying to fool? What about your affair with that *Malayali* fellow, Kirakos? Others may not know anything, but I have been watching all your secret meetings."

Armine wanted to counter the allegation but then thought the better of it. Her outrage returned.

"Let me go, you brute! You fool! You drunkard!" she shouted in anger.

When he released her hands, she scrambled to sit up straightening her clothes.

"You have no idea of what you have done. You have committed an unpardonable crime. You have forced me also to commit a big sin. How will I marry your brother Armen now?"

"Marry Armen? Don't pretend you don't know. Why do you think he has not come back? He has married a white woman. That's why he is not coming."

Armine's world crumbled down around her. She did not know if Vilen was telling the truth. But it was a possibility. Armen had not written in weeks.

Wordlessly she arose, brushed the grass and leaves from her hair and walked home. Once she was inside, the dam broke. She cried in torrents flagellating herself and pleading to God for forgiveness.

Then she went to the rear of the house, drew water from the well and scoured herself with soap and *loofah*.

Walking back to the house after the bath she recalled the lines from Macbeth.

> *Here's the smell of the blood still; all the perfumes of Arabia will not sweeten this little hand.*

She also remembered Goldsmith and briefly contemplated killing herself.

> *The only art her guilt to cover,*
> *To hide her shame from every eye,*
> *To give repentance to her lover*
> *And wring his bosom, is – to die.*

Once she was indoors, there was a remarkable change. Suicides would not get a Christian burial in the Orthodox Church, she remembered. The abject self-pitying a little earlier, metamorphosed into steely determination. She reasoned that what had happened was not brought on at her instigation and hence she was not to blame. But, for the sake of protecting the honor of her family and of Armen, she decided not to tell Mayrik about what happened.

This would be the first time she had kept anything secret from her mother. It grieved her to have to do this, but she did not see an easier option. Only if she became pregnant would she tell her mother; and if that happened, she knew it was the end of her dreams. She would have to marry the illiterate lout Vilen and be a farmer's wife for the rest of her life.

Chapter 18: Two Confessions and a Reversion

The following Sunday Kuriakose went, as usual, to the Pentecostal church for worship. But somehow it did not seem the same anymore. When the beats of the gigantic drum rose to a crescendo and others started speaking in tongues all at once and shaking their bodies, the old fervor was absent in his heart. The frenzy of worship seemed so removed from the quiet demeanor of Ter Samvel.

When it was time to share their blessings Kuriakose pondered for a moment if it would be wise to tell everyone about his trip to Delhi and the miraculous healing of Andranik. He decided to speak the truth but did not share any details of the family he had assisted.

After the service, the pastor and Geevarghese quizzed him about the family but he was adamant.

"I have not taken their permission. It would not be right to tell you any details," said Kuriakose sticking to his guns.

"Are they believers?" asked the pastor.

"If you mean, are they Pentecostals, no. But they are Christians and they believe in God and the Bible."

"The devil does too. Don't forget what the Bible says," admonished the pastor.

Kuriakose had had enough of the moralizing rigidity and the holier-than-thou attitude. He longed to find the true church and stick to it.

On his way home from the worship service Kuriakose considered leaving the Pentecostal church and returning to the Orthodox Church.

However, he had to have a heart-to-heart talk with Ter Samvel first and he would have to wait till Saturday to travel to Nor Garni to meet him.

***

At the service the same Sunday, it was a painful confession for Armine. She arrived at the church earlier than usual to meet Ter Samvel privately before the service began. Armine sobbed uncontrollably as she narrated what had happened.

Inwardly he was disconsolate but outwardly he kept calm as he gently patted her hand and asked, "Have you told Hayrik and Mayrik about this?"

"No, Ter Hayr, I don't have the heart to tell them. They will be beside themselves with sorrow and grief. They will not be able to bear this on top of the dam. Hayrik is drinking himself to death already."

"This is very serious, Armush. What Vilen did was heinous—a terrible crime. It is like the story in the Old Testament of David's son Amnon who raped his half-sister Tamar. You are the only daughter. On the night we celebrated the happiness of Andranik's return alive, Vilen did this despicable act. It is the work of the evil one. You may or may not be pregnant. But don't worry about it now. Whatever happens is the will of God. The whole family will support you."

"It is my fate, Ter Hayr. Why did God let this happen to me? I did nothing to tempt Vilen."

"Armush, I don't have an answer to that. Maybe after many years God will reveal it to you."

"I ask myself if I did enough to stop Vilen. Did I resist enough? Did I give in too easily to sensual pleasure? I don't know. There was no pleasure, really. But I still feel guilty."

"You should not feel any guilt at all. Perish the thought. Vilen took you by surprise and he took you by force. He overpowered you. You did not tempt him. You did not allow him to seduce you. Banish any thought of guilt from your mind."

"It is not easy, Ter Hayr. I will try."

"I am placed in a very delicate situation. I am not only your priest but also your uncle. Shall I speak to your parents?"

"No! Please don't tell Hayrik and Mayrik what happened. They will be devastated. I am confessing to you only as my priest."

"No, I would never tell them unless you wanted me to on your behalf. If you were ashamed or embarrassed to tell them yourself, I will help. This confession is between you and God in my presence. I cannot reveal what you confessed to anyone. I am only concerned if, God forbid, you become pregnant. Your parents will be deeply hurt that you kept them in the dark."

"I will pray about it, Ter Hayr. I will pray with tears that I will not become pregnant. But I want to wait till I am sure. If I am pregnant, I will tell them.

If not, what happened will remain a secret till I die. If I have conceived and bear a child, I will bring up the child as God's gift to me and our family."

"I will pray for you, Armush. You are a strong girl. I will support you through this."

As Armine sought the blessings and returned to the rear of the Church, she felt an immense burden lift away. Her heart was at peace.

***

The wait till the Saturday following was excruciatingly painful for Kuriakose. He longed to meet Ter Samvel and bare his soul to the priest. It was all he could do through the week not to run pell-mell through the cave of death to Nor Garni to Ter Samvel's house.

It was a troubled and fidgety Kuriakose that arrived at Armine's house on Saturday afternoon. For a change, their roles were reversed. The normally loquacious Kuriakose was taciturn and no amount of cajoling by Armine, who tried to forget her own secret sorrow, could make him relent.

"Are you terminally ill? Have you killed someone?" asked Armine sarcastically. He was neither amused nor angered.

"No, I am all right. I need to meet Ter Samvel."

With that he left, refusing, for the first time, coffee and Armenian refreshments.

Ter Samvel guessed straight away that something was seriously amiss and ushered Kuriakose into his study without any ado.

"There is something you want to talk about, Kuriakose jan?" asked Ter Samvel gently.

"Yes, Ter Hayr. Something happened to me while I was at the hospital in Delhi with Andranik, Ter Hayr. He had a physical injury, but I had a far more serious soul injury I did not know about before."

"What happened? Did you have a spiritual experience of some sort?" asked Ter Samvel.

"Yes, Ter Hayr. I did. I found God ... no, no, no! ... He found *me*! At that hospital, the wretched Ram Manohar Joshi hospital ... the façade and the name that hid the foulness and the degradation and the filth within ... that's where He found me." Kuriakose paused, overcome by his painful recollection.

Ter Samvel did not speak. He only looked with a kindly smile as he waited for Kuriakose to continue.

"That first night as I slept sitting beside Andranik, a rat nibbled at my foot. When I awoke, it scampered out through a hole in the wall and I discovered rotting human body parts in a plastic bucket in the same room where Andranik lay. Oh, Ter Hayr how God opened my heart and mind that day! I saw in the rat the temptations that gnaw at my soul. And in that plastic bucket lay the putrefying results of my sins, my own flesh ripped from my body by the evil one. The terrible sins not thrown out of my life but still held on to and given pride of place."

"I did not know that the hospital experience was that traumatic. Son, you have been through a lot," Ter Samvel said with empathy.

"No, Ter Hayr, my pain was nothing compared to Andranik's. I would have gladly switched places with him. Hope you will forgive me for saying this. I felt for Andranik that day like a father feels for his own son. I know I am not that much older than him to be his father. Should the feeling have been as an elder brother?"

"It does not matter. In God's kingdom relationships are not based on age differences. You can be the father or uncle to someone older than you just as much as the other way around. It was God who put the concern and affection in your heart. Andranik is my son. But you can continue to love him like a son or a younger brother. I will not mind that at all. Instead, I will thank God for bringing you into his life."

"Ter Hayr, you are matchless. I am not even an Armenian and you treat me like family." Kuriakose was overcome with emotion. He covered his face with his hands sobbing.

Ter Samvel walked and put his hand on Kuriakose's shoulder. "We are all one family in God. It does not matter whether we are Armenian or Indian or English. As long as we are Christians – especially Orthodox Christians – we are one family."

Kuriakose only sobbed.

Ter Samvel continued, "I thank God for bringing you into our lives in this miraculous way. Without you, where would Andranik be now? Without the affection and the care that you bestowed on him, he would not have survived. We owe you his life."

That stopped Kuriakose's sobbing. "No, no, no! I did not do anything. When I saw Andranik grimacing in pain as the nurse jabbed him with a needle, when I saw the bloodstained bandage on his head, I prayed to God. I said if God would save Andranik I would become Orthodox again."

Ter Samvel smiled. "You bargained with God?"

"No, I know it sounds incorrect. But I prayed earnestly for Andranik's recovery. I was willing to make any sacrifice for seeing Andranik well again."

"And God heard your prayers."

"He is kind and merciful. I am an idler and a sinner. Ter Hayr, I want to keep the vows I made to God. I want to rejoin the Orthodox Church again."

"There will be rejoicing in heaven, Kuriakose jan Can you imagine how happy your father and mother will be? I am happy too. I am almost as happy as I was when Andranik came back."

"Thank you, Ter Samvel. My cup of joy is full. God is kind to me."

"I have one request to make, Kuriakose jan," said Ter Samvel with a faint smile.

"Anything you ask, Ter Hayr," Kuriakose said with much anticipation.

"Will you accept me as your godfather?" Ter Samvel asked.

The tears streamed down Kuriakose's face in torrents a second time as he jumped up reflexively to hug Ter Samvel.

"It would be the highest honor to have you as my godfather. I still cannot believe that you treat me, a non-Armenian, as a member of your family."

"It is my turn to share a story. We Armenians keep to ourselves in the foreign lands we live in. We can be very insular. At the Orthodox theological college in Kottayam, I spurned the friendship of a brilliant classmate. He was a *Malayali*. Just because he was not an Armenian, I was cold towards him. God forgive me, I even secretly despised him when he offered his help. Years after we had gone our separate ways God convicted my heart in the middle of my homily—right in front of all the parishioners. I was speaking on the parable of the Good Samaritan when I realized that the two characters were not of the same race—one was a Samaritan despised by the Jews and the race of the other, the injured, we do not know. A priest and a Levite walked by without helping. I was convicted. I saw myself as the hypocritical priest and the pretentious Levite. The very next day I left Nor Garni in search of that batch-mate I had wronged. Through the seminary, I traced him to faraway north Kerala, in a small village in Wynad district where he was the priest of the Orthodox Church. I confessed my sin to him and sought forgiveness and he forgave me."

"You are a godly man, Ter Hayr. I admire what you did. A lesser man would have overlooked what had happened years ago and done nothing—or confessed only to God. Will you hear my confession how, Ter Hayr?"

"I will, my son. There will be much rejoicing in heaven today."

At the end of his confession, Kuriakose mentioned the love he felt for Armine, Ter Samvel's niece, and her response.

There was deep sadness on Ter Samvel's face as he listened.

Finally he said, "I say this with a heavy heart. Love has to be reciprocal. I know what a fine young man you are. But if Armine does not feel the same way towards you there is little that can be done. As you know, she has been promised. That is a uniquely Armenian tradition. It is something like being betrothed. We haven't heard from her fiancé Armen in a long while. It would be wise not to fall in love with Armine. You might end up hurting yourself."

"I wish it was that easy, Ter Hayr. To be fair to her, she warned me from the beginning and never once encouraged me. I steeled my heart from the start not to have any feelings for Armine, but she is such a wonderful person, I could not help it. I will confess that I have looked at her beauty and been wounded in my heart."

"Do not fall into that temptation, Kuriakose jan. Pray for the protection of the Theotokos when such feelings arise in your heart."

"If I could only be near Armine all the time … I would be the best Orthodox Christian in the world. Just her company, her presence—nothing more."

Ter Samvel looked at Kuriakose for a long minute with deep pathos on his visage as he recalled Armine's confession the preceding Sunday.

"I will pray that God's will be done in your life, son," he said finally.

Having no inkling of the misfortune that befell Armine, Kuriakose mistook Ter Samvel's sadness to be empathy for his unrequited love.

***

Kuriakose was a changed man. On the way back, he stopped at Armine's house.

"Armine jan, I have something to tell you."

"You have suddenly become very talkative again," she replied in her usual disinterested tone.

"I have decided to rejoin the Orthodox Church!" Kuriakose said joyfully.

For once Armine let her guard down and unreservedly showed her happiness.

"That is the best news I have heard!" she cried holding out her hand for Kuriakose to shake.

"I have one other news. Ter Samvel will be my godfather!"

"This calls for a celebration," Armine said running to the kitchen.

She came back with *lavash* and *tzhvzhik.*

"Mayrik is not well. She is sleeping. Father is taking a nap."

This time Kuriakose waited for Armine to fetch the prayer book and he stood while she read the prayer before food. After crossing himself Kuriakose sat down to taste the food.

"We also have the exact same dish! Tastes exactly the same!" he exclaimed. "We call it spare parts curry."

"Spare parts?" asked Armine crinkling her forehead.

"It is made from chicken gizzards and liver, isn't it? Those are the spare parts," explained Kuriakose smiling broadly.

Armine did not smile. Instead, she said solemnly, *"Tzhvvzhiki patmutyun sarkyel."*

Seeing the puzzled look on Kuriakose's face she added, "Don't make a story about *tzhvzhik.* That's what it means. It is a line from a classic short film of the same name—*Tzhvzhik.*"

"How did you see the movie here in Nor Garni?"

"We saw it on 16mm home projector. Actually, the film was an adaptation of a famous short story by a writer with the pen name of Atrpet. Single name—like Saki."

As they talked and shared the food, Kuriakose's passion resurfaced. He looked at her with yearning. But remembering the rat and the rotting flesh he tried to banish the feelings of tenderness he felt.

Armine, on the other hand, inwardly lamented her plight. Kuriakose was now of the same faith but her own destiny had been despicably violated.

"Kirakos jan, I just remembered something. The hall-ticket for the bank test came. It was lying at the check-post for several days."

"Where is your exam center? Which college?" asked Kuriakose.

"Raja's College in Ernakulam. And yours?"

"Mine is the same! What a coincidence! We could go together." Kuriakose was delighted.

"If Hayrik does not take me himself. We will see. Time will show."

"My university exams come before the bank exam. Two whole weeks in the second and third weeks of July. The bank exam is at the end of July. The heaviest part of the monsoon would be over by then."

"If we decide to go to Ernakulam on the day of the exam, we would have to catch the first fast passenger bus from Pathanamthitta. How will we manage that?" Armine said dejectedly.

"There is plenty of time to find a solution for that. We will figure out a way. But now I need to go home and study," he said rising. After thanking Armine for the hospitality Kuriakose pedaled furiously in the direction of the cave of death.

*** *

During the evening meal that night he cleared his throat nervously before speaking up.

"Appacha, there is something I want to tell you. I have come to realize that leaving our Church was a big mistake. I apologize to you and Ammachi for my error. I have decided to rejoin our Orthodox Church."

Appachen let his guard down and beamed broadly.

"I knew you would come back to the fold. Ammachi and I have been praying for you," Appachen said gravely. "Never leave the Church ever again."

Ammachi stood on the sidelines making signs of the cross, murmuring prayers, and wiping her eyes with the edge of the white cotton cloth that she always had over her right shoulder.

"Go and meet Ouseph Achen (priest) tomorrow," said Appachen rising to wash his hands outside on the *verandah*.

Chapter 19: The Onset of the Monsoon

The skies got grayer and murkier by the day. The winds slowly gained momentum. There was a change in the air, the anticipation of the annual event of the southwest monsoon. Once the rains started in earnest the cave of death would be impassable for weeks. Kuriakose longed to see Armine one more time before the monsoon set in.

Two days later Kuriakose went to meet the priest. Ouseph Achen, the priest, who had roundly berated him for leaving the Church the last time they met on the road, was prim and proper this time. Appachen had already told him about Kuriakose's decision to come back to the Church.

"I'm happy that good sense has dawned on you and you are returning to our Church. You know, our Church traces its origins to St Thomas and the Apostles. This is the right church to be in. This is the only church to be in. Can you tell me what caused your decision?"

"Achen, it is difficult to explain. Some days ago, God convicted my heart of its sinful nature. I want to worship God and to walk in the footsteps of our Christian forefathers." Kuriakose found it difficult to open up as he had with Ter Samvel.

"God moves in mysterious ways. I'm happy you are back. Please be active in the youth wing as you were before. Come to the Saturday vigil for confessions. Since you left the Church once, you will need to undergo Chrismation. We will do that before the service on Sunday and after that, you can partake of the Holy Communion."

Kuriakose wondered if Achen would express his regrets for the harsh words of their previous encounter but Achen did not even refer to that.

As he walked back home, he stopped by the culvert over the creek to look towards his favorite grove in the distance and the spot on the opposite bank where he had first seen Armine astride Qurkik-Jalali. Just then the rain began to fall, and he ran all the way home drenched to the skin.

Kuriakose's news journal recorded the continuing genocide in Cambodia. The *Khmer Rouge* captured the US merchant ship *SS Mayaguez*. The *Pathet Lao* progressed inexorably in neighboring Laos, and repeating the history of Anatolia sixty years ago, they called for the extermination of the *Hmong* people. The Suez Canal was reopened after eight years. Junko Tabei of Japan became the first woman to climb Mount Everest. India, following the example of other powerful countries, shamelessly annexed the tiny princely state of Sikkim on its border.

***

Appachen sent him on an errand to the government office at Pathanamthitta that Saturday and he could not go to Nor Garni. He would not see Armine for a whole month because the heavens opened up that Monday, the second day of June. After he returned from Pathanamthitta in the afternoon, he went for the Saturday night vigil. During the confession with Ouseph Achen, he could not unburden himself as freely as he had with Ter Samvel. It was more stilted and formal but Kuriakose cautioned himself not to fall to the temptation of judging his own priest.

The Chrismation ceremony before the service on Sunday took only fifteen minutes. After he partook of the Holy Communion, he felt a great sense of inner peace.

He walked home with Appachen after the service. They walked mostly in silence except for a brief chat about the weather when Appachen looked up at the sky and predicted the monsoon would start the next day.

Although he had been taught not to study on a Sunday, Kuriakose resumed cramming for the examination immediately after lunch. He lay on the coir-strung cot, the cotton pillow doubled up under his head, and began to read. The Telefunken radio played BBC's *A Jolly Good Show* presented by Dave Lee Travis. He dozed off after a while. When he awoke, he did not leave the room but resumed his reading.

His studies were interrupted by Ammachi who came to say, "Somebody has come to see you. He looks like your classmate."

Kuriakose scrambled to his feet and ran his hands through his hair as he walked to the *verandah* wondering who it could be.

It was Geevarghese. 'I should have anticipated this,' thought Kuriakose.

"Praise the Lord! You did not come for worship today. I came to see if you are sick," said

Geevarghese, implying by a twisted smile that that was not indeed the case.

"No, I am not sick," said Kuriakose. He wanted to tell the truth but was unsure how the discussions would go.

"Then why didn't you come for worship?" Geevarghese's voice rose as he asked.

Kuriakose did not like the tone of the question. He decided to tell the truth bluntly.

"Geevarghese, I will not be coming any more to your church."

Geevarghese's mouth fell open in surprise.

"I rejoined the Orthodox Church," added Kuriakose.

Geevarghese found his voice. "You did not tell me."

"It happened very suddenly."

Ammachi intervened, "Son, are you not going to invite him in? Are you going to let him stand on the *verandah*?"

"No, I won't come in," said Geevarghese. "I will not enter the house of a backslider. I will shake off the dust from my slippers when I leave." Then turning to Kuriakose he said, "A dog goes back to its own vomit."

"Don't speak to my grandson like that. Each person has the right to choose his own religion. You cannot force your beliefs on my grandson."

Geevarghese immediately apologized. "Forgive me, I did not mean to be insulting. Anyway, I don't think there is any point in continuing this discussion. Your mind has already been made up. Good luck for the examinations!"

With that, Geevarghese turned and walked away.

***

The sky darkened with steel gray clouds that coagulated into black aerial mountains, through which ran slivers of silver lightning accompanied by deafening thunder. Though he had experienced the monsoon every year of his life, yet the first day continued to overawe him. 'How could any atheist look at the ferociousness of the monsoon and say there is no God?' he asked himself, thinking of the anarchist Edakiruku. The first downpour turned the ground into a muddy swamp. The deluge continued through the night. A clap of thunder shook the cot so violently that he almost fell out.

He woke up early in the morning while it was still dark to discover that there was no electricity. The rain had not let up. He stumbled to the kitchen to find a kerosene lamp. In the feeble light that flickered in the wind, he studied for the final MA examinations.

The monsoon was a blessing in that it was tantamount to house arrest, away from all distractions. Confined at home except for the twice-daily dash in the rain to the cowshed to feed the cows, Kuriakose was compelled to focus on his studies. Without electricity, the old valve radio would not work. The torrential rain had by the second day caused the fields that surrounded the house to become a muddy mess with large pools of water. Only the raised pebbled courtyard around the house did not have any standing water. He knew that the water level in the stream would have risen and the cave of death would have become impassable by now and would stay that way till the monsoon eased and the waters abated.

Kuriakose crammed tirelessly for the upcoming examination. He read Eliot and Joyce, Donne and Herbert, Milton and Blake, Hemingway and Faulkner, Tennyson and Browning, Owen and Sassoon, and all the others in the syllabus. Whenever thoughts of Armine entered his mind, he took a break. He stared wistfully out of the window and wondered how Armine and her parents were coping with the rains. This would be their last rainy season in Nor Garni. He wondered where they would go and if he would ever see Armine again.

By the third day, the pools of water in the fields had slowly joined each other. It was now one shimmering mass of water that surrounded their raised homestead. Appachen walked barefoot through the ankle-deep slush to the cooperative bank. The rainfall that night was the heaviest so far. It was as if buckets of water were being poured from the heavens. There was no let-up. By the fourth morning, the water in the fields had risen. On the footpath to the main road the muddy water had climbed higher than Appachen's calves. The rain continued to fall, and the skies remained black and foreboding. Even during the day, he had to light the kerosene lamp several times to read his books. But Kuriakose stuck to his exam preparations with single-minded determination. He knew a good result would be his deliverance.

Water surrounded the church and there would not be any more services till the waters abated.

By the sixth day, the waters had risen waist-high on the path to the main road. Appachen took down the canoe and paddled to the cooperative bank. When he came back, he brought a big sack of rice, and lentils, potatoes, and onions. Kuriakose wanted to take the canoe out to see the extent of the floods but Appachen dissuaded him.

"You might catch a fever or cold. We cannot take any risks. Your examinations are only three weeks away," said Appachen dissuading Kuriakose.

"Appacha, this will be the last floods we will have. Next year the dam would be up and there would be no more floods here."

Appachen was unrelenting. "Good marks are more important than enjoying a boat ride."

The waters continued to rise. By the middle of the second week, the water level had risen chest high. The waters began to lap at the edge of the raised parapet that surrounded the pebbled courtyard of the house. For three days, the intensity of the rain seemed to diminish a little. But on Sunday the monsoon struck again with renewed vigor. Lightning hit the tallest of the coconut trees and clove it neatly down the middle. The clap of thunder shook the house like an earthquake.

The next day Appachen allowed Kuriakose to use the boat to go to Kozhencherry to buy provisions. Kuriakose thoroughly enjoyed paddling the boat. All the hollows and undulations of the ground had vanished. There was only one even level of muddy brown water, more perfectly level than any artisan could have made. Instead of following the circuitous footpath he could now paddle diagonally across the submerged paddy fields. He marveled at the fact that irrespective of the depth below the boat stayed at the same level.

The grocery store owner had created a raised wooden scaffolding across half the shop. He climbed a ladder to get to the rice, lentils, onions, and potatoes that had been moved up there for safe keeping from the rising flood waters. Kuriakose went next to the kerosene dealer. They needed kerosene for cooking and lighting. It would take several weeks for the wet firewood to dry again.

He took a different, longer route to return home. He stopped to buy fresh-caught fish from a man on another boat. If he did not have exams, that is what he would have done, he thought—fish all day. The fish from the Pamba River were now swimming all over the countryside. The buses and trucks and the few cars and taxis that the town had had all vanished. There were only small boats in their place. The muddy, murky water covered the face of the land. Now he knew why there was a wall around the well. The flood waters were muddy and undrinkable. It registered on him what the ancient mariner of Coleridge felt.

> *Water, water, everywhere,*
> *Nor any drop to drink.*

Fortunately, that was as high as the waters would rise. The next week it started to recede. Submerged plants started to reappear. When the level fell further the paddy fields looking unkempt and bedraggled were exposed. When the puddles separated from each other, Kuriakose ran out to catch fish that were stranded in them. He found many small fish but none big enough.

***

One more week and the month of June would be gone. Armine was counting the days. Four more days till the day of reckoning. She could not bear the suspense. Her life hung by a thread. Although she missed meeting Kuriakose she was glad that the monsoon had providentially kept him away from her through this difficult time. If anyone, Kuriakose was the only one who would have suspected that something was seriously wrong. Her father and mother attributed her gloominess to the weather. Armine was glad that the floods had prevented Kuriakose from coming because she would have been irritable and crotchety and caused him even more pain than usual.

Armine's periods were always painful. They made her dizzy and weak and the abdominal cramps caused her whole body to ache for three or four days. But this Tuesday she was elated when it arrived right on schedule. She covered her head with her pillow and sobbed with joy. She would not have to bear the child of the half-wit Vilen, she told herself. She was free. It was like rebirth. A fresh new lease of life. In spite of the menstruation, she was radiant as she went about her house chores later that day.

The only thing that weighed on her mind as she watched the pouring rain from her window was that this would be their last monsoon season in Nor Garni. The dam under construction seemed as unfair as life itself. The areas that now were flooded would no longer have floods but Nor Garni that had had no floods at all would forever be under water. She knew that the threat of the looming disaster was eating into the health and happiness of Hayrik and Mayrik. There was nothing she could do to turn the tide. Like an unstoppable juggernaut, the reservoir created by the dam would roll over their beloved Nor Garni smothering it into oblivion.

During Sunday's confession, she shared with Ter Samvel, who was visibly relieved, that she was not in the family way.

***

For Kuriakose the ordeal of the final university examinations began in the second week of July. He had nine papers to take covering the entire syllabus of two years. Many a time during the preparations he had wished for semester or at least annual examinations. But, no, the university, in its own wisdom, decreed that two years of learning would be assessed in a period of two weeks on alternating days. Kuriakose had written examinations of three hours each on Chaucer, modern literature (four papers), Shakespeare, the history of the English language, American literature, and literary criticism. He wrote voluminously, almost thirty pages on an average for each examination. At the end of each examination, his right arm was stiff and sore. But he soldiered on. Whenever his courage failed, he reminded himself, 'This is your salvation. Once you get past this you can start a new life.'

The month of June was a pivotal month for India. Indira Gandhi, the Prime Minister, refused to accept the high court ruling disqualifying her election. She declared an emergency and imposed draconian measures suspending civil liberties and imprisoning seven hundred political opponents. Indira Gandhi ruled the country with an iron fist. Elsewhere in the world, in Mozambique, Samora Machel was sworn in as the President of the newly independent country. In another Portuguese colony, Angola, civil war broke out four months before independence.

Chapter 20: The Dual Test

Since the morning bus from the check-post was only at nine o'clock, and the bank test would start at ten o'clock at Ernakulam, which was at least three and a half hours away by bus, it was decided by Hayrik that he would pay for Kuriakose to come by taxi from his village to the check-post. From the check-post, he and Armine would travel together in the same taxi to Pathanamthitta to catch the first fast passenger bus of the day from there to Ernakulam.

So it was that Kuriakose got up at three o'clock in the morning on the day of the examination. He was not surprised to discover that Ammachi had woken up ahead of him and had prepared a breakfast of *idli* (fluffy, steamed rice-cakes), *sambar* (red lentil curry) and eggs fried sunny side up. He was so anxious and excited about the examination and about traveling such a long distance with Armine that he could eat only one *idli*, though he normally consumed as many as five or six. He gulped down the hot coffee, blowing into it to cool it. He remembered then that he would need a light to get back home in the dark and packed Appachen's long four-cell flashlight into his shoulder bag. Appachen also got up before he left and prayed for Kuriakose's success in the examination.

Kuriakose knew that passing this examination could change his life forever. He knew that his whole life depended upon it.

The taxi was almost a half hour late. Kuriakose fumed in helpless anger. Sensing the urgency, the driver drove at pell-mell speed and made up some time getting to the check-post. While the taxi waited, Kuriakose pedaled furiously to Nor Garni. As expected of a former government official everything was ready at Armine's household. Armine's father and mother watched as Kuriakose and Armine mounted their bicycles to ride in the dark to the waiting taxi at the check-post. Once they got on the highway the taxi driver drove at breakneck speed to make up for lost time. Dawn was breaking as they pulled into the bus station at Pathanamthitta. They made it just before the departure of the express bus. Kuriakose was delighted to get seats for them together on the two-seater side of the bus by the door.

It was only then, as the sky lightened, that Kuriakose really noticed the color of the dress that Armine was wearing. It was a bright red. In his eyes, it bordered on the garish.

"Why are you dressed like this? Are you going to a party?" blurted out Kuriakose.

"What is wrong with my dress? I like red. I will wear what I want. This is an exam, not a fashion parade," Armine retorted.

"Exactly! You will stand out prominently instead of blending with the crowd."

"What is wrong with that? Are you ashamed of me?" asked Armine.

"No, I am not. You are already so different from everyone else. You are as fair as a *madamma*. When you wear flashy colors, you become even more conspicuous."

Armine was about to respond when the conductor rang the bell and slammed the door shut catching Armine's left hand. She gasped in agony. Instinctively Kuriakose took Armine's hand in his and gently massaged it. The thumbnail had turned blue. The conductor did not apologize. Kuriakose wondered if he had done it on purpose because of Armine's flashy dress. The moment Armine realized Kuriakose was holding her hand she snatched it back wordlessly and stared out of the window.

"If we can both pass this test ..." Kuriakose began hopefully.

Armine cut him off. "You will pass. I am not good at math. I am coming only because Hayrik insisted."

"I wish you would be a little bit more positive. This job can change our lives. You ... we ... can go to a big city with Hayrik and Mayrik. The new dam will not affect you," Kuriakose tried to explain.

"I don't want to talk about this. You are ambitious. You want to get this job and escape from the village. Go ahead! But leave me out of this. I don't want any false hopes." Armine was adamant.

That was the end of their discussions. Armine nodded off to sleep. Kuriakose kept turning his head to look at her marveling how much more beautiful she looked in sleep. When the bus passed by the backwaters of Vembanad Lake where his parents had drowned, he was glad Armine was not awake to witness his discomfiture. He said a silent prayer for them and for success for both Armine and him in the examination.

On arrival at Ernakulam, they took an *autorickshaw* to the venue of the examination. There was only time for a quick cup of *Kerala coffee* at the vegetarian restaurant nearby. Finding their rooms in the sprawling college was not easy. There were at least five thousand candidates, Kuriakose estimated, all anxiously searching for their assigned room and seat. Kuriakose noticed with unease that many were eyeing Armine lecherously. He wished again that she had worn something less eye-catching.

A slap on the shoulder spun him around. It was RK; and with him was Geevarghese. Kuriakose was taken by surprise.

"You won't introduce us to your companion?" asked RK with a wink.

Kuriakose blushed. He stammered, "She is a friend ... kind of a neighbor," he stammered.

"Does she have a name?"

Kuriakose collected himself. "Her name is Armine. Armine Hovhannisyan. She lives in the next village." Then turning to Armine, he continued, "These are my classmates Radhakrishnan Nair and Geevarghese Tharakan."

Armine spoke up. "Nice to meet you," she said with a smile but did not offer her hand.

Kuriakose hastily intervened. "We need to find our seats. Meet you both after the test."

Kuriakose, with Armine in tow, hurried away to the noticeboard. Their seats were not in the same room. Kuriakose helped locate Armine's desk first and then went to his room.

Geevarghese and RK caught up with him.

"So, this was your secret? That's why you were asking so many questions about Armenians. You are a deep one. I never would have imagined you to be capable of this," RK said with barely concealed admiration and a trace of jealousy. Geevarghese, as before did not say a word, but only glared disapprovingly.

Kuriakose was saved by the bell—literally. The college bell signaled the start of the examination and they went to their separate rooms.

Kuriakose prayed earnestly as he waited for the examiner to distribute the test booklets. Before the booklet was handed to him, he laid his watch on the table to serve as a timer. When the test began, he shut the whole world out of his mind and began to attack the three objective test components of English, General Knowledge, and Reasoning. When he discovered that the questions at the beginning of each paper were more difficult than the rest, he started from the middle and came back to the first section after he had done the rest. Carefully monitoring the time, he was able to answer almost all the questions.

On Enver Pasha's orders, a large contingent of the Turkish forces attacked Sardarabad with the avowed aim of annihilating Armenians and wiping Armenia off the face of the earth. After the conquest there would only be Turkey. Armenia would have ceased to exist. Church bells tolled for days exhorting all men to enlist in the defense. Women and children helped with supplying food to the defenders. It was a do or die battle for the survival of Armenia. The Ottoman forces were entrenched in the heights. Using a flanking manoeuvre the vastly outnumbered ragtag group of patriots

> attacked the aggressors from the rear in addition to repulsing them from the front causing the Ottoman army to abandon their invasion and flee. The shrewd tactics of the Armenian generals saved the day and won the Battle of Sardarabad.

As soon as the three-hour test ended Kuriakose rushed to Armine's room. Armine agreed to Kuriakose's suggestion that they have lunch before returning home. Instead of the vegetarian restaurant where they had had coffee before the test, they walked to the center of town where the bus station was located and found a restaurant close to it. As they walked into the restaurant towards the empty table, the natural choice for Armine would have been the seat nearest to her facing the door. But unexpectedly she moved diagonally across to the other side of the table that was closer to Kuriakose. Puzzled, he stepped aside for her to move in and sit down. As he walked around to the place opposite her, he casually noticed three young men at the table behind him. Two were facing away and he could not see their faces. The one who sat alone on the opposite side, he quickly noticed, had the looks and air of a dandy Malayalam film star, with coiffured hair and a man-of-the-world mien. But Kuriakose did not give it another thought.

"What will you have?" he asked Armine while looking down at the menu placed under the glass table top.

"The examination was terrible. I am hungry."

"OK. Shall we have rice or *paratha*?"

"Eh ..." was the only response he got.

When he looked up surprised to ask Armine what the matter was, she quickly turned her head towards him, away from whatever she was looking at behind him.

"What did you say?" she asked in a confused manner.

"You didn't hear what I asked?"

"You were looking down at the menu and mumbling," she charged.

"OK. I'll try again. I was asking if you will have rice or *paratha*?" he repeated.

"I think I will have *paratha*," she replied.

"What curry do you want to go with it?" he asked looking down at the menu again. "Beef or chicken?" Even as he asked Kuriakose sensed that she was looking again at an object behind him. When he looked at her reflection on the glass tabletop, his suspicions were confirmed. But the moment he raised his head to look at her she turned away to look out of the window.

"Order anything. I don't care," she said distractedly.

"But what do you prefer?" he asked again.

"Just order something! Don't make such a big fuss," she snapped.

He was flabbergasted. The sudden change in Armine's mood was inexplicable. But he knew by now better than to press the issue. He beckoned the waiter and ordered *paratha* for her, rice for him and beef curry for both.

They both fell silent. Kuriakose noticed again that Armine was not her normal calm and collected self. She seemed nervous and fidgety, instead of being in control as she always was. She avoided looking at him and instead seemed magnetically drawn to some point behind him. Whenever he looked at her, she turned her head away to stare at the blank boundary wall outside the window.

The food was quick in coming. He was hungry and fell upon it with gusto. He expected Armine to do likewise considering her earlier statement that she was hungry. But Kuriakose noticed her making the sign of the cross distractedly, quite unlike her usual reverential fashion, and then peck at the food desultorily.

When he looked up to ask what the matter was, he saw her riveted in the same direction behind him with the spoon half-forgotten at her lips. But more than the inattention, it was the look in her eyes that astonished him. It was naked lust. The only time he had seen that look before was the time when he had instinctively embraced her, and she had pushed him away in confusion after only a few seconds. He intuitively realized that she was eyeing the imitation film actor behind him. That fop was the focus of her attention and the cause of her distraction. The food turned to ashes in his mouth. Kuriakose was crushed. Not only had she been lukewarm at best towards him, she was now openly flirting with a stranger while they were dining together. 'What has happened to my incorruptible angel?' he wondered in the pain of disillusionment.

Although he had lost his appetite, his grandfather's dictum of not wasting food while half the world starved came back to him. Half-crazed and angered he resumed wolfing down the food. He looked up again to see Armine squirm in her chair with a sensual look in her eyes. When she realized he was watching, she looked at him, but she immediately turned her head away, with a guilty flutter of the eyelids, to the window, where there was nothing to be seen except the blank boundary wall.

Just then he heard the chairs scrape behind him. The three young men walked past their table on their way out of the restaurant. Kuriakose looked at them and saw the film actor type leading the way swaggering like a rake, flicking his *mundu* with a stylized gesture. None of the three turned to look towards them as they left the restaurant.

"Were they at the table behind me?" Kuriakose asked.

"Why do you ask?" countered Armine.

Kuriakose wanted to retort: 'You don't think I'm blind, do you?' But he bit his tongue.

Then, realizing that the brusqueness of her answer could give her away, she quietly added, "Yes."

The tension miraculously evaporated with the exit of Armine's distraction. Although he could not get out of his mind what had just happened, he did not press the issue and Armine reverted to her former self. Her hunger appeared to resurface as she turned her full attention now to the food. Kuriakose watched her from the corner of his eye. Instead of anger, a wave of pity, for her and for himself, washed over him. There was no further talk as she finished her food.

'What had happened to his angel on the pedestal? The princess who could do no wrong? The fair damsel who was perfection personified?' He had no answers.

When they reached the cashier's desk to pay the bill, he half expected her to reach for her purse, but she did not show any inclination to do that.

"Use the balance from the taxi fare Hayrik gave to pay for my share," she said.

Kuriakose did not want to do that because the money given was expressly for the taxi fare. Fortunately, the cash his grandfather had given him was enough to pay for both their meals. As they walked to the bus station the feelings of despondency and betrayal came back to him. 'How could she be so callous as to flirt with another man, and a total stranger at that, while she is with me?' he fumed inside.

She looked at him questioningly but did not inquire into the reasons for his bad humor.

The bus to Pathanamthitta was already half full but they got seats together again. Armine made a show of ensuring she was not too close to Kuriakose and there was enough space between their bodies. Nevertheless, the mere proximity of his angel, after a stressful day, mollified Kuriakose.

"Do you think you will pass?" he asked Armine.

"Who knows? Time will show," was her noncommittal answer.

"Still, what do you think?" he persisted.

"I am not a walking encyclopedia or a math whiz like you."

"I am not an encyclopedia. I keep a daily journal of news and current affairs just to be able to do well in such tests," Kuriakose explained.

"You keep a news diary?" Armine was amused.

"Yes. How else can one remember all those unfamiliar names of people and places?"

Armine did not respond. She only looked at him as if he was crazy to keep a diary of world news.

"I made two mistakes in the test of reasoning," he volunteered.

She did not seem interested in talking about the test or anything else. She stared out of the window at the darkening landscape oblivious of the presence of Kuriakose or the other passengers on the bus. When the conductor came for the tickets, he paid both their fares. She did not seem to notice or care.

After getting off the bus they walked to the check-post from the main road and then pedaled to her hamlet on bicycles with Kuriakose leading the way. The kerosene lamp on his cycle was only a feeble glow that lit a short distance ahead. He stopped to take out the flashlight from his bag. The four-cell flashlight shone as bright a headlamp.

Armine's father was waiting at the edge of the courtyard. And standing a step behind him to his left was Vilen.

"*Inchu yek ush?* (Why are you late?)" Hayrik asked, almost shouting in anger.

"Hayrik jan!" pleaded Armine, her shoulders visibly drooping, "We came directly from the test. We did not go anywhere. We stopped only for lunch after the examination."

Her father did not reply as he stomped back into the house visibly upset. Armine turned to say, "*Bari gisher!*" to Kuriakose and then climbed the steps to the house. Armine realized that Vilen, the viper, must have poisoned her father's mind again.

Kuriakose got back on the cycle and rode it all the way to the tapioca plot. From there he walked wearily up the hill to the cave of death. He was glad he had remembered to carry the flashlight. The beam threw scary dancing shadows on the dark walls of the cave as he splashed wildly to the other side.

It did not matter to him that she did not thank him. Close family members never thanked each other. What rankled in his mind was the incident at the restaurant. It was painful for him to realize that Armine was as fickle as the other women he had read about in books.

'I must have imagined it. Armine would never do anything like that,' he told himself over and over.

Then larger doubts assailed his mind. 'Was her faith and devotion to the Orthodox Church just a charade? Was all the praying and devoutness that she displayed just a sham?'

***

When he closed his eyes, all he could see was the seductive face of Armine that he had glimpsed at the restaurant at Ernakulam earlier in the day. The sultry glance ... the knowing smile ... the covert look of wanting that only lovers shared ...

He tossed and turned all night long yearning for Armine to look at him with the same gleam in her eyes; for her to squirm with pleasure in his embrace as she had done at the restaurant while looking at the rake. The pangs of jealousy stoked in him not just anger but also lust which would not be quenched. All he saw in his mind was Armine twisting in her chair, flirting coquettishly with an amorous glint in her eyes.

> *Strange fits of passion have I known:*
> *And I will dare to tell,*
> *But in the lover's ear alone,*
> *What once to me befell.*

He would not be able to wipe that image off his mind for weeks; maybe months. Perhaps it was etched and engraved on his psyche forever.

When he woke up next morning, he knew that everything had changed. He felt strangely liberated. The previous evening had been the last straw. The love he had secretly nurtured had died. So did the hope which he had once thought would never die. All that was left in his heart for Armine were the platonic dregs of friendship at the most mundane level.

He remembered Heywood's seventeenth century play *A Woman Killed with Kindness*. No, he knew, he could never bring himself to be that cruel to Armine. If she ever needed his help, he would not refuse, no matter what. But he no longer harbored any fanciful thoughts about playing second fiddle, let alone a self-sacrificing Sydney Carton, to Armen or to anyone else.

Chapter 21: Hope Grows Fainter

The rains slowly decreased in intensity and the water level in the creek crept down to much lower levels. Kuriakose did not go to Nor Garni the following weekend. But try as he might, when the following Saturday came around, he could not keep away any longer. He decided, in the Orthodox Christian tradition, to forgive Armine's indiscretion. The unsuspecting Ammachi at his request again cooked food for him to take. This time it was a thick omelet (*parinjil appam*) made of fish roe and grated coconut and *elayappam* (dumplings of rice with a filling of seeded jackfruit). His story was that he was going fishing to the Pamba River.

"Since when did you take up fishing?" she asked him in surprise. "You always called fishing a cruel sport of man trying to bait a species of inferior intelligence."

"Now that the university examination and the bank test are over, I want to relax. I will be back by evening before it is time to feed the cows."

Armine was in the flower garden watering the plants. She came over to the shoe-flower tree as he was leaning the bicycle against it.

"I have brought you something you will really like. Not spicy at all!" he said.

Her response took him by surprise.

"I am going to Pathanamthitta on Monday to do something."

"To do *something*?" asked Kuriakose in surprise.

"Yes. To do something."

"What is it that you are going to do there?" asked Kuriakose.

"Why do you want to know?" Armine shot back stone-faced. Then after a short pause, she added, "Some work for my father."

"Can I come with you to help?" Kuriakose could not help offering.

"No. If I depend on you for everything, I will never be able to do anything by myself."

"I am not offering my help to make you dependent on me," replied Kuriakose a trifle indignantly.

"Then why can't you take 'no' for an answer? Why do you keep pestering me for every single thing?"

"I am not pestering you, Armine jan. Why do you take it like that? I don't want you to get into any trouble with rowdies."

"Since when have you become my protector and bodyguard?" she asked turning to stare at him piercingly, anger writ large on her face.

Kuriakose was stumped.

"I am just happy to be with you. Why can't you understand that?"

"I told you not to hope. The real reason is that you suspect me. You want to know everything about me. Where I go, who I meet, what I do. "

"That is not true." Kuriakose's voice dropped to a near-whisper, "It is just that I am concerned about your safety. You will be safer if I am with you when you are in town."

Armine did not respond. Her blue eyes showed no mercy, her jaw was clenched firm, her lips a determined straight line.

His shoulders drooped. In a gesture of despair, he passed his right hand from his forehead to the back of his neck. Armine turned away.

He knew there was nothing more to be said.

"I am going," he said and waited expectantly for a change of heart from Armine. There was no response. Armine did not utter a word. She did not even turn around.

"I am leaving," he said once more before dragging himself despondently to the bicycle leaning against the shoe-flower tree.

Once on the cycle, the pent-up frustration combined with despair to produce rage—a helpless rage that expressed itself in furious pedaling. Standing almost upright on the pedals, he strained himself to the utmost, speeding to the top of the ridge and, once over the top, careening at near-reckless speed down the winding track before climbing again in the direction of the cave of death. When he parked the bicycle in the tapioca plot he realized he had completely forgotten about the *parinjil appam* and the *elayappam* in the cloth bag slung over the handlebar. Chiding himself for his temper he carried the bag to the big rock overlooking Nor Garni and, not one to waste food, slowly consumed all of it. When he had finished, the futility of his friendship with Armine hit him and he fought a losing battle to hold back the tears of rejection. The wind stung his eyes as he quickened his pace and tears streamed down his cheeks unchecked.

We look before and after,
And pine for what is not:
Our sincerest laughter
With some pain is fraught:
Our sweetest songs are those that tell of saddest
thought.

***

But there was no wind to blame for the tears that flowed down Armine's face from under the hands that covered her face as she sobbed soundlessly, her shoulders heaving as she crouched down on the pebbles in the backyard.

Her mother called out from the *verandah*.

"Armush, is everything all right? Why is it taking so long?"

"Mayrik jan, it will take only a minute," Armine replied hastily straightening up and getting back to the pots and pans she was scrubbing.

The lead weight of the secret of her rape and the loss of her virginity, the silence and uncertainty of Armen, the specter of soon becoming displaced, and, most of all, the shame of succumbing to temptation at the restaurant, even if only mentally, all combined to depress Armine beyond measure.

Tears, idle tears, I know not what they mean,
Tears from the depth of some divine despair
Rise in the heart, and gather in the eyes,

***

Kuriakose lay on his bed staring up at the thatch. In one fell swoop, his happiness had been snatched away most unexpectedly and all his hopes crushed. He wracked his mind for a probable cause. He could not recall any incident or action that could have been the tipping point.

Then a thought struck him. 'Maybe she is having an affair with that oaf, Vilen,' he thought. The more he considered it, the more plausible it appeared to him. 'Why else was he waiting with Hayrik when they returned after the bank test at Ernakulam?'

Jealousy and anger possessed him. 'Vilen lives next door to Armine and they can meet whenever they like.' 'With an alcoholic father and a sick mother who kept indoors weren't they free to do whatever they wanted?' 'And what is more, he is Armenian, and I am not.' Thoughts like these churned his mind into a whirlpool of jealousy and anger.

Then his feverish mind conjured up another more sinister possibility. 'Maybe she did not want him to accompany her because she had a rendezvous with that rake with whom she had flirted in the restaurant?'

His jealousy and anger snowballed till he could bear it no longer. Then he remembered Shakespeare. 'So, this is what Othello felt?' The irony of the thought did not escape him. He had not known what jealousy felt like when he answered that essay question in the examination. 'If I am Othello, Vilen is Iago and that dandy is Cassio,' he thought. 'No, they don't fit the characters and I would not kill Desdemona anyway.'

***

He did not go to confession on Sunday. He knew the priest Ouseph Achen would not understand and what if he asked him about the identity of Armine? That evening as he lay on his cot stewing in envy, self-pity, and jealousy, he had an idea.

He decided he would go to Pathanamthitta and catch Armine red-handed in the company of Vilen or the fop. The thought of confronting her and exposing her treachery appealed to him. At the same time, pangs of doubt struck him. 'Is it right to spy on Armine?'

On Monday morning, he told Appachen and Ammachi that he was going to the college for a career seminar but instead caught the bus to Pathanamthitta. He reached there before nine o'clock. He knew Armine's bus from the check-post would not arrive for another thirty minutes. He had a cup of coffee and waited. Time hung heavy. He was impatient to have irrefutable proof of Armine's duplicity.

As it got closer to the arrival of the bus, Kuriakose bought a copy of the *Malayala Deepika* newspaper. Then choosing the best location from which to view the passengers exiting the bus, he held the opened paper in front of him and waited. Nine thirty came and went. And then nine forty. There was no sign of Armine's bus. When the bus did not show up even at nine fifty Kuriakose was about to give up. Just then the bus lumbered into view. Quickly unfurling the paper to cover his face he peered over the top expectantly. Armine was among the last to get off, after all the standing passengers had first disembarked. She wore a light-blue half-sari and a spotless white blouse looking as much a college-girl as any other. Only her fair complexion and auburn hair gave her uniqueness away. Armine was alone. There was no sign of Vilen. He waited till all the passengers had got down to make sure Vilen was not on the bus.

Jealousy is an emotion that is not amenable to reason. Even though his first conjecture had been proved wrong his confidence in the second proving right only increased. He was sure she was here to meet the pseudo film actor. He quickly ran in the direction she had gone. It was not to the Sub-Divisional Office where they had gone the last time but to the Land Records Office that she had hastened. He waited outside in the searing heat for twenty minutes. When the heat became unbearable, he moved to the shade of the nearby banyan tree a short distance away.

Armine did not come out even after an hour. He decided to go in and investigate. He knew he ran the risk of Armine seeing him but jealousy overpowered reason. It was in the fourth room down the hall that he saw her. She was seated in front of a heavily powdered, dark complexioned woman sitting behind stacks of brown government files tied with strings. On seeing Kuriakose at the door, the official looked up from her files and Armine followed her look turned her head in his direction. Kuriakose quickly pulled himself back from the doorway and exited the building in haste. He was not sure if she had seen him or not. He went back to the banyan tree and waited. The pangs of hunger attacked him at noon. But he did not want to give Armine a chance to slip away. The hunger made the wait seem interminable.

Finally, at three-thirty she came out. He hurriedly held the newspaper up as he had done before. He saw her look around before unfolding her umbrella and walk briskly toward the bus stop. He followed her at a distance. She stopped in front of a small shop to drink a glass of lemon juice. Soon she reached the bus stop and boarded the waiting bus.

She had not come with Vilen nor had she met the rake. She had obviously come for some work relating to their relocation or land compensation.

He felt ashamed for doubting her and for snooping on her. Sheepishly he caught the bus home.

***

He went to Nor Garni on Saturday to meet Armine. This time he could not bring himself to ask Ammachi to cook anything special. Instead, he wrapped a large portion of banana chips that she had just fried and left to cool.

Armine was aloof and distant. Without a word, he handed over Saroyan's *The Daring Young Man on the Flying Trapeze*.

Armine looked at the book and then at him quizzically.

"Did you do this on purpose?" she asked.

"Did I do what on purpose?" he asked in a puzzled voice.

"You did not know that William Saroyan is Armenian?"

"No, I did not. He is not in our syllabus. I picked it up because I liked the title of the book. But now that you mention it, the name does sound Armenian."

"He is one of the most underrated of authors," said Armine. "He really deserved the Nobel prize."

William Saroyan was placed in an orphanage at the age of three after his father died. Some years later his mother found work in a cannery and reunited the family. His interest in writing was kindled when his mother showed him some of his father's writings that she had preserved. Saroyan was a troubled soul who wrote about the confused and uncertain life of the immigrant. His first love was unrequited. He married another. That marriage ended in divorce, remarriage, and divorce again a second time. He won the Pulitzer Prize for The Time of Your Life *but refused to accept it on the grounds that that play was not greater or better than any of his other works. In life, Saroyan was literally the daring young man on the flying trapeze.*

Armine brought coffee and *dolma* (grape leaf rolls stuffed with minced beef). When she looked at him questioningly, he wondered for a fleeting moment if she knew of his trip to Pathanamthitta trailing her.

Kuriakose decided to restart the conversation with a safer subject.

"How is Andranik doing, Armine jan?"

"Andranik is fine. His healing was so fast that he went back to school last week."

"Armine jan, I feel a great attachment towards Andranik. I was with him during his most difficult time. He is an angel. He is a very special boy," said Kuriakose.

"Don't get too attached to Andranik."

Armine's words took Kuriakose by surprise. He struggled to explain his affection for Andranik.

"There is a love that binds us closer than our families. It is a blessing from God to have affection like that in our lives. Sometimes we cannot find such deep love even in our own families. The friendship of David and Jonathan is the best example."

"All that may be correct. But I still say, don't get too attached to Andranik. He will grow up, have his own friends, and lead his own life. Don't set yourself up for disappointment. You will be disillusioned later."

That brought the conversation to a standstill. Kuriakose wondered why Armine would dissuade him from his friendship with Andranik. He thought about it for some time but could not come up with a satisfactory answer. Instead, his thoughts went back to Armine's solo trip to Pathanamthitta.

Ultimately, Kuriakose could not hold it in any longer.

"Did you go to Pathanamthitta on Monday?" he finally blurted out.

"Why do you ask? Why do you want to know?"

"No reason. Just like that. The last time you told me you were going. I was only asking if you actually went."

"Kuriakose, this idle curiosity is not good for you. You have your life and I have mine. I told you from the very beginning not to expect anything. I told you not even to hope."

"Armine jan, I do not expect anything. But I can hope, can't I?" asked Kuriakose.

"No. Don't even hope," Armine said evenly. "How many times have I told you that?"

"How can you stop me from hoping? How can anyone prevent anyone else from hoping? How can a living human being not hope?" argued Kuriakose passionately like a defense lawyer. "As long as there is life ..."

Armine cut him off.

"It is not difficult. Just do it. Don't say you will try. Just do it." Armine's response was as devoid of emotion as that of an impersonal, impartial judge.

"Armine jan, I told you already, I don't *expect* anything. Your harsh words have killed all of that. I have no expectations left, OK? None at all! But how can I keep my heart from hoping? As long as we are both alive and unmarried my heart cannot stop itself from hoping."

"Are you an idiot? Don't you understand anything of what I'm telling you?" she asked testily.

Kuriakose would not give in. "Hope springs eternal in the human breast ..."

"Don't recite poetry to me," she snapped. "Fine words and real life are two different things. If you have any sense at all, you will listen to me. There is no hope. Forget this foolishness. I am saying this for your good."

Kuriakose looked at her wordlessly. Her blue eyes showed no mercy. The auburn hair seemed like a ring of fire.

"For my good only? This does not affect you in any way?" he asked in a pleading voice.

"Me? No! I told you that from the very beginning. We Orthodox we believe in free will. Relationships are based on free will."

"Armine jan, can't the free will change?" implored Kuriakose.

"Not in my case. It maybe because of my past experience. It maybe because of my current situation and obligation."

"What past experience? What current situation? What are you talking about?" Kuriakose blurted out and immediately regretted it.

"See? Idle curiosity! You want to know everything about me! I told you many times, you have no right to know anything about me." After a pause, she added emphatically, "Nothing! Nothing at all!"

"I'm sorry. I didn't mean to pry ..." his voice trailed off.

Armine got up to bring some more coffee. Neither Hayrik nor Mayrik came out to the sitting room.

When Armine brought *ekler* along with the coffee there was silence for several minutes. Undeterred, Kuriakose opened the can of worms again.

"Armine, I am not asking for anything. Only for us to be friends. That is all. Is that too much to ask?"

"There cannot be friendship between a man and a woman." Armine was adamant.

"Even platonic friendship?" asked Kuriakose piteously.

"There is no such thing as platonic friendship between opposite sexes. There just cannot be."

"You don't know what you are talking about," Kuriakose retorted. "Literature is full of them.

Wordsworth and Dorothy. Sartre and Simone de Beauvoir. Pushkin and ...... I could go on."

"You are the one who is wrong. Wordsworth and Dorothy were siblings—brother and sister. Sartre and Simone de Beauvoir were lovers—not platonic friends. And you know what happened to Pushkin."

"You are probably right," conceded Kuriakose. "But there are other examples that I cannot recall now."

"But none of that is going to change anything between us. What am I saying! There is *nothing* between us. There never will be," Amine added decisively.

"I don't know what to say. Is being friends a crime?" argued Kuriakose unwilling to give up.

"Let us not argue about this. It will not get us anywhere. Just accept what I told you. We are NOT friends. Platonic friendship is possible only between persons of the same gender—not between a man and a woman."

Kuriakose was crestfallen.

"What are we then?" Kuriakose asked plaintively.

"Neighbors. Maybe just acquaintances," Armine said.

"Neighbors? With a dense forest and five kilometers (three miles) between us?" asked Kuriakose sarcastically.

"Far removed neighbors. Or distant acquaintances. Do you know, there is only one step, one very small step from love to hate?"

Armine's tone was not in the least bit conciliatory.

"I can never hate you, Armine. Never! I may despise or hate myself someday, but I can never hate you."

It was finally clear to Kuriakose that there really was no hope.

Chapter 22: Onam and the Boat Race

He did not go to Nor Garni the following Saturday. He did not go to the Saturday evening vigil at the Church either. On Sunday, he skipped confession and Communion yet again. He longed to unburden himself to Ter Samvel who was sympathetic and non-judgmental. Kuriakose believed that he was the only one who would understand his plight. But he could not go to Nor Garni and not see Armine—and he was not prepared to face her.

But when Onam (the Hindu harvest festival of Kerala that transcended religious barriers) came around, Kuriakose decided to make one last-ditch effort at winning Armine's heart or at least saving their friendship. Onam was the ultimate festival of the Malayalis of the state of Kerala. Hindu families invited their Christian and Muslim neighbors to their sumptuous Onam feasts. Although the festival had become something of a secular institution in recent times, with even a four-day public holiday, it was, to Kuriakose's grandparents, a pagan Hindu festival that they would never celebrate.

The other Onam tradition was the annual boat race. Hundreds of boats assembled on the Pamba River and tens of thousands (maybe more than a hundred thousand) spectators lined the banks or watched from bamboo bleachers in paid enclosures.

The highlight of the day was the race of the snake-boats (*chundan vallams*) at nearby Aranmula, where stood a temple dedicated to the Hindu gods Krishna and Arjun. The uniquely constructed snake-boats with narrow bodies as long as forty-five meters (one hundred fifty feet) and tails that tower six meters (twenty feet) over the water raced each other in pairs of two. Bare-chested oarsmen wearing fancy turbans sat in two parallel rows pulling oars to the rhythm of the chants of the leader who stood in the center of the boat with four helmsmen aft. Each boat had three large decorated ornamental umbrellas amidships.

Kuriakose had come early that morning with poetry books from the library and Salinger's *The Catcher in the Rye*. As usual, he had also brought Armine some food in his tiffin box. This time it was rice and beef *olathiyathu, parippu curry* and *parinjil appam*.

They went to the grassy knoll behind the house picking up the *dhurrie* off Qurkik-Jalali on the way.

"Is this the Onam feast?" she asked mischievously.

He looked up from the aluminum tiffin he was setting down on the *dhurrie*. "How many times must I tell you I am not a Hindu? I don't celebrate their festivals," he replied in an irritated tone.

She laughed. He knew immediately that she had tripped him up again.

"But seriously how many dishes make up the traditional Onam feast?"

"Nine," he answered. "But what I have brought is never part of that."

"I like this omelet. What is it made of?" asked Armine.

"It is made of fish roe and grated coconut. I brought it for you the last time but forgot to give it to you because you made me angry. Luckily the fisherwoman brought roe again this morning. We get roe only two months of the year."

"I like this. We make something with fish roe but without coconut. But I like this."

Seeing that she was in a good mood, and not as aloof as she was the on the last two occasions, Kuriakose made bold to ask.

"Have you ever been to the snake-boat race known as *vallam kali?*" asked Kuriakose expecting a snub in response.

Instead, to his surprise she replied. "No, but I have always wanted to go."

Kuriakose could not hide his happiness and hope.

"The snake-boat race is tomorrow. I can take you to see it. It is really beautiful. Very unique."

He half-expected her to fly off the handle at his audacity and humiliate him. Kuriakose wondered if he had pushed too much. Armine looked at him steadily.

"I would like to go but I have to ask Hayrik and Mayrik for permission first."

Kuriakose was overjoyed.

They went back to the house and while Kuriakose waited in the sitting room Armine went into her father's study. She was out quicker than he expected.

"Hayrik has agreed. Mayrik was in pain when we left and she is still sleeping. Since Hayrik has agreed, Mayrik will also surely agree. We can go tomorrow."

"I am so happy. I will come early tomorrow morning."

It was a happy Kuriakose who cycled back to the cave of death. Unexpectedly Armine had become friendly again. There was nothing that could have pleased Kuriakose more.

***

By ten o'clock the next day they were in Pathanamthitta. The town was full of people headed to the boat race at Aranmula. Taxis, buses, and even trucks carried people to the site of the *vallam kali.* Kuriakose and Armine managed to squeeze into a bus headed to the boat race. After getting off the bus near the famous temple they walked to the river bank where the viewing stands made of bamboo had been erected. Kuriakose thought of buying tickets but the bleachers were overcrowded. Instead, he led Armine through the milling crowds to a spot from where they could see unobstructed the boats in the river if they could only get closer to the front. As they inched their way forward through the crowd, three young men dressed in casual *lungis* ogled Armine and laughed lewdly. Kuriakose ignored them.

"They are hooligans—*goondas.* Don't pay any heed to them," said Kuriakose to Armine.

The noise was deafening. The chants of the boatmen from the river were drowned by the cheering crowds who filled every space available, with some even perched on trees and nearby housetops.

Each race had two boats in competition. They watched two races and were engrossed in the third when it happened without any warning. One moment they were on their toes, craning their heads above the spectators in front, as the two *chundan vallams* slid through the water neck and neck, the crowd joining in the rhythmic chants of the oarsmen, and the next Armine had spun around, her face flushed and angry.

"What happened, Armine jan?" asked Kuriakose anxiously.

"Those same men ..." she spluttered in anger pointing at the three men walking away guffawing loudly. "They touched me from behind ... those animals ..."

Kuriakose did not wait. He took off after them. Before the three knew what was happening, he had caught up with them. Reaching out he grabbed the left arm of the leader, the one in the middle, and spun him around.

"Why did you touch her? Don't you have sisters and mothers?" shouted Kuriakose.

The leader only smirked as he slapped Kuriakose's hand away.

"Who is she to you, this albino? Your kept woman?" he laughed derisively.

This infuriated Kuriakose to such an extent that he lost all self-control. Even as he looked, the hooligan seemed to morph into the dandy at the restaurant who had flirted with Armine behind his back. With both hands, he grabbed the shirt front of the antagonist and shook him vigorously.

"How dare you talk about her like that, you bastard?" Didn't your father teach you manners?" screamed Kuriakose in righteous indignation.

The other two thugs stepped forward to shove Kuriakose violently backward. The lapel of the ruffian's shirt tore as Kuriakose refused to let go.

The leader scowled in anger and raising his hands brought them down heavily on Kuriakose's shoulders. As Kuriakose stumbled backward, the man swung wildly. Kuriakose tried to duck but caught a glancing blow to the head. The leader and his cohorts stepped forward menacingly. Kuriakose was not about to give up. He swung upwards hitting the leader in the solar plexus. When the leader doubled up, his two accomplices jumped forward and grabbed Kuriakose by both arms.

It was when the leader straightened up with an ominous look on his face, that Armine, who had rushed up behind Kuriakose, jumped in. She slapped the leader on the face and shouted, "Police! Police! Catch this molester!"

The commotion and Armine's cry caused bystanders to turn in their direction. It was not clear whether the gang feared the fury of the mob or arrest by the policemen on patrol, but they suddenly let go of Kuriakose and took to their heels.

"Let them go," said Armine. "Let's go home. I've had enough."

The Russian poet and playwright Alexander Griboyedov's Georgian wife Nino was only sixteen when they married. Just months after the wedding he was sent to Persia as the Ambassador of Russia. Two Armenian women who had escaped from the harem where they were kept sought refuge in the embassy. When the Persian mob incited by the mullahs surrounded the embassy and bayed for blood, Griboyedov stood firm refusing to release the Armenian women. The crowd stormed the embassy through the roof and killed Griboyedov. After decapitating him they dragged his body through the streets. His body was recovered days later and taken to his beloved Georgia. On the way in Armenia, Pushkin, who was on a visit to the Caucasus, met Griboyedov's body. A memorial was erected there. 'Here A.S. Pushkin met A.S. Griboyedov.' Nino, lived another twenty-eight years. But faithful to the end, she spurned all suitors, and never remarried.

When they were some distance away from the crowd and had crossed the temple at Aranmula, Armine turned to Kuriakose.

"Kirakos jan, are you OK? Did they hurt you?" she asked solicitously.

"Forget about me, Armine jan. Did they hurt you?"

"I am all right. I didn't expect anybody to take liberties with me like that."

"I could have killed them," Kuriakose said his anger again rising.

"Thank you for defending me. You took a big risk attacking the three of them," Armine said.

"I am a pacifist but if anyone hurts you I will risk my life to protect you. I shouldn't have taken you to such a crowded place."

"No, it's all right. I enjoyed the boat race. Those snake-boats are beautiful."

"Yes, they are. We didn't stay for the final race. The winner gets the Nehru Cup."

Armine looked at Kuriakose in admiration.

"You surprised me. I never thought you would go after them," said Armine softly.

Armine's gratitude and appreciation delighted Kuriakose beyond words.

"It was nothing," he said. "Let's go home."

"God will bless you for what you did today. I had better not mention this to Hayrik or Mayrik."

"Yes, I don't mean to suggest keeping secrets from your parents, but they would be very worried if they came to know what happened today," agreed Kuriakose.

"By the way, I have been forgetting to tell you that even your friend who we met at the bank test has an Armenian name," said Armine.

"Really? Who? Radhakrishnan?" asked Kuriakose.

"Don't be silly! The other man, Geevarghese."

"I thought that name was a pure Kerala Christian name," said Kuriakose with a smile.

"The Armenian equivalent is Kevorkian. It is the same name."

When they reached home, Armine insisted that he stay for dinner. Mayrik smiled wanly at him as he and Armine sat at the table. 'She's looking very sick,' thought Kuriakose. *Lavash* and *kharcho* were served for dinner.

"This Armenian curry is very nice," said Kuriakose appreciatively.

Armine translated for Mayrik and they both laughed together. Kuriakose was perplexed.

"This is neither Armenian nor is it curry. It is Georgian lamb soup. The closest Armenian equivalent is the *bozbash*," explained Armine.

"I think this is the first time I've tasted lamb," said Kuriakose blushing. "We get only mutton or goat meat here in Kerala."

"Mayrik is happy that you like it," said Armine.

"*Shnorhakalutyun!*" said Kuriakose thanking Mayrik in Hayeren.

As usual, Armine walked with him up to the shoe-flower tree where the bicycle was. Dusk was deepening when Kuriakose reached home.

Chapter 23: The Test Results

The following afternoon Kuriakose and his classmates met at the college to discuss their career options and the forthcoming selection tests for government jobs.

It was Geevarghese who broke the news.

"The National Bank results are out!" he said brandishing the *Hindustan Express* newspaper that had arrived at Kozhencherry from Madras just before noon.

"Do you think anyone from our backwater pond will be selected? No. Not a chance! There are all those high society fellows from Delhi, Bombay, and Calcutta. Born with silver spoons in their mouths," ranted Radhakrishnan.

Geevarghese was less pessimistic. "Don't be so negative. Let us see how many have been selected from Ernakulam?"

"The results are not center-wise. Difficult to tell. The percentage of success? Maybe one in a thousand, maybe even one in two thousand. What chance do we paupers have?" continued Radhakrishnan.

"Here, give me the paper. We can tell by the first three digits," Kuriakose said holding out his hand.

When he saw the results he immediately froze. There was his number staring back at him. It was unmistakably his. He knew it by heart. There were only two others with the same three first digits of the Ernakulam exam center. Only three out of about five thousand had passed the test. Armine's number, which he also knew, was not on the list.

"My number is there," Kuriakose said trying to hide his excitement. "There are three from the Ernakulam center."

The others looked at him open-mouthed.

"Are you sure?" asked Radhakrishnan in a startled tone.

"Congratulations!" Geevarghese said graciously.

"When is the interview?" asked RK collecting his wits.

Kuriakose looked at the advertisement again. "It says here in four weeks' time. That would be by the end of October."

"When are you treating us?" asked Radhakrishnan.

"This is only the interview stage, RK. If I get the job, I will definitely treat you both and even the whole class. Can I keep the paper?"

Kuriakose ran all the way home. He stopped at the cooperative bank to show the result to Appachen.

"I am happy but are you sure this is your number?" asked Appachen.

"Yes, Appachen. This is mine."

"Go home and check it carefully against your hall-ticket. Only then can we be sure."

Appachen was right as always. He should not have announced his success without confirming first. On reaching home he pulled out the hall-ticket. The numbers tallied. He told Ammachi of the result and that he was going out for a short while.

The rains were not heavy but the water level in the creek had risen a little. He pondered for a moment whether to take the risk. He decided the news could not wait and splashed through the cave of death. The cycle was there by the tapioca plants.

Armine met him at the door.

"Barev, Kirakos jan. What happened?" she said but made no move to stand aside for him to enter.

"Barev, Armine jan! I have some good news. Won't you let me come in?"

"What is the news?" asked Armine not moving.

Kuriakose realized that she was not going to welcome him into their house. He was disappointed but tried not to show it.

"The National Bank results are out."

"You passed," she stated matter-of-factly.

"Yes, I did. Only three passed from the Ernakulam center."

"I had no hopes of passing. So, I am not disappointed," said Armine.

"Sorry. I was hoping you would pass."

"God knows what is best for me. Don't be sorry for me."

Kuriakose did not know whether to stay or go. Armine resolved the dilemma by opening the door wider and inviting him in.

"We must celebrate your success," she said.

Hayrik was closeted in his study. Mayrik smiled broadly and shook his hand, congratulating him over and over, saying "*Shnorhavorum em!*" which Armine translated as 'congratulations'.

In a short while, they had brought for him chicken cutlets and coffee. Kuriakose told Armine of the tentative date of the interview.

Armine translated what her mother said, "When you become a big man will you still remember us?"

Kuriakose was cut to the quick. "Please don't say that. I will forget my own name before I forget you. How can I ever forget you all?"

Mayrik's smile was sad and wistful when Armine translated.

"Mayrik jan, the rains are starting again. I will probably not be able to come and visit you till after the interview."

Only after he uttered these words did Kuriakose realize that he had for the first time addressed Armine's mother as Mayrik and both Armine and Mayrik had accepted it naturally.

Near the door, Kuriakose paused a moment to request Armine.

"Armine jan will you pray for me? Will you pray for my success in the interview?"

"I pray for everyone," Armine replied.

The vague and indefinite response to his earnest appeal jarred Kuriakose.

"Everyone? You pray for everyone?" asked Kuriakose plaintively.

"Yes, everyone," was the stoic, unyielding reply.

Before returning home Kuriakose went to Hayr's house and sought his blessings.

"Never forget that we ourselves we can do nothing. But with God all things are possible."

"Thank you, Ter Hayr, I will always remember that."

"Armine is going through a difficult time. As her priest and confessor, I cannot share more details with you. I cannot even share it with her family. Our whole family appreciates the support you are giving her, although sometimes it may not appear so to you."

"I will always do whatever I can for her. She has been as much of a help to me as well. Without Armine's support, I would never have returned to the Orthodox Church. But there are times when I think she dislikes me," said Kuriakose.

Ter Samvel smiled. "Sometimes it is difficult to understand women. We may never understand them completely. You need to keep in mind that she is promised … betrothed … to Armen."

"That I will always remember. I can never forget that," Kuriakose said resignedly.

"Did Armine tell you? Andranik is doing well in school. He still has the steel plate to protect his skull and he cannot play any kind of sports. But academically he is back to normal. His memory and cognitive ability have not been affected. God worked a great miracle. We will always be grateful to you for your help," said Ter Samvel.

"Please don't thank me for anything, Ter Hayr. I was only doing what little I could do. It is all God's mercy."

After he received the blessings of Ter Samvel for the trip and for the interview he hurried back home.

***

The call letter for the interview arrived the following week by registered post. The postman guessed somehow that the letter had to do with a job, and he lingered till he was given a tip.

The interview was in Bangalore and the bank would pay first class rail fare and board and lodging expenses at a flat rate per day. Kuriakose had never traveled by upper class in his life.

But first, he had to buy a tie. None of the shops in Kozhencherry stocked them and he had to go all the way to Pathanamthitta to find a musty old one that had lain unsold for years. Since there was no one to ask for help, he spent several hours trying to figure out how to knot the tie through trial and error.

***

First class travel was sheer luxury, with only four passengers in each compartment that would have taken twenty in second class. Stuffed leather seats and a fold-out berth, with pillows and sheets provided by the attendant.

Bangalore was the next surprise. It was cool, almost cold. Kuriakose enjoyed wandering around the posh Brigade Road window-shopping, a far cry from the village of Maramon and the small towns of Kozhencherry and Pathanamthitta.

Kuriakose was remarkably confident during the interviews and the group discussions that he faced over the next two days. After the last interview on the second day, the clerk took the onward first-class ticket that Kuriakose produced and reimbursed him twice the amount to cover the to and fro first-class fare and also paid him the per diem to cover the board, lodging, and other expenses.

For Kuriakose it was a lot of money. He had been frugal in eating at the cheapest restaurants and not spending money on anything else. He decided to travel back by second class and with the savings buy Armine a present. He changed into the more comfortable *mundu* and sandals for the overnight journey. Kuriakose walked around gawking at the shops near the railway station but could not be sure what Armine would like. In the end when he was just about to give up hope he had an idea. He hurried to the biggest and most brightly lit cloth shop nearby and bought what he thought would be enough red georgette for a dress for Armine.

The unreserved second-class compartment was cramped. There were five passengers on every seat meant for three, three more on the side and two each on the luggage rack above. Those who could not find a seat squatted in the vestibule and the passageway. Gingerly picking his away to avoid stepping on anyone Kuriakose found a place in the middle with barely sufficient space to sit down. The congested conditions caused the knees of the passengers facing each other to almost touch. He slid his airbag under the seat and waited in the suffocating heat for the train to move to get some fresh air.

It was then that Kuriakose noticed the young woman, who must have been a year or two younger, staring at him. She sat directly opposite him on the facing seat, flanked by two passengers on either side. He discovered from the conversations he heard later that the two men who sat on either side of her were her father and uncle and the woman who sat next to her father on the window side was her mother.

A short while after the train started moving the cool night breeze and the accumulated stress of two days of interviews combined to put him to sleep. To avoid falling asleep on the shoulders of the passengers to his left and to his right, he leaned forward, crossed his arms over his lap and placing his head on his folded forearms, promptly fell asleep.

The train ran through the night while Kuriakose slept a fitful sleep. It was about an hour and a half later that he felt the touch. Somebody's foot was touching his. He moved his foot away slightly, but the other foot returned. He moved his toe away again but to no avail. It then dawned on him that the contact was deliberate. Without straightening up he opened his eyes slowly to look down at his feet. They were not visible. The *sari* of the young woman opposite covered his toes. In the guise of adjusting his posture, he looked at the faces opposite. The mother had fallen asleep leaning against the window, her gray hair fluttering in the wind. The father and uncle, ever watchful, stared straight ahead sternly. The young woman gave him a flushed, conspiratorial look. He then realized what was happening. Sleep left him and he became wide awake.

Kuriakose was excited by the audacity of their action right under the noses of her father and uncle. In a society where it was forbidden for unmarried young men and women to even meet unchaperoned, let alone have even the most innocuous of physical contacts, this was daring in the extreme. He laid his head down again in his lap as if to sleep but he was never more awake. His toes dueled with the toes of the young woman opposite. Unbeknownst to her chaperones, their toes wrestled and intertwined with each other with gentle tenderness alternating with wild insistence. He tickled the soft palm of her foot with his big toe. She was no less demanding.

The twelve hours of train travel passed in this fashion. Before they knew it, the train had reached Ernakulam, the end of the broad-gauge line. Kuriakose tried to catch the woman's eye but she resolutely avoided looking at him and disembarked with her parents and uncle without even a glance in his direction.

Kuriakose changed to the meter gauge line that took him to Thiruvalla from where he caught a bus to Kozhencherry.

When he reached home the enormity of what he had done hit him. Armine had only flirted with her eyes; he had sinned through physical contact with a stranger and that too a non-Christian. He was overcome with remorse.

***

August was a big month for news headlines. The President of Bangladesh, Sheikh Mujibur Rahman, and his entire family were assassinated in a coup d'etat. The Helsinki Accord was signed which recognized European national borders and human rights but also ratified the Soviet annexation of Latvia, Lithuania, and Estonia. After Vietnam and Cambodia, Laos became the third Southeast Asian nation to fall to the Communists. The incarcerated Emperor of Ethiopia, Haile Selassie, died in captivity. Agatha Christie's fictional character Hercule Poirot died in *Curtain*.

Chapter 24: Kappa and the Cows

Kuriakose pedaled with high expectations to Armine's house. Over coffee, *lahmajun* and *khachapuri* he gingerly took out the gift-wrapped package from the shoulder bag which he had carefully placed next to him on the sofa.

"I have a small gift for you from Bangalore," he said holding out the wrapped package.

"Gift? I cannot accept any gift from you," Armine said bluntly.

Kuriakose's face fell. This was completely unexpected. He had expected Armine to be thrilled to receive the present he had brought for her.

"Why would you not accept a gift from me? It is a present. There are no strings attached."

"Why should I accept it? It must be expensive."

"Please don't worry about the price. It is a token of my appreciation. If you don't accept it there is no one I can give it to," Kuriakose pleaded.

"You bought it without asking me and now you are compelling me to accept it because there is no one else to give it to?" Armine was unrelenting.

"I'm not forcing you, Armine jan. Accepting a gift is the natural thing to do."

"I don't think so."

"I cannot believe this!" Kuriakose said. "I feel as if I am demanding a gift from you instead of me giving you a gift!"

"What is in the packet?" Armine asked.

"Please open it and see," Kuriakose said with hope.

"You treat me like a toy," said Armine petulantly.

Armine's words wounded Kuriakose to the core. He wondered why she would have said that and if she could not see how precious she was to him, almost as dear as life itself.

Armine received the packet with studied reluctance. When she opened the wrapping carefully and saw the shimmering red cloth, she blushed as red as the cloth that lay in her lap. Kuriakose was relieved to detect a trace of happiness in her eyes.

"Where did you get the money for this?" asked Armine.

"The bank paid me return first class fare but I traveled by second class. I also saved more than half the daily allowance," Kuriakose explained.

"This is the same red color that you disliked when we went for the written test," Armine reminded him.

"Red suits you, Armine jan. It matches your reddish-brown hair and fair complexion. That day we were going for an examination and not a wedding."

"You have now become a fashion advisor?" countered Armine.

Kuriakose smiled embarrassedly.

Armine continued, "Since you've already purchased it and you have no one else to give it to, I will keep it. Let me bring you some more coffee."

Armine went to let Hayrik know Kuriakose had come. Hayrik came to the door and beckoned Kuriakose to come in.

"Congratulations! Well done! I didn't get to meet you before you left for your interview," he said loudly, holding out his hand. It was clear that he had had one too many.

"Thank you," Kuriakose mumbled in embarrassment as he shook hands with Armine's father. "I don't know how I passed the written test, Sir."

"You are a hardworking, intelligent young man. I saw that in you the first time you came here. How was the interview?"

"I did my best. There were interviews and group discussions."

"You will pass. You will be selected. Mark my words!" predicted Hayrik.

Kuriakose blushed when he remembered Hayrik's anger the night they had returned home from the bank test in Ernakulam.

As if reading his mind Hayrik continued, "I was not angry with you on the day of the test. I know you will not harm Armine. But as a father, I have to be protective towards my daughter. She is my only child. You understand?"

Kuriakose nodded.

"A glass of wine to celebrate?" offered Hayrik.

"No, no, no. I will not drink alcohol. I'm having coffee."

Hayrik went to the table to pour himself a tall glass of red wine and took two large swigs.

"We Armenians we love our wine. The other thing we love is to travel. Our nation is a heaven on earth, but we still go searching for comfort in other places."

"Armine told me about how Armenians came to India," said Kuriakose.

"Armenians never colonized—NEVER! We went to all the same countries as the British, the French, the Dutch, the Spanish, and the Portuguese. They looted the wealth of the countries they colonized and subjugated the people. Armenians never did that. The others forced the natives to convert to their religion. Armenians never did that. They only built churches for themselves wherever they went," said Hayrik warming to the subject.

"Armenians went to all those countries?" asked Kuriakose.

"Yes. You take India. The British were the main colonizers. The Portuguese had Goa, Daman, and Diu. The French were in Pondicherry, Chandernagar, Mahe, Karaikal, and Yanam. The Dutch had bases all over the coastline of India, on both the west coast and the east coast. Armenians were in all the same places, but they did not rule. We traded, we did business. We treated the indigenous peoples with respect, as equals. We did not have the superiority complex of the Europeans who treated the natives like dirt."

"What about the rest of Asia? Did Armenians go to other places too?"

"We went everywhere! Armenians were an adventurous, seafaring nation. It is a pity that we are a landlocked country now. In olden days, our trading ships took us to every distant port— Singapore, Indonesia, Malaysia."

"Were Armenians liked by the locals, I mean the natives?"

"By and large, yes. But there were those who were jealous of our prosperity, mostly the ones who were lazy and not as industrious as us."

> *Julfa thrived on the banks of the Araks river. When the Shah of Persia came to visit, he marveled at the prosperity and the entrepreneurial abilities of the Hayks. His wicked mind saw only one way to instill these qualities in his own slothful and unenterprising people. He ordered his soldiers to demolish the entire town within three days, forcing the Hayks to abandon their beloved Julfa. The deceitful Shah then made a pretense of inviting them to Ispahan where he offered them land on the outskirts. The hardworking Hayks built a town there, which they aptly named New Julfa. Their new abode became an important feeder point for trading the goods they procured from India which they sent through the Silk Road. The route from New Julfa was first to the port of Basra on the Euphrates from where they sailed by sea to India. The wealth and riches of the enterprising Hayks provoked the envy of a subsequent Shah and the Hayks had to again flee with their possessions stealthily in the dead of the night."*

"How unjust! How unfair!" Kuriakose was outraged.

"The malice and meanness of the Persians were nothing compared to the brutality and ruthlessness of the Turks. They mercilessly killed two million of our people, including women and children and liquidated our intelligentsia."

> *The news came from Van.* "Ermenleri hep kesdiler—hep gitdi bitdi!" *("The Armenians all killed—all gone, all dead!") The three gendarmes of Husein Pasha stood guard at the gate while the Pasha walked in to ask for the fourteen-year-old younger daughter for the Sultan's harem. The options were to either sell or hand her over or, failing both, face the consequences. This was the third visit. The sell option was not offered this time—only give; to become the nineteenth Christian concubine in the Sultan's harem. All that was needed to make it legal was for the young girl to renounce Christ and become a Muslim. From her room on the first floor, she heard her father's tortured voice refusing the Pasha. The Pasha offered protection to the entire family if the daughter was given. But the father said, "God's will shall be done—and He would never will that my child should sacrifice herself to save us." The fourteen-year-old was willing to pay the price to save her family. But her mother and elder sister held her firm till the soldiers came and tore her away from their hold.*

"The genocide was a blot on humanity. All occupiers were generally cruel to the local people," said Kuriakose.

"The Dutch in Batavia were the most cruel ..."

Before Hayrik could complete what he was saying, Vilen burst into the room in an agitated state.

"The cows are all dead! The cows are all dead!" he wailed.

On hearing the commotion Armine and Mayrik rushed in from the kitchen.

"Calm down. Tell us what happened. Speak clearly!" commanded Hayrik.

"The cows got into the tapioca garden. They have all fallen on the ground—dead," Vilen said.

"All the cows?"

"Yes, all. Yours, mine, Ter Samvel's, and Mher's. I had gone to the other side of the hill to look for the sheep."

"Tell the truth? Where were you?" thundered Hayrik.

"I was ... was ... asleep. Only for a few minutes ..." Vilen confessed.

"You idiot!" shouted Hayrik. "Twenty-two cows! What a loss!"

Kuriakose stepped in. "Are the stomachs of the cows swollen? Are you sure they are dead?"

Vilen sneered, "What do you know about cows?"

Armine jumped into the fray. "Kirakos jan, don't help if he does not want your help!" she said in anger. "Just mind your own business."

Though he knew that there was no love lost between Armine and Vilen, Kuriakose was surprised at the intensity of her anger.

"But your cows are also there, Armine jan!"

Armine walked out of the room without saying a word.

"Their stomachs are all swollen like big balloons. They are all lying on the ground. None of them are moving," said Vilen.

"Do you have an iron stake? The one you tether a cow to?" asked Kuriakose.

"We have one in our cow pen," said Hayrik.

Kuriakose said to Vilen, "Let's go. We do not have a minute to lose."

Hitching up his *mundu* he started running towards the cow pen. Vilen followed with loping strides.

The stake had been driven into the ground near the entrance to the cow pen. Kuriakose tried in vain to pull it free. Vilen grabbed it from him and with one mighty heave pulled it out of the earth. With Vilen carrying the heavy wrought iron stake in his right hand they set off again, Vilen leading the way this time. It was not the tapioca garden on the way to the cave of death but another that was in the opposite direction.

The mayhem was visible from afar. The normally upright tapioca plants were pointing in different directions, flattened, bent or broken. It was as if a giant dinosaur had stomped through the garden. They dove into the garden through the break in the fence through which the cows had entered.

Kuriakose snatched the stake from Vilen and rushed towards the nearest cow. The cow lay with glazed eyes, froth oozing out of its mouth. Kuriakose knelt by the cow to confirm it was alive. He ran his hand over the swollen stomach that seemed on the point of bursting. Then standing up he held the stake with both hands as high as he could and rammed the sharp edge down on the stomach of the motionless, supine bovine.

The stake pierced the skin and sank in. When Kuriakose let go for a moment, the vertical stake quivered like a thick needle in an overstuffed cushion. Then with one swift move, he yanked it out. With a loud whoosh, the bottled-up gas erupted along with blood and bodily fluids. The enormously bloated stomach collapsed like a punctured balloon. Kuriakose waited a minute to see the cow's condition. The glazed, wide-open eyes shut and reopened. The ears twitched. The breathing returned to normalcy.

Kuriakose did not waste another moment. He ran to the nearest and then from one cow to the next till they all were breathing again. Drained by exhaustion and the adrenaline Kuriakose slumped to the ground and surveyed the scene. A few were already on their feet milling around unsteadily. Vilen was assisting a struggling cow to get back on its feet.

"Leave it alone! Get them all out!" screamed Kuriakose to Vilen. "Get them out before they eat the tapioca leaves again. Make them walk around. They need the exercise."

He wanted to lie back and rest. His arms felt like deadweights. The muscles on his back ached for relief. But looking around he realized Vilen alone could not get all the cows out in time. He staggered up to help herd the cows to the pasture outside.

The cows seemed in no condition to walk all the way back to their cow pens for the night. They were sluggish, drowsy, and disoriented.

Kuriakose sat down on the grass winded, the bloodied stake by his side. He saw Hayrik and Mher talking to Vilen in the distance. He took off his *madras* shirt and sleeveless vest and lay back bare-chested on the grass and closed his eyes.

When he opened them again, he saw Hayrik and Mher looking down at him. He had not heard them walk up silently on the grass. Kuriakose scrambled hastily to his feet in spite of their protestations.

"You saved all our cows," said Mher. "We did not lose even one. We are very grateful."

"If you were not here, they would all be dead," Hayrik added.

Vilen stood a step behind and did not say a word.

"It is nothing," said Kuriakose. "I was present in Nor Garni quite by chance."

"How did you know what to do?" asked Hayrik.

"I have been through this before. As you know, we don't let our cows roam free. So, we don't need to fence our tapioca areas. Once, two of my grandfather's cows that were tethered to the same stake somehow managed to pull the stake out of the ground and went on a rampage in the tapioca field. My grandfather deflated their distended stomachs with an iron stake."

"Vilen told us how you did it. Initially, he was worried you would kill them."

"I thought the same when I saw my grandfather do it," Kuriakose replied.

"What actually causes it?" Hayrik was curious.

"Tapioca leaves react with the acid in the cow's stomach and produces hydrocyanic acid. It is basically cyanide poisoning which kills them. The swelling of the stomach with gas creates so much internal pressure that their vital systems also shut down."

"Our forefathers knew that tapioca leaves were poisonous. That is why we fence our tapioca plots. But I don't think they knew of this drastic remedy," said Mher.

"They need to be fed jaggery or molasses once they get home," reminded Kuriakose.

"Let us go home. Let us feed ourselves too! This calls for celebration," said Hayrik.

"Before we go, the fence needs to be mended. Otherwise, cows or sheep might enter again and get killed," said Kuriakose.

Hayrik directed Vilen to repair the fence. Kuriakose walked home with his shirt and vest in his hands, Hayrik and Mher flanking him.

Mayrik and Armine were waiting outside. When Armine saw Kuriakose's hairy upper torso she thought he looked more Armenian than he ever did. On reaching home, Mher narrated the story to Armine and Mayrik, who were anxious to hear of the fate of the cows. Mayrik beamed with happiness and profusely thanked Kuriakose.

"Shnorhakalutyun! Shnorhakalutyun!" (Thank you! Thank you!)

But Armine's face was impassive. She did not utter a word. She wordlessly brought a towel and a bar of bathing soap. Kuriakose went to the outhouse at the rear to bathe.

Hayrik had brought out a bottle of homemade wine. Kuriakose was embarrassed to decline but he held firm politely even when Hayrik persisted. He had had a close call the day he brought home Andranik. He did not want to risk it again.

"If possible, I would like a glass of apricot juice," requested Kuriakose.

While Armine went to fetch it Hayrik and Mher moved to the study to drink wine and talk leaving Kuriakose alone in the sitting room. When Armine came back with the fruit juice and a plate of *dolma*, Kuriakose could not restrain himself.

"Armine jan, you don't seem very happy at what happened?"

"Why should I?" was Armine's swift response.

"Your cows were there too."

"If the fool had taken care of the cows all this drama would not have been necessary."

Kuriakose was disappointed by the ingratitude. He scowled as he sipped the apricot juice.

"It is difficult to please some people," he muttered sarcastically.

"My parents already thanked you. What more do you want me to do? Bow down before you and touch the earth?"

This only made Kuriakose angrier. He fumed but did not respond.

Armine then surprised him by saying, "What you did actually made me very happy. You saved our cows."

Kuriakose was puzzled by the faint, mysterious smile on Armine's face as she added, "You also heaped burning coals on his head."

Bel came with his hordes to vanquish Hayk and his people and bring them under his authority again. Hayk was not easily threatened. He rallied his people to defend themselves and repulse the attackers. Bel was taken by surprise and turned tail and retreated. Hayk did not let them get off so easily. He and his people pursued them. An arrow that Hayk the skillful archer let fly pierced the armor of Bel killing him. He fell to the ground dead with the quivering arrow standing vertically upright.

Hayrik and Mher came out of the study.

"We have a question for you," said Hayrik in a slurred voice. "Do you think Emergency is good for India?"

"Sir, that is a difficult question. Trains run on time, government offices are more responsive, there is less bribe-taking ... but there is also less freedom, especially freedom of the press. All newspapers are censored. The Indian government even expelled three British journalists," replied Kuriakose.

"Who cares about freedom in this country? Only the rich have freedom. They have freedom to do anything they want. The middle-class and the poor are not worse off under the Emergency," said Hayrik.

"Sir, that may not be completely true. There is a lot of latent opposition to the Emergency. It is slowly building up ... especially against the Young Turks ..."

Hayrik froze. "What did you say?" he roared.

Kuriakose immediately realized he had made a huge faux pas. "I meant the younger leaders of the Congress party of Indira Gandhi, like Ghulam Nabi Azad. They are known by that name in the newspapers ..." Kuriakose tried to explain.

"I don't care what the newspapers say. The Young Turks are directly responsible for the Armenian Genocide. Don't ever use that term in this house. Do you understand? Is that clear?" Hayrik was livid.

> *Talaat, Enver, and Djemal Pasha were the leaders of the secretive CUP (Committee of Union and Progress) also known as the* Young Turks *or in Turkish* Jön Türkler or Genç Türkler. *Their strong nationalist tendencies received public support amongst the Turks, and they seized power in 1913. The triumvirate was directly responsible for the genocide of the Armenians, which they instigated and actively implemented with inhuman cruelty. They also supported Germany in World War I. In November 1918, the three Pashas fled the country, but they could not escape justice. Fittingly, they were served their just desserts; Talaat by Soghomon Tehlirian in Germany; Djemal by Stepan Dzaghikian, Bedros Der Boghosian, and Ardashes Kevorkian in Georgia; and Enver was killed by the Red Army in Tajikistan.*

The news journal of Kuriakose recorded the two assassination attempts, both by women, within days of each other on President Ford, who was unhurt in both incidents. A big earthquake in

Turkey killed three thousand people in Diyarbekir. In boxing, Muhammad Ali defeated Joe Frazier in Manila. Andrei Sakharov won the Nobel Peace prize but did not receive permission to travel out of the Soviet Union to receive the prize.

Chapter 25: The Big City

The telegram arrived out of the blue. Kuriakose's thoughts went back to the wire that brought him news of Andranik's accident and he received the telegram with trepidation. Only when he opened it did he understand why the postman had a smug look on his face. He expected a big tip for being the harbinger of good news.

The telegram read:

THAZHAKANDATHIL KURIAKOSE MATHEW STOP YOU HAVE BEEN SELECTED AS PROBATIONARY OFFICER STOP REPORT TO CALCUTTA HEAD OFFICE BY DECEMBER FIRST WEEK STOP LETTER FOLLOWS

His joy knew no bounds. He ran to the house from the courtyard shouting, "Ammachi! Ammachi! I got the job!"

Ammachi came out of the kitchen wiping her hands on the thin cotton towel that served as an apron.

"God bless you, son!" Then, seeing the postman waiting near the steps leading up from the road, she said, "Give him some money. Make him happy."

"Where will be your job? At Cochin or Ernakulam?" she asked.

"No, Ammachi. It is very far away at Calcutta. It is three days' journey by train."

All of Ammachi's happiness evaporated in an instant to be replaced by a look of dejection.

She opened her mouth to say something but thought the better of it and went back to her kitchen.

Oblivious of his grandmother's apprehension, Kuriakose changed into decent clothes and ran all the way to the cooperative bank to tell his grandfather.

This was the first time he had seen Appachen so unabashedly happy. He beamed from ear to ear.

"God bless you, son!" he said making the sign of the cross.

But just as quickly Appachen was businesslike again.

"You need to go to Chengannur railway station and book your tickets right now. You have to be there next week. Travel first class. They will pay you when you report for duty," he said giving him money.

Kuriakose left by the next bus to make the reservation. By the time he returned home, it was night. The only reservations available were on the fourth day, which left him just three days to prepare for the trip and the cataclysmic upheaval in his life.

***

The next morning, he went to meet his friends. The shy bookworm was by now a local hero.

"How did you do this? Teach us also!" said Radhakrishnan.

He treated them to Kerala coffee and *halwa* and promised them a big feast at home when he came back on annual leave.

"To collect a big fat dowry and marry a rich heiress?" teased Radhakrishnan. "A bank manager is a big catch. All the millionaires will line up with their daughters and their gold."

'If only I could marry Armine, I would give all my money away,' thought Kuriakose.

He went to the college to pay the fees for the degree certificate to be mailed home when it was issued months later.

On the way back home, he stopped by the only bookstore in Kozhencherry and bought an expensive book, *The Romantic Age of Poetry* as a farewell gift for Armine.

Ammachi waited on him at dinner with even more devotion and affection than usual.

"After how many years will you be eating our food again!" she lamented.

"Don't worry about him. He will soon be eating like a *sayip* (white man)," said Appachen jocularly.

***

The next day he went to bid goodbye to Armine and her family. The joyous news of his success was eclipsed by the news of his imminent departure. He saw sadness in their eyes and the parting itself was awkward.

When Kuriakose presented the book of poetry wrapped in brown paper, Armine accepted it reluctantly and did not open it till he insisted. She did not show any emotion when she opened the package and merely said, "Thank you. I will bring coffee."

"Congratulations! What did I tell you? Didn't my prediction come true? Didn't I say that you would succeed?" Hayrik patted him on his shoulder as they shook hands.

"Calcutta used to be a big center for Armenians," said Hayrik. "There used to be a road called Armenian Street there. But the Communists may have changed it by now to Lenin or Marx."

> *The Englishman Job Charnock's name will go down in history as the founder of the city of Calcutta, which at one time was known as the 'city of palaces' and later as the 'black hole'. But just as the Armenian Mar Thomas had reached the Malabar Coast before Vasco da Gama did, an Armenian was in Calcutta before Charnock ever set foot there. Charnock's tomb in the St. John's Cathedral of Calcutta was considered the oldest European's, but the tomb of Rezabeebeh (wife of Sookeas) in the Armenian cemetery precedes Charnock's by sixty years.*

> *Charnock stamped out the horrifying practice of sati (the mandatory suicide of the Hindu wife on the funeral pyre of her husband) because he was enamored of an attractive young bride about to commit sati. He rescued her and took her home and they lived together until her death many years later. She bore him several children.*

Armine and her mother brought *lahmajun* and coffee.

"Why are you leaving so soon?" asked Mayrik in Armenian and Armine translated.

"They gave just a week's time. The only rail reservation available was the day after tomorrow."

When Armine's parents left the two of them alone Kuriakose asked Armine, "You will write every week, won't you?"

"Do you think we are living next to a post office? This is Nor Garni, a village in the forest, a village that will soon vanish."

"But we will keep in touch through letters?" asked Kuriakose tentatively.

"You already know I am not good at writing letters. Let us not make promises that we cannot keep. Time will show."

"How can you send me away with such heartless words?" Kuriakose said pitifully.

But Armine had no mercy. "Let us be realistic. Who knows what the future holds for my family and me. We do not know where we will go from here. Only God knows where life will take you. If it is God's will we will meet again. If not ..." She left it incomplete.

Kuriakose felt incredibly sad.

As he was pondering over what she had just said, Armine added, "You are so lucky to be alone. You can go where you want to go and do what you want to do."

It was like turning the knife in the wound. 'Does she think I'm lucky to be parentless? Doesn't she know I'd give everything to have Appa (father) and Amma (mother) back again?'

Kuriakose was infinitely tired. Armine went to call her parents. He shook hands gravely with Hayrik and waved goodbye to Mayrik and Armine and left the house. He walked to the garden and took one final look at the *aryunashushan* flower before leaving.

From there Kuriakose went to bid Ter Samvel goodbye. Ter Samvel was effusive in his praise and prayed for success at his new job and for safety in the big city. Kuriakose felt remorseful that he had not brought any candy for Varazdat and Varduhi.

"How is Andranik doing?" asked Kuriakose.

"He has completely recovered. The steel plate was removed. He cannot play sports for another six months but other than that he is the same Andranik he was before the accident," said Ter Samvel.

"I feel sad to be leaving without seeing him."

"God bless you, Kuriakose jan and may others be a blessing to you as you have been to us," said Ter Samvel blessing him.

He shook hands with Ter Samvel and Tikin Karine and hugged the children, Varazdat and Varduhi, before he left.

***

He spent the last full day before the journey at home. In the afternoon when the heat had lessened, he went to his secret grove for one final time. He did not carry any books with him to read. Instead, he savored in silence the quiet wonder of the spot that had brought him solace in his most difficult days. This was also the place where Armine, his unattainable, yet deeply yearned for friend, had first appeared less than a year ago. He listened to the cawing of the crows, watched the kingfisher and the water snake in the stream, and hoarded into the deepest recesses of his soul the impressions and memories of this sacred place that he wanted never to forget.

> *There was a time when meadow, grove and stream,*
> *The earth and every common sight,*
> *To me did seem*
> *Apparell'd in celestial light,*
> *The glory and freshness of a dream.*

When the sun went down, he trudged home in the fading light. From Wordsworth, he moved to Gray.

> *Now fades the glimmering landscape on the sight,*
> *And all the air a solemn stillness holds …*

When he got home, he made the last entry in the journal of current affairs. He would not need to keep this journal anymore. Among the entries for November were the coup and countercoup in neighboring Bangladesh. The Russian-backed MPLA defeated the FNLA and captured Luanda, the capital of Angola. The most heart-wrenching news was the bloodshed and violence that erupted in freshly liberated East Timor, another former Portuguese colony.

***

"Son, never forget God. Always remember the Church. Ammachi and I will pray for you every day. Always keep your promises. Don't promise hastily what you cannot deliver. Never steal anything from the office, things or time. Do your work as to God, not to man," advised Appachen as they waited the next day for the taxi to arrive to take them to the railway station.

Ammachi cried while Appachen prayed before they stepped out of the house. Appachen had never looked more vulnerable. Parting was not easy. He had not hugged them since middle school. Finally, Ammachi could not restrain herself any longer. She quickly hugged him and kissed him on both cheeks.

Kuriakose slung the heavy steel trunk over his back and Appachen helped carry the airbag to the taxi. Appachen had decided to go with him to the station to see him off. Nothing more was said in the taxi or at the station where they waited silently for the Madras Mail to arrive.

"Go with God," said Appachen before Kuriakose boarded the train. When Kuriakose looked out of the window he saw Appachen watching the moving train with a forlorn look.

He did not imagine that he would not see Appachen or Ammachi again.

After twelve hours, the train arrived at Madras Central station the next morning. He would not have cared if it had taken a hundred hours. Traveling by the uncrowded first class was a luxury to be savored. The train from there to Calcutta was in the afternoon. Again, access to the first-class waiting room made the wait easier. The Coromandel Express from Madras took forty hours to get to the Howrah station in Calcutta.

It was biting cold when he stepped out of the train the second morning at Howrah. For someone who had not experienced the seasons in equatorial Kerala, it felt bitterly cold in shirtsleeves. It was the coldest he had ever felt; much colder than Bangalore where he had gone for the interview. The language was different too. Everyone spoke Bengali, a language he had never even heard before. Nobody seemed to understand the accented, broken Hindi he spoke. He shivered in the cold as he bargained with a taxi to take him to the nearest YMCA. The taxi deposited him at the ancient YMCA on Chowringhee Road in central Calcutta. He hurried to get ready to report for duty. To his chagrin, the hot water tap did not work. He quivered like a leaf when the cold water hit him.

When he asked the receptionist for directions, he was surprised to find that the office was within walking distance. He was even more surprised when he discovered that the very next street was called Armenian Street just as Hayrik had mentioned. He saw this as a good omen. The formalities in the personnel department, including a medical test at a nearby doctor's, took all day. That evening when he got back to the YMCA, he wrote letters to Appachen and Ammachi and also a letter to Armine care of the check-post.

***

He bought a sweater the next day and slowly adjusted to the winter weather and the politics of working in an office where direct recruits were viewed with jealousy and suspicion by long-serving clerks. Kuriakose's earnestness and lack of guile slowly won the confidence and the support of the much older employees whom he supervised.

Two weeks later he found long-term lodgings in the nearby Birchmore Mansions, a hostel run by the Birchmore Society, a charitable Anglo-Indian association with branches all over eastern India that helped poor children to get an education.

The accommodation was Spartan and the food pseudo-British. He was puzzled the first time to find only a single potato and a small cup of soup for dinner. No piles of rice and curry as he was used to. But he not only got used to the bland cuisine but also soon developed an affinity for it.

He wrote letters every week to his grandparents and to Armine. No replies came from Armine; but letters from Appachen, with the address painstakingly copied in English and the letters in beautifully scripted Malayalam, arrived every two weeks. There was news of the birth of a new calf, of the dam construction nearing completion, of church activities but only a line at the very end on his and Ammachi's health. The only classmate he kept in touch with was Radhakrishnan, RK. They wrote each other at least once a month. RK could not pass any of the competitive examinations even for clerical jobs and remained unemployed. The despair in his letters made Kuriakose feel guilty.

When he got his first salary, he sent half of it by money order to Appachen and Ammachi. But he was furious when Appachen informed him in his next letter that he had given a portion of that as a gift to Ouseph Achen, the priest. He wrote an angry letter to his grandfather. It was only weeks later during his evening prayers that he was overcome with remorse for disrespecting the office of priesthood. He immediately wrote a tearful letter of apology to Appachen.

His first significant purchase was a transistorized Murphy radio. But his hopes of listening to radio stations from overseas like the BBC and the VOA were dashed to the ground because of high noise and electrical interference. The only station he could listen to comfortably was the local station of All India Radio. He fell in love with the *Statesman* newspaper and read it assiduously every day. From time to time, there were reports of delays pushing back the commissioning of the new Pamba River dam. Kuriakose received news of the delays with gratitude. 'Maybe when he went home on annual leave at the end of the year Armine and Nor Garni would still be there! What expensive gifts would he carry for Armine like Solomon for Sheba!'

After almost five months of silence from Armine, he began registering the letters he sent in the hope that the acknowledgment signed in her own hand would prove that she was well and that his letter had reached her. Unfortunately, this did not work out that way—the acknowledgments were signed by the warden at the check-post where the letters were delivered.

The work at the bank quickly lost its charm. He realized that he was only a glorified clerk, toting up numbers every day and trying to find the errors made by the clerks whom he supervised. The account ledgers were heavy contraptions that required the employment of peons whose job titles were messengers. These messengers carried the heavy ledgers from the counter clerks to his desk and then back to the clerks. The one bright lining was the monthly balancing of ledgers which everyone else hated. He enjoyed playing Sherlock Holmes using his deductive skills to locate errors. But the job itself was not what he had envisioned it to be.

In spite of the poverty and the chaos he saw on the streets every day, he enjoyed the solitary, independent life in the city. Saturdays were half-days and when work ended at one o'clock Kuriakose went habitually to the afternoon matinee. He did not miss a Hollywood movie but scrupulously avoided Hindi and Bengali films.

He soon discovered the seamy side of the city. The trams and the buses were almost always overcrowded. His preferred mode of transport for short distances was the two-wheeled rickshaw pulled by a man. One evening as he was headed back to his lodgings the rickshaw puller kept mouthing *"Lal batti?"* with a wicked leer. Initially, it did not register. But a little later he figured out it meant 'red light'. He found the very suggestion revolting.

Time flew. The weeks and the months sped by. He had completed ten months of probation on the job and was only two months away from confirmation.

Chapter 26: Destiny Comes Calling

He was usually the first to get to the Birchmore dining room for breakfast, but one morning he discovered that a middle-aged white man had got there ahead of him.

"Good morning! My name is Garlow, James Garlow," called out the stranger in a disarmingly cheerful tone.

"Good morning, my name is Kuriakose Mathew," responded Kuriakose a trifle self-consciously.

"Care to join me?" asked James Garlow.

As Kuriakose walked over unhesitatingly to the stranger's table, he could not have imagined the far-reaching consequences of his action.

It turned out that James Garlow was actually Rev. James Garlow, an ordained minister of the Southern Baptist Church of Nashville, Tennessee. He was now the president of a nonprofit based in Washington, DC, called *Aid the Vulnerable* which partly funded the activities of the Birchmore Society.

Jim (he preferred to be addressed thus instead of Rev. Garlow) was soon fascinated by the erudition and skills of Kuriakose (Jim shortened the name to Kirk) and intrigued by the fact that he had returned to the fold of the Orthodox Church. From that first day, they had breakfast together every morning.

On the fourth day, Jim invited Kuriakose out to dinner at the fashionable *Moulin Rouge* on the posh Chowringhee Avenue in the evening. Kuriakose was overawed by the opulent ambience of the restaurant. He turned down the offer of wine or beer and was a little surprised that Jim, an ordained minister, would drink alcohol.

In the middle of the meal, Jim dropped a bombshell.

"How would you like to work for an American organization as a finance officer?" asked Jim.

Kuriakose was stunned. The probationary officer's job that he had in the National Bank of India was one of the plum jobs (other than the government administrative service) that educated job seekers vied for. To leave this coveted and secure job for an uncertain future with an unknown foreign entity seemed rash and foolhardy.

"I need time to think. This is too unexpected," said Kuriakose.

"Kirk, I know what you are thinking. I've been coming here every year for the past ten years. I'm familiar with the Indian situation. In all the ten years, I have not offered a job to anyone. I am doing this because I'm convinced that you are the right person for this job. You do not need to give me an answer right now. Think about it and let me know."

"Why me?" asked Kuriakose.

"I have been cheated and lied to by Christians in this country, including church leaders. Funds meant for orphans and widows were diverted for building private homes for the leaders and for the education of their children in expensive private schools. I need someone I can trust to monitor the proper use of the money we send."

"Jim, I am honored by your trust in me. But I need to think about it. You see, I support my grandparents."

"You need have no fear of not being able to continue with that, Kirk. We will pay you at least four times as much as you are making now. And it will be in dollars. If you perform well there are opportunities to work overseas." Then came the clincher. "This job will be many times more satisfying and rewarding than your present job," Jim said with a wry smile.

***

That day at work the first letter from Armine arrived. Kuriakose was beside himself with joy and tore open the envelope in anticipation. But he was disappointed when he saw the contents. It contained only a brief note of a few lines.

It read:

"Barev! Hope you are well. Mayrik died two days ago. We buried her in the church cemetery. God bless you."

That was all. There was no date. There were no details of Mayrik's passing. Nor any endearing terms or expressions of love that he had dreamt about. It was just an unsigned note without any salutation to him by name. Though the note itself was anonymous, the handwriting was unmistakably Armine's. He was crushed by the cryptic nature of the note and her reticence for sharing information. He felt frustrated and powerless.

The news of the death of Mayrik saddened him and the thought of the effect her passing would have on Armine and her father filled him with apprehension. All he could do was to pray for the departed soul and for the living. He was glad the Orthodox Church permitted praying for those who had passed on.

He made up his mind that night after the evening prayers.

***

Kuriakose beat Jim to the dining room for breakfast the next morning. While they were waiting for toast and boiled eggs to be brought to their table Kuriakose decided to get it off his chest.

"Jim, I have decided to accept your offer. I prayed about it last night and I think this is the right decision."

Jim was overjoyed. "I think so too, Kirk! I'm delighted!"

He rose to hug Kuriakose.

"It is not immediate, of course. I need to complete my probation period, or I will lose the security deposit. There's also a month's notice to be given."

"That's OK. By the end of the year is fine. In the meantime, before I leave, we can discuss the terms and work out the details."

Jim was to return to the US that Saturday. He gave Kuriakose five hundred dollars in cash as an advance to travel to the regional office in Bangkok where he was to be based till his US visa came through.

Kuriakose accompanied Jim to the international airport.

"I won't have to come to India that frequently anymore!" joked Jim before catching the Lufthansa flight to Frankfurt.

***

Two weeks later as he had his Sunday brunch at the YMCA, he saw tucked away in a corner of the Sunday's *Statesman* the news of the Pamba river dam. The construction was nearly complete, and they were giving the final touches for the commissioning and the inauguration by the Prime Minister in three months' time. His stomach churned and he broke out in sweat.

He wanted to get in touch with Armine desperately. He even toyed with the idea of traveling to Kerala to see her. But he balked at the three-day journey time each way by train. Taking leave now would mean the extension of his probation period and thus delay his separation from the bank.

He struck upon a brilliant idea. He would reveal the secret of Armine's location to his trusted friend RK (Radhakrishnan) and request him to go to Nor Garni via the check-post to meet Armine. He rushed to the General Post Office to send a telegram. The next morning, he also sent RK a money order for a thousand rupees, half of it to cover the expenses of the trip and the other half for Armine.

The reply telegram from Radhakrishnan arrived on the third day.

"VILLAGE ABANDONED/EVACUATED TWO WEEKS AGO STOP NO FURTHER INFORMATION ABOUT WHEREABOUTS STOP LETTER FOLLOWS"

Kuriakose wept that night for a love that was lost.

***

As if to compound his woes, a black-bordered letter arrived from Appachen the following week. Kuriakose opened it with extreme anxiety. His worst fears were confirmed when he read the letter— Ammachi had passed away. Appachen's long letter provided full details. Ammachi had developed stomach pains two months after his departure and it had steadily worsened. She refused to go to the hospital for fear she would die there. Ammachi had died at night with only Appachen by her bedside. The cortège the next day wound its way slowly behind the hand-drawn hearse all the way to the Orthodox cemetery quite a distance away.

Kuriakose had a strange dream that night. He was a young boy once again. He sat on the *verandah* and watched the two hired laborers unhusk the huge pile of coconuts collected over several months. Each stood before an iron stake driven into the ground. Picking up each coconut they brought it down on the sharp end of the stake with just enough force to pierce the husk. Then, with a sideways twist the husk was ripped off. The growing mound of husks would be sold to coir factories. Once the husk was off, the man would bring down the coconut hard on the stake splitting it into two, spilling the sweet coconut juice on the ground. All were so sated after the first few coconuts, that nobody wanted the juice anymore.

Kuriakose dreamed of the time Ammachi had scolded him when he had picked up the two split halves of a coconut and placed them together.

"What God has cast asunder, let no man join together!" Ammachi had said.

The coconut halves would be dried on rush mats in the sun till the kernels shriveled and separated from the shell wall. He dreamed of the courtyard carpeted with drying copra.

He dreamed of Ammachi frying the copra in a large wok until the golden oil began to ooze out and slowly fill the pot. After all the oil was extracted Ammachi would fish out with a wooden ladle the crunchy, reddish-brown dregs for Kuriakose. He remembered how, after the first few mouthfuls, the initial deliciousness would turn into cloying satiety.

He woke up with a start from his dream, remembering the love Ammachi and Mayrik had shown towards him.

As he tried to sleep again, he wondered if God had split Armine and him asunder, like the two halves of a coconut, never to join them again.

***

Radhakrishnan's letter arrived two weeks later. It confirmed in greater detail what the telegram had stated in brief. The people of Nor Garni had been threatened with forcible eviction if they did not leave voluntarily by the deadline set by the government. According to the staff at the government check-post, which had been relocated much farther away on higher ground by the main road, the Armenians had sold off most of the cattle and the goats in distress sales at a fraction of the market price.

> *Murderers, thugs, and criminals were let loose from prisons and were each given a rifle, a bayonet, and a dagger—and a license to kill,*

rape, and loot with impunity. The Turkish militia and the zaptiehs came in the morning. Without notice, they drove us out of our home of several decades. Under the pretext of searching for guns, they ransacked our homes and looted our prized possessions and heirlooms handed down from generations, our memories of a lifetime. They tied our men in groups of five and led them out of town. Teachers, bankers, doctors, professors, scholars, physicians, traders, businessmen; they took them all out of town and slew them. They took indecent liberties with our girls and young women. They robbed us of our cherished lace, our bridal veils, lovingly made. The public, our neighbors, lined the street to watch us as they walked us out and the Muslim women sought our jewelry and ornaments for pittances, for piastres.

Since there were no takers for the horses and the sheep, the Armenians had taken them with them by truck. The government had provided one truck for each family for transporting all their personal possessions and livestock.

They waited by the seaside, on the shores of the Arabian Sea at Surat in the Indian princely State of Gujarat. Their ship from Basra had not come in. They waited still, never giving up hope. On the seventh day, an Arab dhow from Yemen brought the bad news. Their ship had sunk off the coast of Karachi. Several Armenian traders were ruined by the loss of goods. There were more calamities in the coming months. Two ships, laden with bales of silk, sailing from Surat to Basra, were waylaid by pirates. Another, bound for Surat from Bengal was captured by the Mahrattas who were waging a battle against the English. Such catastrophes wiped out the entire wealth of many Armenian traders and bankrupted them.

The check-post staff had told RK that some trucks had gone south towards Kanya Kumari and others had headed north towards the district of Malappuram. The public works department had come in after the village had been evacuated, demolishing the houses to make them uninhabitable.

That was all the information that RK could provide.

Kuriakose closed his eyes in utter despondency as he visualized the destruction of the beautiful hamlet that he had seen in its pristine glory. More importantly, he wondered if he would meet Armine ever again. His grief was palpable and unbearable.

***

Kuriakose submitted his resignation the next day. His colleagues suspected the cause to be homesickness and depression. His supervisor, the chief manager, tried to dissuade him from taking such a drastic step He advised Kuriakose to wait for at least three months. But Kuriakose was adamant.

Kuriakose wrote letters to Appachen and to Armine informing them of his decision. He sent Armine's, as usual, by registered post to the only address he had, care of the check-post. He hoped somehow the letter would be redirected to wherever Armine was.

He set about getting the Thai visa and making travel arrangements. Two weeks into the notice period of a month, his MA degree certificate arrived from Kerala University.

A few days after that came Appachen's letter expressing disappointment at his decision to resign from one of the best jobs in the country. He wished Kuriakose had come to see him before taking the decision. He hoped Kuriakose would visit him before he left the country but said he would understand if he could not. He closed his letter by advising Kuriakose not to fall prey to the wiles of strange women and to always trust in God for everything.

***

As Kuriakose stood on the tarmac to board the Singapore Airlines flight to Singapore, and onwards from there to Bangkok, he felt as if he was shedding the pupal cocoon of his existence hitherto and emerging in a brave new form into a world unknown.

Part Two

Thirty Years Later:

Five Days in 2005

无巧不成 [*Wu qiao bu cheng shu.*]
[Without coincidences, there would be no stories.]

(A Chinese Proverb)

Chapter 27: The Dubai Happenstance

The Dubai airport has always been a jumble of contradictions, thought Kuriakose, as he observed the goings on and the glaring disparities of the passengers at the terminal. Menial laborers from poverty-stricken south Asia were sprawled around the terminal floor. Stylish Russian tourists sashayed about, duty-free shopping bags in hand. Upwardly mobile executives toting their ubiquitous laptop bags and cell phones rushed to their destinations.

The five-hour layover en route to Washington from Tashkent was going to be painful. Since he was flying KLM and his elite frequent flyer status was with the competing Star Airlines group, he had no access to the business class lounges this time. Wearily he had taken the first vacant chair he found in the hallway of the terminal lined with electric palm trees. He watched in horror as a laborer returning home stripped down to his underwear as he changed clothes in full view of everyone at the terminal. Another snored loudly as he slept indecently spreadeagled next to his companions.

To while away the time, he watched again on his laptop the *NPR* program on coincidence he had viewed in his room at the Grand Mir Hotel (the old Hotel Russia) in Tashkent. Kuriakose had found the coincidences fascinating and too good to be true— yet true. What are the chances of one's future mother-in-law being among the crowd in a photograph taken at a faraway holiday resort months before the photographer had even met his fiancée? It was almost as if the universe itself was conspiring to help in the many incidents explored in the program. It was divine intervention for all practical purposes. He mentally noted to ask his colleague from Shanghai about the Chinese phrase on coincidences that the presenter had quoted.

He closed his eyes wearily and tried to recollect the last day in Tashkent. The railway museum with its collection of American and Russian locomotives had been fascinating. It was not listed in any tourist guide and he had stumbled upon a well-kept secret quite by accident. He was jolted out of his reverie by someone calling his name.

"Kuriakose!"

He thought at first it was addressed to someone else. The name is not uncommon in Kerala and a good many of the passengers must be from that State—his State many years ago. Out of idle curiosity to see who his namesake was, he turned in the direction of the caller. He was surprised to see a burly Indian waving his arm and moving in his direction. It took several moments for it to register that the man who was coming closer with his right hand raised in friendly greeting was none other than his old classmate, RK or Radhakrishnan. Radhakrishnan had grown much heavier and his once luxurious head of jet-black hair was reduced to thinning gray hair on a balding pate, but he was still easily recognizable. As Kuriakose hastily scrambled to his feet, Radhakrishnan asked in Malayalam.

"Isn't this the same Kuriakose from Kozhencherry? Of Maramon? Have you forgotten me?"

"Radhakrishnan! What a surprise! No, I haven't forgotten you," replied Kuriakose in English

In a second, they were shaking hands and slapping each other on their shoulders.

"You haven't changed a bit," said Radhakrishnan.

"Neither have you!" countered Kuriakose. "Hard to believe it has been thirty years since we graduated."

"Yes, time has flown by. I work here in Dubai for a chemical laboratory. What about you? Heard you had resigned your bank job and disappeared. Where are you now?"

"I live in America. Didn't plan to emigrate. It just happened."

"How did you do it? Who did you marry? A *madamma* or an *NRI* from India?" asked RK with a knowing wink.

"No, I did not marry an American or an Indian expat," laughed Kuriakose. "Actually, I'm still single. Never married."

"How did you do it then? I mean, get to America."

"It is a long story. Towards the end of my first year at the bank, before my probationary period had ended, I chanced to meet an American do-gooder who hired me to oversee the Indian operations. Mostly, orphanages."

"And then?"

"I worked out of their regional office in Bangkok for a year. I must've done something right because a year and a half later he asked me if I was interested in moving to the US and looking after their global operations. That's my life story in a nutshell. What about you?"

"Oh, my story is not a tenth as exciting as yours. I could not find a job in Kerala. Went to Bombay but that was even worse. Out of desperation, my mother mortgaged our land and house and paid a recruiting agency a king's ransom to get me a job here in Dubai. The first two years were not easy. But then later things slowly got better. I paid off the mortgage and repossessed the house before mother died. She died in peace."

"Are you married, RK?" asked Kuriakose, remembering the nickname.

"Yes, as soon as I had a steady job my mother wanted me to get married. Her name is Kamala. We have two children, a boy and a girl. They are twenty-four and twenty-two now. The son works in Abu Dhabi as an office manager. I'm looking for a decent boy for my daughter."

"You have done very well for yourself, RK. You have grown-up children! It feels like yesterday we were at the college. When is your flight? Want to get a coffee?"

"I am flying Air India to Thiruvananthapuram." Seeing the puzzled look on Kuriakose's face he added, "Many names have been changed. Trivandrum became Thiruvananthapuram, Cochin is now Kochi, and Calicut has become Kozhikode. There is about one more hour for boarding. Came early to buy some duty-free cigarettes and booze for my friends," said RK.

"I have a long wait. The flight from Tashkent landed at eight in the morning. The flight to Amsterdam is only at one o'clock."

"I think there is a coffee shop somewhere nearby," said RK.

Kuriakose turned back to his chair to pick up his laptop bag. He had slung it over his shoulder and was reaching for the handle of the carry-on when he heard Radhakrishnan laugh his trademark mischievous laugh.

"You know, when I saw you sitting there, I thought you had come to Dubai for a secret rendezvous with your old Armenian girlfriend Armine."

The name Armine hit Kuriakose like a body blow. He let go of the carry-on, which thudded to the floor, and whirled around.

"What did you say? What did you just say?" Kuriakose asked in a hoarse, manic whisper.

"You look as if you have seen a ghost!" laughed Radhakrishnan.

Kuriakose had no time for levity. He said in a commanding, no-nonsense tone, "Repeat what you just said."

Kuriakose's serious look had a sobering effect on his friend.

"I didn't mean to offend you. I was only joking. Can't you take a joke?"

"It's not a joke, RK."

"I should have simply asked you if you had come to see your friend Armine. Forget the girlfriend part. I am sorry."

"Is Armine here in Dubai?" Kuriakose's voice was deathly calm.

"Yes, she is in Dubai. I thought you knew. Didn't you both keep in touch?"

"Where is Armine?" Kuriakose's almost shouted in anticipation and expectation.

"She is in Jumeirah. Not far from here. We met quite by chance," answered Radhakrishnan.

"How did you meet her?" Kuriakose was like a man possessed.

"Through a strange coincidence, I met her at the Indian Independence Day party at the house of my boss's friend last year. But this is a much bigger coincidence meeting you after thirty years unexpectedly like this."

Kuriakose did not dare ask another question. 'Surely, she must be married to a rich Indian,' he thought, losing all hope.

Radhakrishnan continued, "She is the *ayah* ... what is the word ... nanny. He is a Sardarji. The wife is a glamorous socialite. They have two children. A boy and a girl. Armine came into the living room to introduce the children to all the guests. They sang *Twinkle, Twinkle Little Star.*"

Kuriakose was as if frozen in stone, wide-eyed in disbelief. RK continued, "I got a chance to talk to her when I bumped into her and the children as I was searching for the bathroom. She told me she has been in Dubai seventeen years ... that was last year ... it will be almost eighteen now. When I asked her about her family, she said evasively that she has to take care of the children and walked away."

"Did she say anything else?" asked Kuriakose in desperation.

"Yes, she did. She turned around after a few steps and asked about you. She asked if we were in touch and I said no. She pronounced your name in a funny way ... Koorikos or Korikos or something like that. When she uttered your name, she had a strange look on her face."

"What else did she say?" Kuriakose asked impatiently.

"She didn't say a word more. She looked crestfallen. She pointed in the direction of the bathroom and went in the direction the children had gone."

"Is she a live-in nanny? Does she live there?" asked Kuriakose.

"I don't know. I have no idea."

"Where can I find her? How can I meet her?" the words came tumbling out of the depths of Kuriakose's heart.

"I can get the Sardarji's address and phone number for you. My boss's secretary is a *Malayali*. I can get it for you," offered Radhakrishnan pulling out his cell phone from his trouser pocket.

"Please! Thank you!" said Kuriakose in feverish excitement. He then bent down to take out his notepad from the laptop bag.

"She's going to text me in a few minutes," said RK when he had finished the call.

An uneasy silence hung between them as they waited to hear the ping of the arriving text.

For the Love of Armine

When the message arrived RK said reading from the phone, "His name is Bhupinder Singh Trehan." Then handing the phone over to Kuriakose he added, "Here it is, the address and phone number."

Kuriakose hastily scribbled it all down in his notebook and then tore the page out and put it in his wallet.

He then turned around to a surprised Radhakrishnan to shake his hand. "Do you mind if we had coffee together another time? This cannot wait."

"This coffee is like your bank job celebration that never happened!" exclaimed RK.

"Sorry, RK, sorry. When we meet the next time, I will treat you to the best meal you ever had in your life. I promise." Then suddenly remembering he pulled out his wallet and extracted a business card. "There is my email address and phone number. Now that we have met again, keep in touch. All the best! Safe journey!"

Then like a crazed man Kuriakose gathered his belongings and with a hurried wave rushed away in the direction of the airline counters.

A perplexed Radhakrishnan could only shake his head and watch Kuriakose vanish into the crowds as mysteriously as he had met him after a gap of three decades.

Chapter 28: The Reunion

Kuriakose did not waste any time. He canceled his ticket forthwith, collected his checked-in baggage, and then deposited that and the carry-on in the left luggage. Rid of everything except his laptop bag, he raced to the exit and jumped into the first available taxi.

The driver turned out to be an Indian from Kerala.

"*Ningal malayali ano?* (Are you a *Malayali?*)" he asked in Malayalam looking at Kuriakose through the rear-view mirror.

This was not the time for a longwinded conversation with a country cousin. To preempt that, Kuriakose replied in the best Tamil he could muster, "*Naan oru Thamizhan.* (I am a Tamilian.)"

The rest of the ride was in silence. But the driver kept studying him in the rearview mirror seemingly unconvinced he was not a *Malayali*.

But Kuriakose's thoughts were running faster than the speed of light.

Since the Indian Independence Day was on the 15th of August, it would have been almost nine months ago that Radhakrishnan had met Armine.

'Would she still be there? Should I call first?' he wondered.

After some thought, he decided not to call. What would he say to the Trehans, the employers of Armine, if he called? They might not permit Armine to meet a stranger.

What if it was Armine herself who answered the phone? What if her situation had changed and she did not want to see him anymore? What if she did not want to reopen the past? He had to see her face to face at any cost whatever be her situation.

'No, it is safer to not give any advance notice,' he decided. In any case, he had already canceled his tickets on the spur of the moment. If he only needed to make a phone call that could have been done from the airport and he still could have caught his flight to Amsterdam.

No, after all these years he wanted to meet Armine in person. He ran the risk of being utterly disappointed, even humiliated depending on Armine's current situation and her response to him.

'What was the saying,' he asked himself, 'You can never go back home? But there was also the other one. Nothing ventured, nothing gained.'

Kuriakose did not care. This was too important to be resolved through a letter or a phone call.

The taxi sped on. He glanced out of the window. In the distance, he could see the tallest building in the world, the pencil thin Burj Khalifa under construction. The sail-shaped Burj Al Arab stood tall in the distance. To the right of the road lay the metro line under construction in the open sandy desert with no dearth of land.

He reminded himself that he needed to send an email to his office informing them about the changes to his itinerary.

Soon they reached Al Sufouh. From here, he knew, it was only a short ride to the affluent Jumeirah area. His excitement reached fever pitch. Each second seemed interminably long. He willed the taxi on.

At last, they were there. Kuriakose thrust a credit card at the driver as he studied the impressive façade of the building. It was definitely a building for the well-to-do.

"Add a ten percent tip," Kuriakose told the driver without turning around.

"Sorry, only cash," said the taxi driver handing back his card. Kuriakose did not have any dirhams. He paid in dollars and took the receipt.

Kuriakose practically bolted for the front door of the apartment building. Before he could press the bell, a janitor opened the door. Kuriakose pulled out the notepad to show the address.

"He not in. He already go office," said the Pilipino janitor.

"That's all right, I've already spoken to him on the phone. He asked me to wait at home," bluffed Kuriakose.

The janitor let him in.

The elevator carried him to the fifth floor. There were four apartments at each level. Locating 504 did not take any time at all. It took all of ten steps from the elevator to reach the front door.

His heart beat wildly and his throat constricted as he paused for a moment in front of the door. Then with a trembling hand, he pressed the doorbell.

He listened intently for sounds from within. There were none. He pressed the bell a second time. There was silence still. His heart fell. Had his impetuous actions come to naught?

As he reached out to press again one last time, he heard the muffled sounds of footsteps within getting progressively louder as they approached the door.

Through the intercom came the question in Hindi in a woman's voice.

"*Kaun hai?*" (Who is there?)

His heart jumped. The voice sounded familiar. But on account of the tinny audio of the intercom and the fact that he had never heard Armine speak in Hindi, he needed to see the speaker with his own eyes to believe. He thought rapidly and decided to tell another lie, the second in under an hour, so she would open the door.

"Courier. *Trehan saheb ke liye parcel laya hoon.* (I've brought a parcel for Mr. Trehan.)" He said in Hindi.

The trick worked. There came the sound of heavy bolts being slid before the door opened a fraction but still held by the security chain.

Through the narrow gap, they stared at each other for a few stunned moments, reminiscent of Stanley meeting Livingstone on the shores of Lake Tanganyika. It was Armine who got the words out first.

"Kirakos jan!" she breathed aloud in stunned disbelief, her eyes widened in astonishment.

There was only one person in the whole world who called him that. His heart flew. Ecstatic joy flooded his heart and permeated every fiber of his being.

"Armine jan!" he said softly in open-mouthed wonder.

Other than the gray hair at the temples but she had not changed substantially. She was dressed in a *salwar kameez* and looked every bit a woman from India or Pakistan.

"I never thought I would see you again, Not in this world. Not in this lifetime," said Armine tears welling in her eyes.

"Armine jan! Armine jan! If I were to die this moment, I would die happy," Kuriakose said.

"I cannot believe this! After all these years, you found me," Armine said wiping her eyes with the back of her hand.

"God has His time. Are you going to let me stand at the door and not invite me in like you did in Nor Garni?" asked Kuriakose attempting a smile.

"Sorry, Kirakos jan, my brain is not working. Come in! Come in!" said Armine unhooking the door chain and stepping back a few paces. She appeared to be dazed by what was happening.

He stepped into the room but stood leaden-footed on the coir doormat that said *'Swagat'* ('Welcome'). They looked at each other unable to believe that the other was flesh and blood. Kuriakose wanted to hug her in in sheer relief and dispel the feeling of unreality at the same time, but remembering the botched hug thirty years ago, did not dare take a step forward. Instead, just like in the olden days, he stuck his hand out and she reciprocated in the old lady-like style with only the fingertips.

"Now I know you are real. This is not a dream," said Kuriakose.

Armine stepped back after the handshake and looked down at the carpet. There was an uneasy silence.

"Is the wife home? Are the children home?"

"No, the children have gone to play school and to kindergarten. Mrs. Trehan has gone to her kitty club."

"Maybe I should not have entered," said Kuriakose.

"Why? Because there is no one else in the house? Don't worry about that. But I will come out with you. The children won't be back for another thirty minutes. The driver brings them back. Let me get the keys and my purse," said Armine.

When Armine returned, she had brushed her hair and thrown a *dupatta* over her shoulder.

"We cannot go out anywhere. It is burning hot outside and I don't have a car," said Kuriakose.

"We can sit on the stairs by the lift well," suggested Armine.

The stairs and the floor were uncarpeted. They sat side by side on the mosaic staircase facing the elevator.

"Do you remember the picnics we had, Armine jan? We have no *dhurrie* or the roots of the jackfruit tree to sit on today," said Kuriakose nostalgically.

"Those days are like a dream now, Kirakos jan. A dream ..." said Armine her eyes clouding with sadness.

Kuriakose turned slightly towards Armine so he could watch her face. The auburn hair, now thinner, a lighter shade, and graying at the temples; the face, yet unlined, calm; and the mien, still solemn and aloof.

Armine turned to him and added, "Kirakos jan, we came out of the cave of death. We are still alive. We've met again."

"Yes, Armine jan. It is only due to the ineffable mercy of God that we are meeting again. I can never, never get over this. It is a miracle I have been praying for ever since we parted but never thought would happen," said Kuriakose reverently.

"I prayed for you every day, Kirakos jan," said Armine in a soft voice. "Not for everyone as I once told you when you asked me to pray for your interview. I have been praying specifically for you."

"You remember everything ..." Kuriakose was emotionally overcome and had to clear his throat several times before he could speak again.

"Armine jan, those are the kindest words I've heard in years. Thank you for praying for me. God heard your prayers," replied Kuriakose. Then he added, "I prayed for you every day as well."

Kuriakose looked at his watch. "We don't have much time. The children will be back soon."

"Time for what? You have to go? I didn't even ask you where you live," said Armine.

"I will tell you everything, Armine jan, when we have the time to sit down and talk. There are many things to tell you. I'm sure there are things you may want to share with me too. What time will your work be over today? I can come around and pick you up."

Armine laughed a hollow laugh. "What time will my work be over? My work never ends, Kirakos jan. I am on call twenty-four hours a day, seven days a week. I am a live-in nanny."

"No off time? No vacation?" asked Kuriakose incredulously.

"On paper, I have the weekends off but only on paper. The husband and wife have their own lives to live and it is left to me to take care of the children even on weekends. I get two weeks of vacation each year as per the agreement. But I have nowhere to go, Kirakos jan."

"Armine jan, you are practically a slave! This is unfair. It is nothing but exploitation." Kuriakose was affronted.

"Kirakos jan, I don't have to spend anything for food and accommodation, and they pay me one thousand per month. It is not as bad as you think it is."

Kuriakose did some mental math. "One thousand dirhams is approximately two hundred seventy-five dollars. That is nothing, Armine jan."

"One thousand dirhams is equal to twelve thousand rupees. It is a lot of money in Kerala. I don't spend anything on rent or food and nothing on clothes or cosmetics."

Kuriakose moved two steps down and sat sideways so he could face Armine.

"Armine jan, we are running out of time here. Can I be direct? Can I ask you a very personal question?"

"Yes, Kirakos jan," replied Armine.

"Are you married, Armine jan?" asked Kuriakose.

"Kirakos jan, what a question! I said just now that I have nowhere to go. I am not married. Who will marry me? I came here after Hayrik died. I have no one left in this world. I remember I once envied you for being alone. Now I know what it means. My words have come back to haunt me."

"I was afraid to ask you. Don't tell me about Armen. We can talk about everything later. Do you trust me?"

"Kirakos jan, I always trusted you. I trusted you from the first day I met you. My hands were tied then, and I had other obligations and duties to fulfill."

"If you trust me, Armine jan, will you leave this job?"

"Leave this job? When? I have to give three months' notice. And what do I do after leaving this job?" Armine asked skeptically.

"Armine jan, please trust me. It is God who brought us together again. Not you, not me. I will do everything I can to take care of you."

"What about your wife and children?"

"Armine jan, I am single—like you."

"That actually makes it more difficult," responded Armine thoughtfully.

"I know what you are thinking. It is nothing of the sort. You said you trust me. I will take care of you. You are nothing but a slave. Please resign today."

"*Today?* You are still the idealist you were then. If I do not give three months' notice, I have to pay six months' wages as compensation. I do not have that kind of money to give away. Are you out of your mind?"

"Armine jan, you said you trust me. Why do you doubt me then? I will take care of the payment. Do you trust me enough to leave this job? Just tell me."

Armine looked at Kuriakose steadily with a deadpan face for a long while.

Finally, she said, "Thirty years ago, I was impulsive and reckless. The cave of death did not hold any fears for me. I risked my father's wrath and continued to meet you outside our house." She paused. "Why should anything scare me now? I have nothing to lose. I don't know what I am doing but I trust you. I will leave this job."

"Thank you, thank you, thank you, Armine jan! Where is your passport?"

"My passport is with them. They hold it as security, so I don't run away. Don't make a face. Every employer does that here. That is the norm."

"Call Mr. Trehan right now and tell him you are resigning. Pack your things, get your passport from them, and be ready by evening. I will come back to pick you up. I need to go to the airport."

"Airport? Where are you taking me to?"

Kuriakose smiled. "We are not going anywhere. At least not just yet. My luggage is at the airport."

"Tell me first. How did you find me?" interrupted Armine.

"I ran into my classmate Radhakrishnan at the airport two hours ago. What a stroke of luck!"

"Radhakrishnan ... was he the classmate of yours who we met at the bank test at Raja's College in Ernakulam?" asked Armine.

"Armine jan, I must hand it to you. Your memory is unbelievable!"

"That was an unusual trip we made. How could I forget?"

"Armine jan, there is so much to talk. But first, we need to get your freedom. Let's go back to your apartment. I will stand outside while you call Mr. Trehan. Once he agrees to release you, I will go over to his office and make the payment. And then I will come to fetch you in the evening. Agreed?"

"I don't know what I'm doing. My whole world has turned upside down in the last twenty minutes."

Kuriakose waited in the hallway while Armine called her employer. A few minutes later she came out shaking her head.

"He did not agree. He does not think I can pay the penalty."

"Give me his office address and office phone number, Armine jan. And please call a taxi for me. Before I go I need to do one thing. Do you have Wi-Fi here?"

After Kuriakose had connected to the Internet, he transferred ten thousand dollars from his home equity line of credit to his checking account. Then he left promising to return.

Chapter 29: The Release

When the secretary enquired about the purpose of the meeting Kuriakose thrust out his business card. The ploy worked. The Washington, DC, address got him into Mr. Trehan's office without a wait.

"Have you come to ask for a donation for *Aid the Vulnerable?* We run an export-import business here," began Mr. Trehan after the introductions.

"No, I did not come for donations. I came here to ask for the freedom of Armine Hovhannisyan your servant."

"Freedom? No one is holding her against her will. Who are you to demand her freedom?" asked the burly, turbaned Mr. Trehan, stroking his beard haughtily. "Armine has signed an agreement with us, and we will abide by that."

With studied deliberation, Kuriakose withdrew the bank envelope from his laptop bag and placed it on the table.

"There is your money, Mr. Trehan. Now let her go."

Mr. Trehan reached for the envelope with unseemly haste and carefully counted the cash.

"Six thousand dirhams? This is only half the money. Where will I get an *ayah* at short notice to replace her?"

Kuriakose had had enough. "Now look here Mr. Trehan. If you want to play hardball, I'm game. You have broken every labor law of this country. You have made her work round the clock every day with no breaks or weekend offs. Now look here. I am paying you the full six months' wages as per the agreement, even though I consider it unfair. If you do not release her, return the money. I will call my company lawyer in Washington and he will file a labor complaint here in Dubai against you and your wife. You will both go to jail and end up paying Armine a small fortune in overtime wages. I promise you, my attorney will take you to the cleaners."

The threat had the desired effect on Mr. Trehan who abruptly changed his tone. "Come, come, don't get agitated Mr. Kuriakose unnecessarily. We can work something out amicably. Why do we need to involve third parties, eh? Are you taking her to America to work for you?" asked Mr. Trehan.

"No! She will never be my servant," Kuriakose said emphatically.

"Then, are you her brother or relative?" persisted Mr. Trehan with a sly look.

"None of your business," Kuriakose said evenly. "I will come around after seven o'clock this evening to pick up Armine."

***

Once outside, Kuriakose searched his phone for the number of the hotel apartment where he had stayed the previous year for a month while supporting the audit of the Afghanistan office. He had no idea how long the stay would be this time. After making an initial reservation for two weeks, Kuriakose took a taxi to the airport to retrieve his baggage. Before going to the left luggage office, he sat for some quiet moments, following the dictum of his Russian priest, thanking God for all that had happened in his life, both the pleasant and the unpleasant. The events of the day had been most startling, unexpected, and completely unforeseen. Life had yet again pulled the carpet from under his feet.

He went to the Irish bar and swilled a drink of Haig, his favorite scotch. The name reminded him of the Hayks he had grown fond of over the years. The alcohol calmed his feverish brain. He remembered that he had forgotten to inform his office of the change of plans. A CFO going AWOL was not good form. He phoned the president of *Aid the Vulnerable* to tell him about his delayed return, completely forgetting the time difference of eight hours between Dubai and Washington. The call predictably went into voice mail. Though he left a message, as added insurance, Kuriakose shot off an email seeking a month's vacation citing pressing and urgent reasons and delegating his authority to the director of accounting. He knew this was going to raise many eyebrows at headquarters because he had seldom, if ever, taken a real vacation. He then spent the next two hours responding to emails and providing suggestions to the director on issues that could not be completely resolved.

He pondered over all that had happened and the plans for the future. For someone who meticulously planned his actions, the decisions he had taken today were outrageously impulsive. He had just committed himself to taking care of another individual without considering the implications.

Since they were not related, she would not be eligible for a green card for living in the US and it was equally unlikely that she could stay in Dubai without a sponsored job. Even if she could, the cost of housing and other expenses would be prohibitively high. Maybe he had to go back to his roots in Kerala (the part of his life that he had subconsciously shut out from his mind) and set up a second home there for Armine to stay. But no option was satisfactory if it meant seeing Armine for only for a few days a year. After this miraculous second encounter, he was loath to be away from her even for a day for the rest of his life.

He even contemplated resigning from his job. He still remembered vividly the consternation of his colleagues when he had quit the bank job thirty years ago. It would be the same all over again if he resigned from the CFO's position now. His plans, till yesterday, were to work until he was eligible for full Social Security benefits. All that had changed in a trice. He could support both Armine and himself with his savings if they lived in a less expensive third country.

He soon realized that there were far too many imponderables for him to resolve the problem on his own. He needed help and guidance from above. He took out his prayer book and prayed. He prayed that, if nothing else, he would always be in the same town as Armine for the rest of his life.

He checked his watch. With the evening traffic levels, he calculated that if he left now, by the time he got to Armine's apartment either of the Trehans would have returned.

He collected his luggage and took a taxi to Jumeirah. The traffic was worse than he had imagined. Thinking ahead, he jotted down the number of the taxi as he would have to leave his luggage behind with the driver when he went up to Armine's apartment.

It was a stunningly beautiful Indian woman, who looked more like a Bollywood film actress, who opened the door.

"Hello, I am Asha. Mrs. Trehan," she purred with a big smile.

"Mr. Kuriakose!" called out Mr. Trehan from near the television, above which hung a picture of the Golden Temple of Amritsar. "Have a drink and stay for dinner. After all, it is Armine's last day with us."

Kuriakose was in the middle of politely declining the offer citing the taxi waiting below with his luggage when Armine entered with the two children. Clearly, they were both attached to Armine.

Armine had changed from the *salwar kameez* of the morning and had transformed herself into an elegant Western lady in a navy-blue skirt and a pale pink top. But she neither smiled nor said a word to him. She went back inside to bring her two bags one by one. Her baggage consisted of an old-fashioned hard-shell suitcase and a smaller bag.

"Is that all?" asked Kuriakose.

"Isn't it enough?" retorted Armine with a rueful smile.

Kuriakose swung his laptop bag to his back and took hold of Armine's bags, one in each hand. After perfunctory goodbyes to the Trehans, they left the apartment and headed towards the elevator.

"I did not want to stay a minute longer than necessary in that apartment," said Kuriakose when they were in the elevator.

"Why? They are nice people as employers go," said Armine.

"I have nothing personal against them, but you were practically their slave. I wanted that chapter in your life to end once and for all. That's why I was in a hurry to leave."

When they reached the taxi, Kuriakose set the bags down near the trunk for the driver to load. He held the rear door open for Armine and was about to go around to the other side when he noticed Armine pointing to the front seat next to the driver.

He was nonplussed. He thought to himself, 'After canceling the flight to meet her and after making all the sacrifices to rescue her from her predicament, why would she not want me to sit in the back seat with her? Did she not trust me?' He began to fume inwardly the more he thought about it. But just as soon, he began to chide himself. 'You do not know what she has been through. Be patient. It is not a big deal. This is only a short ride,' he told himself.

Soon they were at Dar al Saada, the apartment hotel in Bur Dubai. While checking in Kuriakose held his hand out for Armine's passport but she insisted on handing it over herself to the counter clerk. Kuriakose did not understand that either. 'What secret could be there in a passport? I already know her date of birth from the bank application years ago,' he wondered.

***

Armine walked around their suite inspecting everything closely; the kitchenette, the bedroom, the washing machine, the bathroom, and the balcony.

When the bellhop had left, she turned around to Kuriakose and said, "Everything is fine. But there is only one bedroom."

"Armine jan, I made the reservation only today. We are lucky to get even this. Don't worry. Have no fear. I will never harm you, Armine jan. Didn't you tell me you trusted me? The bedroom is for you. I will sleep on the sofa in the sitting room."

Armine did not reply but only twisted her lips in an expression of disapproval and skepticism.

"One minute," she said carrying the smaller bag to the bedroom.

She came back with a small gift-wrapped package in her hand.

"It is my turn to give you gifts, Kirakos jan. This is for you."

"Armine jan, you do not need to give me any presents," Kuriakose responded in confusion.

"Now you are the one reluctant to receive gifts as I was once?" was Armine's caustic response.

"No, no, I will never refuse anything you give me Armine jan," Kuriakose replied hastily accepting the packet.

When he carefully opened the wrapping without tearing it, he stared openmouthed at the book inside.

It was *Armenian Poems* by Alice Stone Blackwell.

"Armine jan this is a treasure!" Kuriakose exclaimed. "It was published in the year 1917 in Boston, Massachusetts. This is a very rare copy of the book. It must have cost a lot of money."

"The value is more than the cost, Kirakos jan. I found it in a second-hand bookstore in Bombay about twenty years ago. The moment I spotted it in the pile of books on the floor, I remembered you and your love of poetry. It had your name written all over it. I did not know if I would ever meet you again, but I kept it carefully for you—in memory of the year we shared in Nor Garni and Maramon."

"I am touched, Armine jan. Not merely because this book is priceless but more because you kept it safe all these years in the hope of our meeting again. I have no gift to give you."

"Kirakos jan, don't make me angry. Why do you have to give me anything in return? Why don't you accept it as my gift to you?" Armine said reproachfully. "You paid a fortune for my release. I will never be able to repay you that."

"Armine jan, this world does not have a present I could give you to match the happiness I feel in meeting you again."

Armine walked over to the luggage lying by the television and attempted to carry her larger suitcase. Kuriakose immediately jumped up and grabbed it from her hands.

"Please. Don't carry anything when I'm with you."

As he lifted the bag, he turned and told Armine, "There is something I must tell you. I have been to Armenia. Not once but many times."

That brought Armine out of her shell. "No!" she cried in wonderment. "You need to tell me about my Motherland. And you must tell me about yourself. Obviously, you don't live in India. If you did, you couldn't have afforded the payment you made to Mr.

Trehan. Where do you live? What do you do for a living? What happened in your life during the past thirty years since you left Kerala?"

"Armine jan, I will tell you everything," said Kuriakose with a smile. "But first let me put this bag in your bedroom."

"Actually, I know where you live. You are an American citizen living in America, in Washington, DC."

Kuriakose was stunned. "How did you find that out?"

"Elementary, Kirakos jan! You have a pronounced American accent although you have been trying to hide it. You need to have lived long enough to pick up the accent. And if you stayed long enough in America, it is an absolute certainty that you would have chosen naturalization and become a citizen. You were always interested in foreign countries through books and the radio."

"Well done, Armine jan! What about Washington, DC?" How did you guess that?"

"Mr. and Mrs. Trehan mentioned Washington several times. They were speaking in Punjabi and I didn't understand a word they said but since you had visited him in his office today, I put two and two together."

Kuriakose shook his head in wonderment. "You will never cease to amaze me."

When he returned after placing Armine's bag in the bedroom, they sat on the two sofas facing each other and Kuriakose told her about his life; the bank job near Armenian Street in Calcutta; his fortuitous meeting with Rev. Garlow; the tenure in Bangkok; the move to Washington, DC; his travels around the world; and his rise over the years to become the CFO of *Aid the Vulnerable.*

Armine listened with rapt attention.

"I think I have bored you," said Kuriakose looking at his watch. "I completely lost track of time. You must be hungry. What shall we do for dinner?"

"The refrigerator is empty. If you can buy something from the supermarket nearby, I can cook dinner."

"Armine jan, I don't want you to do any work. You can cook another day. Today, though, I am taking you out for dinner."

"It will be expensive, Kirakos jan."

"The fatted calf! The fatted calf!" chortled Kuriakose.

"So now I am the prodigal daughter?" was the lighting fast riposte from Armine.

Kuriakose looked at her dumbstruck. "You haven't changed one bit. As I said many eons ago, you will make a good lawyer."

***

They walked out to the street and hailed a taxi. This time Armine moved over and gestured for him to take the seat next to her.

"What kind of food are you in the mood for?" enquired Kuriakose.

"Anything—as long as it is not spicy."

"I remember that." Kuriakose shook his head and smiled. "So, Indian food is out. French or Italian?"

Armine settled for Italian. Kuriakose asked the driver to take them to the Dubai Mall.

When they reached the restaurant, Armine was quite the lady allowing Kuriakose to pull back the chair for her to sit down.

"Will you have some wine?" asked Kuriakose.

"You have changed a lot, haven't you? I remember you passing out after a single glass of wine now you drink whiskey!"

"How did you know that?" Kuriakose was flabbergasted.

"I smelt it in your breath in the elevator. Why do you think I asked you to take the front seat in the taxi? You came into the apartment with bloodshot eyes looking like a drunkard."

Kuriakose could only smile sheepishly.

Armine chose chardonnay and chicken marsala and Kuriakose settled for pinot noir and Italian meatballs. He could not help remarking as they sipped their wine and waited for the food to arrive, "You seem to be quite at home in a posh restaurant!"

"What did you take me for? A country bumpkin?" she shot back with a straight face.

Kuriakose blushed and stammered.

With an impish smile, Armine replied, "Use your head. I had to accompany the family when they went out to dinner to take care of the children. Where would I have the money to splurge going to a restaurant on my own?"

The dinner was a silent affair. As they waited for the dessert Armine asked Kuriakose, "What are your plans?"

"Plans?" Kuriakose seemed to have forgotten all about their predicament. He seemed perturbed for a second. Then he laughed such a hearty laugh that Armine asked him, "Are you all right?"

Kuriakose had to make an effort to control his laughter before he replied, "Who cares! I don't mind living like this for the rest of my life!"

"Are you drunk?" was Armine's response.

"I am not drunk with wine, Armine jan. The heady happiness of your presence has lifted my spirits to the seventh heaven," was Kuriakose's reply.

***

When they got back to Dar al Saada Kuriakose asked, "Do you want to sit and talk for some time?"

"We can talk tomorrow," was Armine's curt reply.

She brought a bed sheet, a pillow and a comforter from the bedroom. Despite Kuriakose's protests, she made the bed for him on the three-seater sofa.

Kuriakose lay in the dark staring at the ceiling. His thoughts went back to the first time he saw Armine across the stream and how he had lain on the rope bed gazing vacantly at the thatched ceiling of his grandparents' home in Maramon. That now seemed like another lifetime.

When realization hit him that Armine and he were under the same roof for the first time ever, he got goose bumps. He quickly scrambled to his feet and prayed the evening prayer that he knew now by heart.

So much adrenaline coursed through his veins that sleep was not easy to come by. He finally fell asleep past midnight. He woke up with a start two hours later. It was freezing cold. The air conditioning had not been set right.

'If I feel so cold even with a comforter how much colder would Armine feel?'

He tiptoed to the bedroom and tried the door handle. To his surprise, it was unlocked. He went back to the sofa and got the comforter. For a moment, he wondered if he was doing the right thing. Then he turned the handle and stepped into the bedroom.

There lay Armine on her stomach fast asleep. In the streetlight seeping through the blinds, her peaceful, child-like face had taken on a cherubic look. He stood mesmerized for a few moments looking at her beautiful form. A deep yearning took hold of him. But firmly banishing the emotions and the passion that swirled within him, Kuriakose gently covered the sleeping Armine with the comforter and quickly stepped out of the room locking the door shut behind him. Surprisingly, sleep came to him almost immediately and he slept like a lamb.

Chapter 30: The Morning After

Kuriakose woke up disoriented. It took him a few minutes to comprehend where he was and why he was sleeping on a sofa and not on a bed. When he surmised where he was, he jumped up and looked around for some visible evidence that he was not hallucinating. There by the door next to his sneakers and shoes were neatly placed three pairs of ladies' shoes.

He was not dreaming! Armine was indeed in the next room! He hurried to the bathroom for a quick shave and shower. Then, suitably freshened up, he brewed coffee.

He switched the television on and watched the BBC news on mute with subtitles so as not to disturb Armine. As he sipped his coffee, he looked at the shoes by the door, Armine's and his, lined up together. A wave of emotions suddenly came over him. Quickly he grabbed his notebook from the laptop bag and penned his thoughts down. As he walked to the kitchenette for a refill of coffee, the thoughts he had just jotted down rearranged themselves in his head into a poem. He was astounded. He quickly returned to the sofa and set to paper the poem that had just spontaneously formed in his head. Kuriakose lay down on the sofa to think of possible improvements or additions to the poem and in a few minutes, he was asleep again.

About an hour later he was awakened to his name being called softly.

"Kirakos jan! Kirakos jan!"

He opened his eyes to see what he thought in his drowsy state was an angel looking down at him.

"Kirakos jan, I made some Armenian coffee for you."

Kuriakose scrambled to his feet. "Sorry, Armine jan, I had woken up earlier, but I fell asleep again."

Armine smiled. "That's all right. You don't have to go to the office today."

Kuriakose smiled as he shook his head. "You won't believe this. I have never had a true vacation in over fifteen years. Emails and phone calls were part of my leave. But this time they will not be."

Kuriakose switched the television off and they both sat down. Armine looked at him with a faint smile, over the brim of her coffee cup.

"I'm happy to see you happy but what is funny?" asked Kuriakose.

"Nothing," said Armine shaking her head.

"Tell me. Please," pleaded Kuriakose.

"I was wondering how the quilt walked in by itself to my bedroom," she said with a twinkle in her eye.

Kuriakose laughed. "It was cold last night. The air-conditioning had been set too low. But I have a small surprise for you." He reached into the laptop bag and carefully pulled out a sheet of paper. "Here. This is my gift for you."

Armine thanked Kuriakose and looked at the sheet of paper with curiosity. It read:

The Dream of Soles

There are our shoes in a neat row by the door;
Mine never dreamt they'd ever get lucky
To lie next to yours all night.

Armine looked at him quietly for a moment.

"Reminds me of metaphysical poetry. Means more than it says. Since when did you start writing poetry?" asked Armine.

"Since this morning!" said Kuriakose laughing heartily. "I always loved poetry but never did write a poem myself. Even this one, I really did not write. It just popped into my head."

"Unrequited love is the best inspiration for poetry and literature," Armine said deadpan.

"I would contest that. Love reciprocated can also produce good literature."

"Name one!" challenged Armine.

"The Brownings!" answered Kuriakose triumphantly.

"Enough of this talk! What will we do for breakfast? You insisted on buying only coffee on the way back yesterday."

"Armine jan, I already told you. I don't want you to do any work—not even cooking. Relax!" said Kuriakose with a smile.

He was completely unprepared for Armine's flare-up.

"Don't ever use that word in my presence. *Ever!* You use it once more and I will leave you. I will go back to being a slave."

She turned away, covering her face with both hands.

Kuriakose was contrite.

"I didn't mean anything, Armine jan. It is just an ordinary word. But I will never use it again if you don't like it. I'm sorry I upset you," apologized Kuriakose rubbing his forehead with this right hand.

Fear gripped his soul. Would he be able to handle temperamental reactions like this from Armine whom he loved more than life itself? Was she still distrustful, secretive, and irrational as she was earlier? He knew right away that he was willing to pay any price to be with Armine.

Of its own accord, his mind went back to the secret grove where he had first espied Armine.

Just as quickly Armine was herself again.

"Let's go for breakfast," she said. "I am hungry for Armenian or Kerala food. I'm tired of Punjabi cuisine."

***

Kuriakose did not know of any Armenian restaurant but he knew of the Kerala coffee shop named *Kappi Kada* at the nearby mall.

"Tell me about Armenia," Armine said after they had ordered. "I want to hear all about my Motherland."

"I fell in love with Armenia from the time I got off the plane. But let me start with the cave of death."

"The cave of death? Don't remind me of those days again, Kirakos jan. But what has the cave of death got to do with Armenia?"

"I found a tunnel in Armenia that reminded me of the cave of death—except it was the tunnel of life," said Kuriakose.

"Really? Tell me about it!" said Armine excitedly.

"Sorry. It is not that similar really. This one was two kilometers (a little over a mile) long with a two-lane road."

"Then why did it remind you of our cave of death?"

"Remember how surprised I was the first time I followed you through the cave of death?"

"Yes, you were staring open-mouthed at Nor Garni as if you had seen a fairytale castle," Armine said smiling.

Kuriakose smiled too. "That was exactly how I felt when traveling to Stepanavan from Yerevan. Till the car entered the tunnel it was hot and arid with not a tree in sight. Then we enter the tunnel and come out at the Vanadzor end and it was an entirely different world. Lush green vegetation, so cool and pleasant. I think I was as open-mouthed as the first time I saw Nor Garni."

"Tell me, why were you going to Stepanavan?"

"This was after the 1988 earthquake of Gyumri. A very sad event in the history of Armenia, Armine jan. I visited Vanadzor and Spitak too which were badly affected. It was tragic. Twenty-five to fifty-five thousand people lost their lives and about a hundred and fifty thousand were injured. Tens of thousands of homes were destroyed."

"I wonder where I was at that time?" wondered Armine aloud.

"You don't remember?" asked Kuriakose surprised.

Armine's face suddenly blanched. "I think my mind has shut it out. I don't want to remember." Armine clapped her hands over her ears. "Don't ask me! Don't ask me! Don't ask me!"

Kuriakose froze. "Sorry, Armine jan. I did not mean to upset you."

Armine got up and rushed to the restroom.

***

The food had arrived by the time Armine returned. Armine's choice was *palappam* with chicken stew and Kuriakose had ordered *paratha* and egg curry cooked Kerala style.

Armine continued from where she had left off but not a word was said about the incident.

"You were saying about the earthquake?"

"Yes, I was saying it was a horrendous natural disaster. It happened less than two years before Armenia declared sovereignty and three years before Gorbachev's perestroika and glasnost policies broke up the Soviet Union. On the positive side, the terrible earthquake opened the doors for the first time to Western NGOs to enter Armenia and commence their relief work. That is how *Aid the Vulnerable* got in too."

"How long did you stay there?" asked Armine.

"We are still there, Armine jan. We moved from relief to development. We help children in the health and education areas."

"At what places are you working now?"

"We are still focused in the area hit by the earthquake. Spitak, Vanadzor, Stepanavan, and Gyumri. We have an office too in the capital Yerevan, where more than a third of Armenia's population lives."

"Someday, I hope to see all those places. Which is the place you like best?"

"Without a doubt, Stepanavan. I fell in love with it at first sight. Quaint and pastoral, it stands on the banks of the Dzoraget River. There is a memorable bridge over the river with a spectacular view. The town was named after the Bolshevik Stepan Shaumyan."

"They didn't change the name after the fall of communism? Like the Indians did—Trivandrum to Thiruvananthapuram, Cochin to Kochi, Bombay to Mumbai, Madras to Chennai, and Calcutta to Kolkata?"

"Not Stepanavan! But Gyumri was earlier Alexandropol and Leninakan and Vanadzor used to be Karaklis and Kirovakan. You know, I even got to visit towns that were entirely Russian once. The one I found most unforgettable was Privolnoye. It was earlier called Sverdlov. It broke my heart on my last visit to see it crumbling and in ruins. The majority of Russians had moved back to Russia. Another Russian village I wanted to visit – but couldn't – was Pushkino."

"Take me with you when you go again. I remember you mentioning Pushkin when you talked about platonic love. Pushkin was anything but platonic!"

"I won't argue that," smiled Kuriakose. "By the way, here's another link with the past. Remember the Pushkin memorial you told me about? Where Pushkin met the body of Griboyedov's body being taken to Tbilisi? That memorial is just outside the tunnel on the Vanadzor side. Before the tunnel was built, the only route was the pass two thousand five hundred meters (eight thousand two hundred feet) high that went over the mountain. It is called the Pushkin Pass."

"You actually went to the places and saw the things I told you about!" Armine said in awe.

"I was lucky. It amazes me how the past we shared connects with everything that came after it and even with the present and maybe even the future."

When Kuriakose had paid the bill, Armine surprised him by saying exuberantly, "Let's go to the Gold Souk!"

As they were rising to go, Kuriakose had a sudden inspiration.

"Armine jan, I hate to disappoint you, but can we go to the Souk later?"

"Why not now, Kirakos jan?"

"I just had a brainwave. Let's go to Armenia!"

"*What!*" Armine was incredulous.

"Yes, Armenia! You have always longed to go there, and I never tire of traveling there. Let's go!"

"This is crazy, Kirakos jan! You are the still the dreamer!"

They rushed back to Dar al Saada for their passports.

Kuriakose hired a taxi to take them to the Armenian Embassy located in Abu Dhabi. The drive took an hour and forty minutes. When the two passports were presented at the embassy, the official looked at the US passport of Kuriakose and said the visa could be collected tomorrow. But he said the visa for the Indian passport would take up to three weeks as it required the approval of the Ministry of Foreign Affairs in Yerevan. This was disappointing news for Armine and Kuriakose. They picked up the visa application forms to fill them out in the next room. They returned a short time later with the filled-in forms.

When the official looked at Armine's form he was startled.

"*Hovhannisyan? Armine?*" he repeated aloud. "*Duq hai eq?* (Are you Armenian?)" he asked in Hayeren.

"Yes, I am Armenian, but I am a citizen of India," she replied.

"You don't need a visa. Sorry. Since I did not open your passport earlier, I didn't see your name. I didn't know you are Armenian," he apologized. "But since Mr. Mathew needs a visa which will be issued tomorrow, we will issue a visa for you from here to save you time at the airport in Yerevan."

Their former dejection disappeared. Kuriakose and Armine were elated.

"We must celebrate! This is a sign!" said Kuriakose in the taxi back to Dubai.

"Sign of what?" asked Armine.

"I have no idea!" said Kuriakose smiling broadly.

When they reached the hotel the first thing Kuriakose did was search online for tickets to Yerevan.

"The earliest tickets are three days from today. Can you wait that long?" Kuriakose asked with a smile.

"I cannot believe I am going to Hayastan. Never in my life did I think it even remotely possible. They were only dreams," said Armine.

"Remember the line from Milton that we shared? They also serve those who stand and wait. Now let us celebrate. We will first go where you wanted to go and then we will celebrate."

***

That evening they took the *abra* (ferry boat) across the Dubai Creek to the Gold Souk on the other side. As the boat chugged its way to the opposite shore Armine's auburn hair streamed in the sea breeze exposing the nape of her neck. While Armine watched the imposing buildings and the churning water, Kuriakose could not take his eyes off Armine's arresting face.

Unable to restrain himself, he said sotto voce, "You have a beautiful nose."

"Don't start that again, Kirakos jan," Armine admonished him swiftly in a harsh whisper.

Kuriakose muttered a hasty apology and clammed up. Looking at the water he was reminded of the monsoon floods he had experienced at his grandfather's home in Maramon. With immense sadness, he remembered his grandparents, Appachen and Ammachi, and Armine's parents, Hayrik and Mayrik, who were no longer in this world.

Soon they were on the other side. They wandered around the crowded Souk, Armine window-shopping and Kuriakose just enjoying Armine's presence, completely oblivious of the surroundings.

"Will you let me buy you something?" asked Kuriakose.

"No, Kirakos jan, thanks." Then she astonished Kuriakose by saying, "I cherished the red georgette cloth you presented me after your interview. I did not accept it gracefully then. Sorry."

Kuriakose was visibly touched. "You haven't forgotten anything."

"I would like an ice-cream, though!" said Armine.

"You can have anything you want, Armine jan. Anything I can afford is yours."

From the Souk, they went to the Deira City Centre Mall. Despite Kuriakose's pleas, Armine steadfastly refused his offer to buy her something. So, it was again only window-shopping.

"This is my first real holiday, Armine jan," said Kuriakose. "No work at all."

"Don't forget, Kirakos jan, it is my first holiday too!"

As they walked past the Taj Mahal restaurant Kuriakose noticed an older Western man in shorts and a T-shirt at the outer table half stand up and stare open-mouthed at Armine. Armine realized that Kuriakose had noticed. She turned to look at him with an enigmatic look and shrugged her shoulders professing innocence.

"What was that all about?" asked Kuriakose with a smile.

"That man smiled at me. I smiled back. That's all."

"There was nothing more?" persisted Kuriakose.

"What could there be? He is a pleasant looking middle-aged man and we smiled at each other acknowledging each other," Armine seemed a bit peeved at Kuriakose's questioning.

"Are you sure that was all?" Kuriakose would not give up.

Armine stopped to turn towards him.

"Kirakos jan, you are reading too much into this." As she looked at him Armine intuitively knew that Kuriakose was thinking about the incident from thirty years ago.

"I know what you are thinking about! You still haven't forgotten that lunch in Cochin after the bank selection test, have you?"

Kuriakose blushed and stuttered.

Armine's face turned serious.

"Kirakos jan, I am not an angel. I'm a human being. I made a mistake that day. I didn't do it to spite you. I was frustrated with my performance in the test. I knew I wouldn't get through. My future looked bleak. Not that it is rosy now. And I was coming to terms with something that had happened in my life that I could not tell you then. That I did not tell anyone, except my priest, Ter Samvelyan— not Hayrik or even Mayrik with whom I shared everything in my life."

Kuriakose was speechless. Finally, he said, "Armine jan, I am surprised that you remember what happened that day. I didn't even know whether you were aware I was upset."

Armine smiled. "It does not a take a psychologist to know your feelings. You were never a good actor!"

"Armine jan, I always told you the truth. I lied to others—even to Appachen and Ammachi. But I never lied to you. You hurt me badly that day."

"Kirakos jan, I tell you again. I didn't do it to spite you. It just happened. The fellow winked at me behind your back. I was flattered by his attention. I shouldn't have responded, but I did. I am human. Now thirty years later I am asking for your forgiveness."

Kuriakose was touched. His voice cracked as he said, "There is nothing to forgive. Only God forgives. I also made mistakes then."

Armine's curiosity was kindled. "*You*? You made mistakes?" Armine laughed incredulously. "What mistakes Kirakos jan? Tell me! I want to know!"

"Armine jan, I'm ashamed to tell you what I did. I can tell this to no one. But to you, I will. Let's find a place to have dinner. A celebratory dinner for our success at the Armenian Embassy."

Kuriakose narrated the incident with the Hindu girl in the crowded second-class compartment on the train coming back after the interview in Bangalore.

Instead of being upset Armine seemed to be genuinely amused. Kuriakose was puzzled.

"You physically flirted with a girl right under the noses of her father, uncle, and mother?" I never would have imagined you to be capable of that!"

"It was a mistake, Armine jan. After the restaurant incident, I was convinced that you disliked me. I thought if you could do it, I could too. I shouldn't have done it."

"Kirakos jan, it must have been the excitement of the moment. That was what it was for me. Now that we have both unburdened our hearts let us bury it forever." Then looking Kuriakose in the eye she added, "In any case, we are not that age anymore!"

"That may be true on my passport, but you have taken twenty years off my age since we met!"

Before Armine could reply Kuriakose added with an amused look. "In any case, what has age got to do with it?"

Armine did not smile. She gave him a searching look before looking down at her hands in her lap. After a moment, she looked up with a smile.

"You know what the Americans call what you did?" asked Armine.

"They have a lot of slang, much of which I wouldn't ever dream of repeating for your ears," said Kuriakose.

"No, this is nothing vulgar," said Armine with a serious face. "The phrase is 'playing footsie'." She smiled shyly when she said that.

Kuriakose burst out laughing.

"Where did you pick that up from?" asked Kuriakose.

"From books. All my masters had shelves of books. They did not love books as Hayrik did. Books were just a status symbol to them. I read voraciously. Books were my escape. They preserved my sanity."

Chapter 31: The Revelation

The next morning Kuriakose woke up to the smell of coffee brewing. Armine had woken up before him and was already at work.

"*Bari luis* (good morning), Kirakos jan!" called Armine from the kitchenette.

"*Bari luis!*" called out Kuriakose.

When he returned from the bathroom he asked, "Armine jan, do you want to hear my *bari luis* story?"

"*Bari luis* story? I'm curious."

"On my very first visit to Armenia, the flight from Frankfurt landed at Yerevan at the unearthly hour of two o'clock in the morning. By the time I got to Hotel Ani Plaza, it was close to four o'clock. There was no time left to sleep with the jet lag and everything. When I came down for breakfast, groggy and disoriented from lack of sleep, the receptionist cheerfully called out '*Bari luis!*' And my stupid response was, 'My name is Kuriakose Mathew—not Barry Lewis! There was a South African cricket player by that name."

Armine doubled up laughing. She laughed so much that tears streamed down her face. This was the first time that Kuriakose had seen her laugh uninhibitedly.

"We need to go to the embassy only by afternoon. Where do you want to go in the morning?" asked Kuriakose.

"Walking around yesterday tired me out. Let's take it easy today. We will see after we collect the visas from the embassy. Let me get breakfast ready. Good thing we bought bacon and eggs on the way back yesterday."

"Sorry, Armine jan. No bacon or eggs for me today, please."

"Why what's wrong? Something you ate yesterday?"

"No, I'm fine. But I don't eat animal products on Wednesdays and Fridays," said Kuriakose.

"Why? Are you dieting?"

"No, I'm not dieting. It is a religious thing."

"Religious? Are you still Orthodox?" asked Armine concerned.

"Yes, by the grace of God I am still Orthodox. But I'm a member of the Russian Orthodox Church."

"Russian?" Armine was stupefied. "Are you ...?" Armine left the question open.

"Am I married to a Russian?" laughed Kuriakose. "No, I'm not. I already told you, I'm single. I was not married to a Russian either. I never married. That is not to say I was celibate or anything. But that's neither here nor there."

"But why did you join the Russian Orthodox Church?" persisted Armine.

"When I moved to DC – that's what we call Washington – I first went to an Armenian Church. But their services were only in Armenian of which I did not understand a single word. Then a friend told me about the Holy Apostle's Orthodox Church outside DC. It belongs to the Russian Orthodox Church, but the services are all in English."

"Are there no Malankara Indian Orthodox churches there?" asked Armine.

"No, I don't think so. Actually, I don't know. I never looked."

Armine shook her head. "You are so strange. You never cease to surprise me."

Just then his phone rang. It was his boss from *Aid the Vulnerable* in Washington calling to find out what had happened to him and when they could expect him back.

They talked for almost an hour. The CEO tried to cajole Kuriakose into coming back right away. When that failed, he tried to push Kuriakose into giving a firm date for his return but Kuriakose would not budge. He would only say that something big was happening in his life but he could not provide more details than that at this time.

When the call ended, Armine came in from the kitchen.

"Do you have to go back soon? Will they fire you?"

"I am not going back till we figure out your future. They can fire me for all I care," said Kuriakose nonchalantly.

"I don't want you to lose your job for my sake," said Armine.

"Don't worry. Things have a way of working out."

"By the way, do you know how you sleep?" asked Armine.

"How I sleep?" Kuriakose was puzzled. "Like everyone else I suppose. Why?"

"I woke up before you today. When I came over to see if you were up, I saw you fast asleep hugging your pillow for dear life," said Armine laughing.

Kuriakose blushed. "You are not supposed to look at a sleeping person. And what's wrong with hugging a pillow?"

Armine only laughed.

"I'm hungry. I have to have breakfast. We should've bought some fruits for you yesterday," said Armine.

"I forgot. I'll have a few slices of bread with some coffee."

Over breakfast, Armine said, "Two things we did not discuss yesterday. One was religion and the other was about your ... what is the right word ... your personal situation."

"Both are touchy topics," responded Kuriakose lightly.

"We talked about religion a little bit today. I didn't tell you about mine, Kirakos jan," Armine said gravely.

Kuriakose was immediately alarmed.

"Tell me Armine jan, you did not leave the Church. I rejoined the Orthodox church because of you."

Armine cupped her chin as she pondered. Then with much effort, she said, "I have not left the

Armenian Apostolic Church, Kirakos jan. But I have not been to church for almost eighteen years. No confessions, no Communion, no liturgy. But I say my morning and evening prayers every day. I read the Bible when I can."

"Sorry, Armine jan. I can still see how much you love the Church."

"Yes, I love the Church and I will never leave it even if I am killed."

"Your work must have got in the way," offered Kuriakose.

"I could use that as an excuse but there is more to it than that. I carry a heavy load of guilt, Kirakjos jan. I have not been to Church since the year of the Gyumri earthquake."

Kuriakose wondered what the earthquake had to do with Armine's faith. She had not been to Armenia and seen firsthand the death and the destruction for her faith to have been weakened.

"Let's talk about something else, Kirakos jan. I cannot go on. Tell me about Armenia. Will it be cold there? Will we have to take warm clothes with us?"

"It gets very cold there in winter. In some places, it goes down to -30 or -40 Celsius (-22 to -40 Fahrenheit). The first few years after Armenia regained its independence were difficult years. The collapse of the Soviet Union in 1991 ended the fuel supplies and economic support. No vehicles plied the street. There was no heating in houses and apartments. People had to make do with what firewood they could find. Many died of the cold. Many more had to have amputations due to frostbite and gangrene in their extremities."

Armine was appalled. "How horrible! Is the situation still like that?"

"No! Yerevan looks like a capitalist city now with cars choking the streets. The old tramline was removed. To get back to the weather. Summers are hot in Yerevan. It can feel as hot as it did in Kerala but without the humidity. Since this is May, we will be fine."

"Tell me about Yerevan. I am so eager to hear more about my own country that I have never seen."

"You will see it in two more days! Be patient."

"No, Kirakos jan, I want to hear something now."

"Yerevan is a beautiful city. I love it! It is a mixture of old and new. The Republic Square has many Russian style buildings. There are also many Russian-style apartment buildings. There are also newer, modern buildings, European-style restaurants, and cafés. Parks. Amazing bridges with bridges below them. Statues. There are statues everywhere."

"Is there a statue of Komitas?" asked Armine.

"There is. But the biggest and tallest statue is Mayr Hayastan in Victory Park. You will like it. They are sculpting a statue of William Saroyan to be unveiled in 2008, the 100th anniversary of his birth. It is not ready yet."

"When you mentioned Mayr Hayastan I remembered Mayrik. I am counting the hours, Kirakos jan, till I touch my Motherland. I will touch the ground for Hayrik and Mayrik."

"Armine jan, Yerevan also has an underground metro. And a huge structure called the Kaskad started during Soviet times is being completed. But the best part of Yerevan is none of these. It is the

319

view of Mount Ararat, Sis and Masis, that captivated me."

"I cannot wait, Kirakos jan. Let us go and get our visas."

"Remember you quizzed me once on the story of Noah and the Ark? The Armenian Coat of Arms has Noah's Ark atop Mount Ararat in the center. But sadly, Sis and Masis are now in Turkey."

***

In the taxi to the Armenian Embassy in Abu Dhabi, Kuriakose said, "Our meeting again is a great, great coincidence. Don't you agree?"

"I completely agree, Kirakos jan. I cannot believe this is real."

"On the subject of coincidence, I have a story to share."

"A fellow parishioner and I were sharing stories of how we had come into Orthodoxy and then he told me about how he met his wife," said Kuriakose.

"And what was the coincidence?" asked Armine.

"His first wife suddenly died of leukemia when she was only twenty-eight."

"How tragic!" Armine's face reflected the pathos she felt.

"There's more. They had four small children. He had to continue working. But he could not work and take care of the children at the same time. And the cost of day care for the children was way beyond his means. He went to the Social Security office to see if they could help in any way," continued Kuriakose.

"And could they?" Armine could not contain her curiosity.

"No, they could not. But the lady who was handling his case directed him to a nearby church that was taking care of women in need. She said he could find affordable day care assistance there."

"And?"

"He did not lose any time. He went up to the church the same afternoon. The parking lot was empty and there was no one around. He was getting back into his car to drive away when a woman came out of the building. When she asked him what he wanted she told him he had come to the right place and led him into the building next to the church."

"The suspense is killing me," said Armine leaning forward in eagerness.

"When they entered the room, the women present started shouting in joy, 'He has come! He is here!' This puzzled my friend quite a bit. He did not know what was happening. In a minute, they brought in a young woman who had clearly been crying. Then they told him the story. The young woman's husband had died two months ago, and she had lost her home, her car ... everything. She did not have a job to support her three small children. The previous evening, they had all prayed for a kind man to come and offer her a day care job which would allow her to take care of her three children as well. They believed earnestly that their prayers had been answered and he was that man."

"Nice story. Obviously, he hired her, and both their problems were solved," said Armine leaning back against the seat thinking the story was over.

"No, wait! Yes, he hired her as the nanny. But the story did not end there. They fell in love. Two months later they were married. She was fifteen years younger than him. They have been happily married for thirty-two years now. Their seven children are adults and have children of their own."

Armine was moved to the point of tears. Wiping her eyes with the palm of her right hand she said, "That's such a moving story. They were both so lucky to find each other. Not everyone is as fortunate as them."

Then she looked out of the window in silence.

After a brief pause, Kuriakose said, "And sometimes we fail to recognize miracles when we are in the midst of them."

Armine did not respond.

***

The passports were ready with the visas stamped. Armine's face glowed as she ran her fingers over engraved visa with reverence.

"One step closer to Hayastan," pronounced Kuriakose with quiet satisfaction. "We must celebrate with Armenian food today!"

From the embassy, they took the taxi back to Dubai to the Ibn Battuta Mall where the *Lavash* restaurant was located. Armine was charmed by the rural Armenian décor with a *tonir* (clay furnace) as the centerpiece and clay and copper cooking utensils of various sizes and vintages strategically placed all over the dining area.

It was too early for dinner and the waiters were sitting together at a table talking boisterously in Hayeren. A young man unhurriedly left the group to attend to them. When Armine addressed him in Hayeren he was taken aback. Armine was delighted that the menu was in English and Hayeren. Armine chose *harisa* and *dolma*. Kuriakose's selections were *tzhvzhik*, *bozbash* and *lavash*.

"I remember how you disliked *harisa* that time in our house," teased Armine.

"No, Armine jan, I did not dislike it. It is just that I loved the other Armenian dishes more," said Kuriakose defensively.

"That sounds like the *Julius Caesar* of Armenian cuisine!" was Armine's retort that made Kuriakose blush.

"Actually, there is one Armenian dish that I really abhor," said Kuriakose with an enigmatic smile.

"*Khash*!" was the lightning fast riposte.

Kuriakose stared at Armine openmouthed. "How did you guess that?"

"It doesn't take a genius to guess that," Armine replied. "Tell me where did you have *khash*? Yerevan?"

"No. Of all places, it was in Tashkent, Uzbekistan. In the summer."

"Wrong time, wrong place. It is really a food for mid-winter. The Armenian tradition is that *khash* is not for months without an 'r'. So, no *khash* in May, June, July, and August."

"Nobody told me that. Remember the story of Khojah Gregory you told me about?"

Armine's forehead crinkled in thought for a minute. "You mean Gorgin Khan?"

Kuriakose beamed. "Yes! The very man! When I went to Uzbekistan to provide aid to the orphans at the Mercy Houses there, I took a trip from Tashkent to Samarkand. The historic buildings of Samarkand reminded me of the domes of the Taj Mahal. Gorgin

Khan had served the Mughals. The small restaurant in Tashkent was called *Sevan*."

"We will go to Lake Sevan, won't we?" asked Armine.

"Of course! We will see everything we can in Armenia. Traveling with you to Hayastan is more like a pilgrimage than a tourist trip."

"Thank you, Kirakos jan."

"Sevan is the most beautiful lake in the whole world. It is at an altitude of over six thousand feet. There is an ancient church by the lake and two old monasteries. Two colleagues from my office in Yerevan treated me to *Ishkhanatsoog* or Prince Fish. It is a special variety of trout that is unique to Lake Sevan. By the way, there is a river in Armenia called the Pambak. It reminded me of the Pamba River."

"Do you remember you called me 'river fish' once?" asked Armine with an impish grin.

"Armine jan, you remember everything!" Kuriakose said in amazement.

"You are not far behind, Kirakos jan!"

"Do you know, I can read Hayeren?" asked Kuriakose.

"No! I don't think you can," said Armine.

"Then cover the English names on the menu and I will read the names in Armenian."

Armine's curiosity was kindled. She covered the English names and pointed to one name in Armenian. Kuriakose studied the name and slowly articulated, "O-jha-khu-ri. *Ojhakhuri.*"

"That is correct!" Armine admitted in surprise. "Try this one," she said pointing to another.

"Cha-kho-kh-bi-li. *Chakhokhbili.* This is beginning to sound like an Armenian spelling bee!"

"I'm impressed! You really know the alphabet," conceded Armine. "I deliberately chose a Georgian dish that I thought you would be less familiar with. Who taught you the alphabet?"

"It is a funny story. I learned more than half the alphabet by myself within three hours of landing in Yerevan for the first time."

"That sounds far-fetched. How did you do that?"

"Remember I told you about the *bari luis* story? Remember I could not sleep? There was nothing to read. All that was there in the hotel room was a menu like this in English and Armenian. By comparing the English and Armenian lists I was able to figure out twenty-seven of the thirty-six alphabets."

"Kirakos jan, you do the most crazy things!"

"The story does not end there. I found an error in the menu. Two names in English had been interchanged. I carried the menu to the office that first day and asked the staff if it was not a mistake. They thought I was a spy! It was my first visit."

The food arrived and both of them made the sign of the cross before eating. Kuriakose tried the *harisa* and said, "It is not that terrible after all."

***

As they walked out of the restaurant, Kuriakose asked Armine, "Where do you want to go now?"

He was surprised when Armine turned to look at him with a somber look on her face.

"What's wrong, Armine jan? Are you not feeling well?"

"I am alright. I made a mistake. I should have told you something before we got the visas and you booked the tickets. Actually, I should have told you before I even agreed to leave my job."

"We can find a place to sit down and talk."

"No, Kirakos jan, let's go back to Dar al Saada. I cannot share this in the open."

The taxi ride was completed in silence. Once they were in the hotel room Armine headed straight for the sofa after taking off her shoes by the front door. Kuriakose followed suit.

Armine took a deep breath and launched straight into her story.

"Now that we are at this stage in life we can talk about past mistakes without embarrassment," began Armine.

"What are you talking about?" asked Kuriakose in a concerned tone.

"Kirakos jan, I am not the angel who you think I am. I am worse than St. Mary of Egypt. You are Orthodox so you know who I am talking about. She is the one who seduced many men, including many men on a ship

from Alexandria on a pilgrimage to Palestine."

Kuriakose petrified, nodded in assent.

"St. Mary repented and became a saint. I am what she was before her repentance. After Hayrik died, I moved to Bombay looking for a job. That's where I found the poetry book. But Bombay is a terrible place if you are not rich. After two years of squalid living working in a factory, I went to a Gulf recruitment agent. He promised me a job in Dubai. It cost me all the money Hayrik had left me. When I arrived in Dubai, I found that I had to work as a maid in an Arab sheik's house. He was a rich man with several houses and wives. Everything went well for the first two weeks. Then he discovered that I was an Armenian and a Christian. He came into my room that night and raped me. He violated me every night. It was like being in a harem. He abused me for being Armenian."

"Stop, Armine jan!" cried Kuriakose covering his ears. "I don't want to hear anymore."

"No, I want to tell you everything. I want you to know who I am. You can cancel the tickets and I can go back to the nanny job if you don't want me anymore."

"Armine jan, nothing will change whatever be your story," said Kuriakose ashen-faced.

"This happened in 1988 that is why I could not remember where I was at the time of the Gyumri earthquake. I lived like that for a year. He held my passport. I could not run away. I think at some deep level, I even secretly enjoyed it. I am so guilty, Kirakos jan. I have never gone to confession since then. I'm a fallen woman," she cried covering her face.

"Armine jan, don't torture yourself. You had no control over this."

"Kirakos jan, I remembered the stories of the Turks abducting even fourteen-year-old girls for their harems and raping them. The Turks raped wives in front of their husbands and mothers in front of their children. I took solace in the fact that I was sharing the suffering of my ancestors. Anyway, after a year he got tired of me and gave me away to his warehouse manager who was a Malayali. I thought I had been saved from my troubles. But when the wife went to Kerala with the children for the funeral of her father, the man ravished me. He defiled me worse than the Arab sheik."

Kuriakose listened in stunned silence, his heart overflowing with sorrow for Armine.

Wiping the tears from her face she laughed bitterly before continuing, "Do you want to hear more, Kirakos jan? I will tell you. Remember the night of celebration when you returned from Delhi with Andranik? That night as I was going back home Vilen seized me and raped me in the fields."

A look of deep anger and hatred came over Kuriakose's face.

"I never told this to anyone except Ter Samvel— not even Hayrik and Mayrik. I mentioned this yesterday. You are only the second person to know. That is the story of my life, Kirakos jan. That is the real Armine. I am not the angel you think I am. I did not want to deceive you. That is why I told you this."

"Armine jan, your story does not change anything. You were the victim, not the offender. Even if you were at fault, it would not change my decision. My sins are far bigger than yours. Armine jan, may I make a request?"

"Even if I said 'no' you would still request," said Armine resignedly.

"Armine jan, I need to make this request."

"Go ahead. I will listen. But I don't promise to respond or act," Armine replied.

"Thirty years ago, you pointed me to Orthodoxy and saved my life. Will you let me do the same for you? When we are in Yerevan, will you go to the Armenian Apostolic Church with me? Will you go to confession and Holy Communion?"

Armine bit her lips trying in vain to prevent the tears from flowing. Then nodding her head in assent, she rose from the sofa and swiftly went to her bedroom and shut the door.

Kuriakose lay back on the sofa staring at the ceiling. When he thought about Vilen raping Armine his mind went to Kalatozov's landmark movie *Letyat Zhuravli*.

Try as he might sleep would not come. He felt that the genocide of the Armenians had at last personally touched him. He thought of his own peccadilloes and sins of passion.

He remembered Armine teasing him at the start of the day about hugging a pillow. He grabbed his notebook and wrote:

> ### Clutching at Straws
> *You mock me for hugging a pillow in sleep -*
> *If you only knew the dreams that I cling to,*
> *As adrift I float 'midst the jetsam of love.*

He knew that he loved Armine so deeply that even if she were guilty of murder, he could not stop loving her.

He turned on his laptop, plugged in the headphones and listened to his all-time favorite Don McLean song from the 70's, *'Castles in the Air'*.

Chapter 32: Nekhlyudov and Maslova

When Kuriakose showed the poem to Armine over coffee the next morning, she asked, "What jetsams are you referring to?"

"Armine jan, what you told me yesterday pales in comparison with my sins. Not that you were the sinner. You were sinned against. I already told you I was not celibate though I never married. I've had several affairs, Armine jan. I'm not saying this to make you feel better. Nor am I bragging about it. We are human beings with fleshly bodies."

"Were you in love with them, Kirakos jan? Or, as you Americans say, were they one-night stands?"

"Armine jan, I was never close to a stranger. They were all friends. But somehow I could not bring myself to consider marrying them except one."

"And she was an Armenian from Yerevan," said Armine with a smile.

Kuriakose looked at her openmouthed. "How did you know? How did you guess?"

There was a twinkle in her eye as she said, "A woman's intuition, Kirakos jan. Never doubt a woman's intuition. Tell me the story."

"I already told you I visited Armenia several times. And many times, I had to stay for several weeks at a time as we were expanding and opening new offices. To save on hotel bills, the office rented an apartment for me on Kasyan Street."

"Is that in the center of the city?" asked Armine.

"Yes, it is. And I lived the life of a workaholic. I did not cook. There was a supermarket across the street that sold hot food. I reveled in *imam bayaldi, salat kraboviy, salat stolichniy, forel zapechennay, strelyal zapechnnnay, zharkoe, salat griboye,* ..."

"Kirakos jan!" interrupted Armine. "Why are you telling me about food? You are trying to evade your confession! And none of them sound Armenian!"

"They are all Russian names. All the shop labels were in Russian. Anyway, to get back to my story. I was leading a quiet life happy to be in Armenia. I went jogging in the morning for two days and then stopped because stray dogs chased me."

"Kirakos jan! You are again going off at a tangent!"

"Sorry. Here's my confession. I was attracted to a young lady by the name of Gohar and I noticed that she was interested in me as well. One day we traveled together to Gyumri for some project work and we were late coming back. It was close to midnight when we entered Yerevan. Everything was fine until I stopped the *Zhiguli* car in front of her apartment on Mamikonyants Street. What was meant to be goodbye hug got out of hand and we ended up at my apartment on Kasyan Street."

"Bravo, Kirakos jan! I never thought of you as a Lothario!" teased Armine.

Kuriakose blushed. "No, Armine jan. We both loved each other. I went back to the States and returned after four months. We were still in love. The supermarket food was traded for restaurant meals. We went sightseeing on weekends. We went to Dilijan to meet her parents. Everything was going well."

"Then what happened? Why didn't you two get married?"

Kuriakose hesitated. "Armine jan, that I cannot tell you."

"Kirakos jan! How can you stop telling the story before the end?"

"It is too personal," hedged Kuriakose.

But Armine would have none of it.

Kuriakose took a deep breath.

"Armine jan, I have a confession to make. Meeting you again in this life affirms my faith as an Orthodox Christian. Just think. What were the chances of our meeting again in this way? One in a million? The odds are so high, maybe one in several billion. Even when you did not love me, even when you made me feel you hated the sight of me, I still loved you, Armine jan. I never stopped. I told myself that our first meeting was so improbable that it had to be God's will. In the past thirty years, I have made mistakes."

He paused to see if Armine would stop him. She looked at him wide-eyed but did not say a word.

Kuriakose continued, "At times when I doubted God's promise, I looked for others. All those relationships fizzled out. I had my heart broken several times. I didn't know at those times that they happened for a reason. It was for meeting you again."

Armine spoke up. "Kirakos jan, what are you saying? We are not of that age anymore. Now more than before, we have to keep love and romance out of this. It is too late for all that. You have a job and a life to live in America. I will find a way somehow to support myself."

"You don't need to marry me, Armine jan, if you don't love me. But let us live together ..."

"Kirakos jan, what are you saying!" Armine exclaimed. "Are you suggesting we live together in sin? What will people say? Will God forgive us? Let us stop this discussion right here. If you want, you can complete the Gohar story but leave you and me out of it."

Kuriakose was broken and seemed close to the point of tears. Then he said with an effort, "Armine jan, you didn't let me complete what I was going to say. I meant, live together in the same town, near each other."

He paused.

"Armine jan, you haven't changed one bit. You are as hard and unyielding as you were. Here is what happened with Gohar. I saw a dream. I know we Orthodox don't believe in visions and dreams, but this actually happened. The dream was after I had returned to America after meeting her parents. In the dream, there were swirling mists against a dark, foreboding sky. You were on a white steed. 'Have you forgotten me?' you asked. When I did not answer, you said, 'I will wait for you forever.' I woke up in a cold sweat and the dream was broken. Right then and there I sat down and wrote an email to Gohar breaking off our relationship. She resigned before my next visit to Yerevan. I heard later that she emigrated to Canada. She left a book for me as a goodbye present. It was Bulgakov's *The Master and Margarita*. She had introduced me to it."

Kuriakose pulled out his notebook and quickly wrote:

All Our Nays

All our nays are only puny mounds
In the face of God's resounding flood;
And the white dove of hope flies away
To Ararat – never more to return.

He tore out the sheet, handed it over to Armine and stalked out of the suite in a huff.

***

'We are Nekhlyudov and Maslova. Like Nekhlyudov I need to let go and start life anew,' decided Kuriakose recalling Tolstoy's *Resurrection.*

Kuriakose came back forty minutes later, completely chastened. He was contrite.

"I'm sorry, Armine jan. I upset you. How are you feeling?"

"I'm fine. I'm always fine."

"Armine jan, forgive me for leaving abruptly. I just had to let off steam. Needed to be by myself. I was too upset. But I am OK now. Got some raspberry cheesecake for you."

"Kirakos jan, before we have the cheesecake there is something I need to tell you."

"You've changed your mind. You have decided not to go to Armenia with me?" asked Kuriakose in trepidation.

"No, that's not it. Our trip stands unless you change your mind. I want you to know the truth. I hurt you because I loved you."

Kuriakose looked at her uncomprehendingly. "I don't understand," he said.

"I'm talking about thirty years ago. I loved you too much then. The only way I could stop loving you was by making you hate me."

"And all the while I thought you actually disliked and even detested me ..." his words trailed off.

"You were always quick to jump to conclusions. I used that against you," Armine said. "Remember, you came to Pathanamthitta spying on me. You thought I didn't see you, didn't you?"

Kuriakose blushed. "I loved you, Armine. One does foolish things when one is in love. I loved you. You don't know how much. You were my world. You have no idea how much it hurt when you started raising the wall of coldness between us."

"I knew. It was hard for me too. Very hard. I cried myself to sleep almost every night. I hated myself for being so hard on you. But I had no choice. I was betrothed. I was promised to Armen. You knew that. Even if I was not, I couldn't have married you. My parents would have never approved my marrying an *otar*, an outsider, a non-Armenian."

"I wish you had told me the truth then. I wish you had told me you loved me but that our love was impossible," Kuriakose said, the pain welling up once again. "Instead you only said not to hope. You were harsh. You pushed me away."

"No, I could not have done that. I could not have told you the truth," Armine said with the old decisiveness. "Medicines have to be bitter. You would have ruined your life if I had not pushed you off. "

"Armine jan, you have no idea ..." began Kuriakose.

"Kirakos jan, I told you all this to set the record straight. I told you the truth because the past does not matter anymore. But, in a way, nothing has changed, either. Let us be realistic. We cannot get married, Kirakos jan. You have your life to live and I will find mine. I do not want to be a burden to you."

"Armine jan ..."

"No, Kirakos jan, it is not possible. I told you of my past life. I need redemption. I need God's forgiveness."

Kuriakose was about to say something but Armine raised her hand and continued. "We will be disappointed. Instead of setting ourselves up for failure, let us be happy in this brief time together. Let us make this pilgrimage, as you called it, to Armenia and then let us part as friends. There is nothing to negotiate."

Kuriakose was silent for a long while. Then, he said with eerie calmness, "I remember a million years ago, you quoted free will. That is still etched in my mind. I see that I cannot change your mind. I will respect your decision. I have no other choice. You hold all the cards."

Armine intervened. "Kirakos jan, let us not discuss this anymore."

"I am not trying to change your mind. I believe in free will too. But I also believe that God has a plan for me. If I have to choose between the two, I will always choose God's will over my free will."

"Kirakos jan, this argument is futile."

"I'm only saying that I thought God had a purpose in bringing us together so miraculously after three decades. But maybe it was not meant to be long term. I agree with you. Let us be happy together. Let's not argue about the future."

Armine's face was wan. "Shall we have the cheesecake now?"

"Of course, Armine jan! I brought it for you. Let us go out again in a little while. If we stay indoors, we will argue again. I need to tell you this. I called my office in Yerevan."

"What for, Kirakos jan? Are you thinking of working while we are there because of our argument?"

"No, Armine jan! I am determined to enjoy this time with you. The first real vacation. I called Yerevan for a different reason. It would be much cheaper to rent an apartment instead of two hotel rooms. We will also use one of the office cars. We will put in the gas."

"Gas?"

"Gasoline. Petrol. Benzene in Yerevan. I asked them to see if they could get us the same apartment on Kasyan Street."

"You are still thinking of Gohar," teased Armine.

"No. Kasyan is very close to downtown Yerevan. Komitas street is only a block away. The Tsitsernakaberd Memorial is within walking distance. The Great Hrazdan or Kievian bridge is on the way there. That bridge reminded me of the Clifton Bridge in Bristol. You will love it."

"I cannot wait to see Armenia, Kirakos jan."

"Me too. I saw Qurkik-Jalali."

"What do you mean? Don't remind me of her. Don't make me cry. I can still feel her gentleness and strength."

"When I was in Yerevan, I took the metro from Barekamutyun station to the Sasuntsi David metro station just to see the statue of the legendary hero. I gazed for a long time at the glorious statue of Sasuntsi David astride Qurkik-Jalali. It brought me such fond memories of you. What happened to Qurkik-Jalali, Armine jan?"

"What a tragedy it was to take her away from Nor Garni! She did not like the new place at all. Neyyatinkara is near the border with Tamil Nadu State and very close to the Neyyar dam. She pined for Nor Garni. In less than a year, she got sick with laminitis of the hooves and couldn't walk anymore. We had to have her put down. It almost killed Hayrik when the butchers came for her. On an impulse, Hayrik gave away the stallion Sevuk also to them. They were surprised when Hayrik didn't accept any money for either Qurkik-Jalali or Sevuk."

"It must have been heartbreaking for both of you."

"It was for Hayrik. He was already depressed after Mayrik's passing. Then the loss of Nor Garni and finally the death of the horses. He drank himself to death. Cirrhosis of the liver. He even sold his coin and stamp collections. A crafty collector cheated him. He promised a large sum and Hayrik gave the coins and the stamps in trust before payment. The cheat denied having received anything of value and paid only a fraction of the amount."

"Terrible. What happened to Vilen?"

"In spite of what he did to me, I did not wish him ill. I did not curse him. Punishment is God's—not ours. He slipped and fell from a coconut tree and broke his back. He died in Nor Garni. His was the last burial there conducted by Ter Samvel."

"I was going to ask about Ter Samvel and his family. Where are they? I would like to meet them again."

"Ter Samvel and his family came with us to Neyyatinkara but within six months they were able to immigrate to Australia. Through the help of some friends, Ter Samvel got admission to a master's course in theology which allowed him to work part-time. I have not been in touch with them since I moved to Dubai. It has been a long time."

"Let us try to locate them through the Internet. We could go and visit them," said Kuriakose.

"We? We are going our separate ways after Armenia. I cannot pay you for even this trip ..."

"Let us not argue again. Don't worry about the cost. Meeting you again is the best blessing I ever received Armine jan. Since we have been completely honest with each other I must tell you that there is something that I've been holding back. I will tell you tonight."

"Is it something I need to worry about?" asked Armine.

"No. I don't want to be mysterious, but after our morning's discussions, it will be just information. No emotion."

Armine only arched her eyebrows questioningly.

When Armine returned from her room a short while later, Kuriakose noticed that she had not changed into street clothes.

"Aren't we going Armine jan?"

"Kirakos jan, would you mind if we didn't go out for lunch? Can we order something from the restaurant?"

Armine's choice was *shawarma* and *hummus.* Kuriakose ordered *pita* bread, *falafel,* and *matchbous.* After a dessert of *esh asarya* and ice-cream both retired for an afternoon nap.

***

Kuriakose woke up to the aroma of coffee brewing. As he lay on the sofa, he thought how wonderful it would be if this idyll never ended. But he quickly banished the thought. After a leisurely cup of coffee, they left for the Festival Centre Mall. Kuriakose noticed while they walked around that one of the movies playing was *Casablanca.* Armine readily agreed to his suggestion to watch the movie. Armine kept dabbing at her eyes several times during the movie. When the lights came on she hurriedly put her handkerchief away.

"This is the most perfect movie ever made," said Kuriakose. "It is my favorite. I have a DVD of the movie at home."

"It is a very sad movie. Rick and Ilsa did not marry."

Kuriakose had turned to look at her as she said this, and their eyes met. They both realized the significance of Armine's words. Armine quickly averted her eyes. After dinner, they took a taxi back to Dar al Saada.

"Since the flight is at ten o'clock, we need to leave the hotel by six thirty," suggested Kuriakose.

"We will finish the packing first and then talk," responded Armine.

When the packing was done, they talked about the future of Armenia.

"My plan was to continue working in the States till full Social Security and then retire in Armenia. It would get me a step closer to heaven while still on earth," said Kuriakose with a wry smile.

Armine also smiled. "There must be a big rush of Armenians returning to Armenia and non-Armenians immigrating there?"

Kuriakose shook his head. "It is the opposite. A friend of mine told me that if American and Schengen visas were easy to come by, Armenia would be empty by noon."

"Why? Why would Hayastantsis leave the Motherland, their own country?" asked Armine in disbelief.

"Your nanny job has kept you secluded from contact with Armenians. Armenia has made much progress after independence. You will see signs of development everywhere. But unfortunately, the economic growth has not been uniform."

"The rich are getting richer and the poor poorer?" asked Armine.

"Sadly, like other newly independent countries, corruption levels are high. Many of my Armenian friends have expressed a feeling of unfairness and injustice. Cronyism is rampant. Without connections and bribes, one cannot get things done it seems."

"That is so sad," said Armine gloomily. "I was secretly hoping for a future for me in Hayastan."

"Who knows! Things might change for the better. The cost of living is high compared to other former Soviet Republics and you can see old people sweeping the streets or begging because their pensions cannot support them anymore."

"Was Armenia better off within the Soviet Union?"

"Good question! An American-educated friend of mine surprised me by saying that the quality of life was better under Russia."

"I hope Armenia changes," said Armine hopefully.

"My dream of Armenia is an egalitarian society with no super-rich ... the breaking up of monopolies and the removal of licenses ... the Armenian Church being the conscience-keeper of the nation ... if all of this happens it will be heaven on earth. But in spite of its problems, Armenia is still the best place on this earth."

"Why do you say that?" asked Armine.

"Money is not everything, Armine jan. You should see the natural beauty of Armenia. But it's more than that. The people of Armenia are its biggest asset. I remember driving from Stepanavan to Yerevan and stopping to take pictures of a mobile beekeeper and his beehives. Not only did he pose for photos but also invited me to his small cabin on wheels and served me, an *otar* who didn't speak a word of Hayeren, *lavash* and fresh honey. What hospitality! What generosity! I still remember his name—Harut."

"Since I was a child, I have been dreaming of seeing Masis before I die," said Armine.

"On a clear day, you can see Mount Ararat towering over Yerevan. It is a pity that the holy mountain now is in present-day Turkey, Armenia's arch enemy."

"How close is Masis to the Armenian border?" asked Armine.

"It is very close. It is hard to believe it is not in Armenia. Masis always reminds me of the genocide which Turkey refuses to acknowledge even today."

"They will never admit it," affirmed Armine.

Kuriakose's face hardened. Lines of anger materialized as he pursed his lips.

"No amount of material compensation will erase the painful memories in the collective consciousness of the Armenians. But the continued denial of a proven historic fact rankles in the mind of Hayks and all right-thinking citizens of the world."

"The Turks will never acknowledge the genocide, let alone seek forgiveness," said Armine emphatically. "That would be tantamount to an admission of guilt."

"Denial of guilt does not result in absolution nor does it cause the crime to vanish," countered Kuriakose.

"Tell that to the fanatics!" laughed Armine bitterly. "But hypothetically speaking what would be a just recompense?"

"Firstly, the return of Sis and Masis to Armenia along with the cities of Ani and Van and half of Lake Van. Secondly, the restoration of all churches, religious buildings, and parochial institutions to the Armenian Apostolic Church. Thirdly, permitting Armenia to have a free trade zone and seaport. Finally, visa-free, open borders for Armenians."

"That is a tall order."

"Yes, it is a wish list. But the main expectation is that they proffer a national apology for the genocide."

Armine sighed and was silent.

"What has happened has happened. Justice comes only from God," she said as she rose and moved to the kitchen. "I will make some good Armenian coffee."

"The remembrance of the genocide always makes me feel miserable and depressed. I need a drink. Armine jan, would you be angry if I had a drink?"

"As long as you don't get drunk and become a nuisance."

When Armine returned with the coffee, she also a brought a glass for Kuriakose. Kuriakose showed Armine the bottle of Haig he had retrieved from his bag.

"I remember you asking me about Nixon's Chief of Staff who was also a Haig, wasn't he?" asked Armine.

"Yes, that was Alexander Haig. You remember everything!"

"So do you!" was the pat reply.

"Here's looking at you kid," said Kuriakose raising a toast to Armine imitating Bogart in the movie.

"To our trip to Hayastan!" returned Armine raising her coffee mug.

"Armine jan, forgive me for remembering Hayrik as I drink this whiskey. It is such a pity that Hayrik and Mayrik passed away."

"Such is life. What about your grandparents?"

"Appachen and Ammachi too are no longer with us. Ammachi died while I was in Calcutta. Appachen died three years later when I was in America."

"Kirakos jan, did you go to Kerala for their funerals?"

"No, Armine jan. Appachen deliberately informed me by letter instead of by telegram. He did not want me to take leave during my probation. I could not have made it in time there anyway. Of Appachen's death, I came to know only several months after his passing. No one in my extended family knew of my whereabouts," said Kuriakose ruefully.

"What about the property?" asked Armine.

"Gone. A second cousin of Appachen grabbed the ancestral home and land. I did not contest it."

"Lost hearths and homes—that is the theme of many an Armenian life," Armine intoned philosophically.

Chapter 33: At the Foot of Masis

Kuriakose did a double take when Armine stepped out of her room in the morning. Armine was wearing the same translucent skirt with the Armenian alphabet that she had worn when they had gone to Pathanamthitta to get certificates for the bank test application.

"I cannot believe this!" exclaimed Kuriakose. "You kept that dress all these years?" Kuriakose was incredulous.

"Again, the same mistake," said Armine twisting her lips. "This is a skirt—not a dress and, yes, it is the same one. I take good care of my clothes since I cannot afford to buy clothes too often. And since I do not go out very often, they last forever."

"Armine jan, this is a sign! I loved this skirt the first time I saw it. That was my first glimpse of the Armenian alphabet."

"Kirakos jan, that is probably not correct. You saw Hayeren captions below the photos on the wall in our home in Nor Garni."

"As I said, I take this as a good omen," Kuriakose said.

"We Orthodox do not believe in omens, Kirakos jan. Did you say your morning prayers?"

"Yes, I did. Let me settle the bills and check with the front desk on our taxi."

Soon they were on their way to the airport to catch the Emirates flight to Yerevan.

After check-in, security, and immigration Kuriakose led Armine to the business class lounge. Armine was awed by the comfort and the exclusivity of the lounge.

"Everything is free here. Any kind of alcohol, soups, salads, appetizers, main courses, desserts … everything."

"It's too early for anything for me. I'll just have a coffee," said Armine.

"I think I'll have a glass of wine," said Kuriakose.

"Fear of flying?" enquired Armine quizzically.

"No!" laughed Kuriakose. "I got over that a long time ago, except when the turbulence is too heavy. The reason for wine now is that I can't resist anything that is free."

"You know what, I will have a glass of wine too," said Armine.

"Really?" Kuriakose was surprised.

"Yes. Really. A chardonnay, please, like the other night. I remember sipping wine at Nor Garni with Hayrik and Mayrik. I will drink to them."

They clinked glasses for the trip and raised a toast to Hayrik and Mayrik.

As they waited for their flight to be announced, Armine turned to Kuriakose. "You were supposed to tell me a secret. You slyly evaded it last night as you always do."

"You did not ask, Armine jan. You are the one who forgot. But don't worry I will tell you in good time. I will tell you today."

Kuriakose decided to test if the wine had loosened Armine inhibitions any.

"Armine jan, now that we have put even the remotest possibility of ... how shall I say? ... non-Platonic love ... behind us can I ask you something?"

"As long as there are no hopes or expectations, go right ahead," said Armine waving her hand magnanimously.

"Do you know when I knew for certain I loved you?"

"When you saw me for the first time on Qurkik-Jalali?" Armine asked with a twinkle in her eyes.

Kuriakose blushed. "I admit I fell for you at first sight. But the certainty came later, much later. Guess?"

"When I sang the love song of Komitas in the dusk?"

"That was beautiful, with the darkness falling. Your singing evoked images of faraway Armenia. But that was not the time."

"I give up. It can't have been the many times when I roasted you," remarked Armine sarcastically.

"My love for you was confirmed on our first visit to your church. I fell in love with you at the church. Armine jan, it was when you lit the candles before the *khatchkar* at the St. Gregory

Armenian Apostolic Church in Nor Garni that I fell for you hook, line, and sinker."

"But all to no purpose, right?" asked Armine. "If you keep talking like this, I will need more wine and we will miss our flight."

Their flight was on time. Kuriakose's frequent flyer status got them through the business class line ahead of everyone else in economy. Before he put his laptop bag in the overhead bin, Kuriakose extracted a manila envelope from it and tucked it in the inside pocket of his traveler's vest.

"How long is the flight, Kirakos jan?"

"We should be there in three hours although the schedule shows the flying time as three hours and thirty. We can hope to be on the ground by one o'clock."

When the plane had reached cruising altitude and after drinks had been served (Kuriakose and Armine settled on another round of wine to celebrate) Kuriakose extracted the envelope and held it out.

"Armine jan, this is for you. This is the secret that I mentioned yesterday. Now that we both know there is no future for the two of us together, the contents of the envelope can be revealed."

Armine was alarmed. "Are you giving me money? I won't take it, Kirakos jan. I refuse to take money from you."

"Armine jan, it is not money. It's only information."

"Is it a will? I am not ready for this." Armine balked.

Kuriakose was beginning to lose patience. "I am not giving you anything. There is nothing in it for you."

"Then why are you giving it to me?" Armine was irritated as well.

"You are making too big a deal of this. Just open the envelope and read what is in it. If you don't like it, you can always give it back to me."

"OK. No need to get upset," Armine said soothingly. "I will open the envelope and read what is inside."

Just then the plane encountered some turbulence and Armine instinctively took Kuriakose's hand. The fasten seatbelt sign came on and the crew made an announcement regarding bad weather en route. The turbulence lasted a few minutes. When it eased, Armine quickly withdrew her hand.

Looking at Kuriakose she said with a smile, "You did the same thing thirty years ago."

"Were we in a plane then?" Kuriakose asked in mock surprise.

"I'm not talking about the plane but about your hand. You did funny things while you were holding my hand just now. You did the same when we shook hands in Nor Garni."

"I did nothing of the sort then or now. I was only holding your hand," protested Kuriakose.

Kuriakose looked at the monitor. "There is Isfahan!" pointing it out to Armine. "That's where the migrants forced by the Shah of Iran arrived to set up New Julfa. We fly over Teheran and the Caspian Sea and over Azerbaijan into Armenia."

"An Armenian's life is full of peregrinations, and in the case of the more unlucky, deportations. Always moving and restarting. Settling down only to be uprooted again," Armine stated with great pathos.

Lunch was served at this point. Kuriakose settled on salmon while Armine chose the minced beef.

"The envelope," reminded Kuriakose when lunch was over and the trays were cleared.

Armine opened the envelope and warily unfolded the letter-sized document.

Armine turned to Kuriakose. "What is all this about? I don't understand. It says DNA ancestry project at the top. What is a haplogroup? I wasn't expecting any of this." Armine handed the paper and the envelope back to Kuriakose.

Kuriakose laughed. "I'll make it simple for you. One day some months ago, I came across this website on the Internet that offered to trace one's genealogy if you paid them a fee and sent them a few swabs from the inside of your mouth. I opted for the paternal or Y-chromosome testing." Kuriakose paused.

"I'm listening," said Armine.

"To cut a long story short, somewhere in my paternal genealogy I have Ethiopian, Syrian, and Armenian blood. And Dravidian—lots of Dravidian. To state it even plainer there is a high probability that my great great grandfather was from Armenia."

"You are Armenian?" Armine was astounded.

"Remember you telling me once that I looked Armenian? You were right. But I don't think it is anything unusual. There were thousands of

Armenians for at least two centuries in the area. Some intermingling must definitely have taken place."

"I am so happy! We are of the same blood."

"I did not want to share this earlier because I did not want you to base your decision on my being Armenian or an *otar*, a non-Armenian. If you loved me, my origins should not matter. But since you have already decided that we should go our separate ways, I thought I would share it with you. The project is not over. I am escalating it to advanced testing."

"Kirakos jan, you are right. It does not change anything between us. It wouldn't have helped even when Hayrik and Mayrik were alive. I was already promised to Armen. But this might help you get Armenian citizenship when you retire."

"That is the idea, Armine jan. That's the plan."

After the plane landed at the Zvartnots airport outside Yerevan, Kuriakose wondered for a moment if Armine would stoop down and kiss the ground. Instead, Armine made the sign of the cross and bent down and reverentially touched the floor as they came out of the aerobridge into the terminal.

At the passport check, Armine dazzled the officer with her fluent Hayeren. Kuriakose's passport check took longer in spite of the US passport he held. As they walked through the duty-free shops Armine looked around in wonder. "This is not the Armenia I imagined," she whispered.

Outside Tigran Harutyunyan from the Yerevan office of *Aid the Vulnerable* was waiting for them. Tigran was speechless when Armine spoke to him in Hayeren.

"Do you want to go straight to the office, or do you want to go the apartment on Kasyan Street first to freshen up?" asked Tigran.

"Tigran, Astghik may not have told you. I am on vacation this time. I will not be coming to the office. At least not today. We will go to the apartment first and from there we will decide where to go next."

Armine interjected. "Let's go straight to Tsitsernakaberd first. That's what we came for! Before we do anything else, I want to pay homage first to my ancestors who died in the genocide."

"We can go there from the apartment after we drop off our luggage," suggested Kuriakose.

Armine was adamant. "Kirakos jan, if you don't want to go now I will take a taxi. You can join me after you leave the baggage at the apartment."

"No, Armine jan, that's not what I meant. If you want to go first to Tsitsernakaberd, that's where we will go. The baggage can stay in the car."

Armine did not say another word during the ride to the Memorial. She looked out of the window at the people and the buildings. The sky was overcast, and Mount Ararat was not visible.

"Let's buy some flowers," suggested Kuriakose taking out some dram he had left over from his earlier trips. But Armine insisted on buying the flowers with her own money. She carefully took out five dollars and bought flowers with that.

When they reached the eternal flame, Armine laid the flowers down and sank to the ground with her head bowed. She remained in that position for many minutes. Then she straightened up and sat on her haunches as she had done on the *dhurrie* many years ago. She stayed unmoving for some time, but her shoulders started to heave as she sobbed, tears pouring down her face. Kuriakose knelt down next to her but dared not intervene.

After a while, the sobbing stopped. Armine wiped her eyes with her handkerchief and stood up.

"Let's go to the museum," said Armine.

Holding her emotions in check, she intently looked at and carefully studied all the exhibits.

"I will be back here again," said Armine as they stepped out.

The sky was still overcast and gray.

"Sis and Masis are on the other side. If we are lucky, we will be able to see it from there. Otherwise, we will have to wait for another time—later today or maybe tomorrow."

They could see the gray clouds change to sheets of rain on the distant Araratian plains. As the rain came down the clouds above began to thin. As Armine watched in open-eyed wonder, the snow-clad peaks of the towering, all-encompassing Mount Ararat majestically revealed itself.

At that very instant, a rainbow formed above the rain.

Armine gasped in wonder at the beauty before her. She surprised Kuriakose by reaching out and taking his hand in hers.

"Remember the rainbow over Nor Garni when you saw my village for the first time, Kirakos jan?"

"Yes, Armine jan. I will never forget that. This is beautiful. A gift from God," said Kuriakose in awe.

"God has given me another gift, Kirakos jan. All the hindrances in my heart have been removed. My soul is at peace. Kirakos jan, please forgive me."

"What are you saying, Armine jan? What is there to forgive?" Kuriakose was so distressed he brought his other hand over and held her hand between both of his.

"Kirakos jan, forgive my stubbornness. Forgive my hard-heartedness toward you. I was being very foolish."

"Armine jan, please stop," pleaded Kuriakose his eyes welling with tears.

"Men don't cry, Kirakos jan," Armine said. "My eyes have been opened. May I ask you something?"

"Yes, Armine jan, please! What can I do for you?"

"This has nothing to do with the paper you showed me on the plane. Even if you were from Mars, I would still be asking you this. Are you ready?"

Kuriakose nodded.

Armine continued, "If it is not too late and if you still want me, Kirakos jan, I want you to know that I will be yours for the rest of my life."

Kuriakose could not believe his ears. Instinctively he drew Armine in a hug. This time Armine did not resist but hugged him back with great ardor.

"I had hoped, prayed, and longed for this moment all my life, Armine jan," said Kuriakose trying hard not to break down, his cheek pressed against hers.

"Armenia changes everyone," Armine said softly.

Abruptly he straightened up and, looking her in the eye, he said with an impish smile, "I never wanted to play Rick anyway!"

Armine was puzzled. "Rick who?"

"The one from *Casablanca*."

Armine laughed and collapsed in his arms.

Glossary

alani	pitted dried peaches filled with walnut and sugar
Ammachi	Grandmother (in Malayalam)
Appachen	Grandfather (in Malayalam)
aryunashushan	a blood-red lily from Armenia
autorickshaw	three-wheeled motorized transport for hire
ayah	a live-in governess or nanny
Ayurveda	the traditional Hindu system of medicine
bozbash	Armenian lamb stew with dried apricots
chapati	flat, unleavened bread cooked on a skillet
chillies	fiery and pungent green or red chili pepper
chundan vallam	the snake-boat of Kerala
dhurrie	An Indian rug made of heavy cotton (also durrie)
dolma	grape-leaf rolls stuffed with meat or vegetables
dupatta	women's upper body scarf
ekler	bread filled with sweetened cream
elayappam	rice dumplings with jackfruit filling
esh asarya	"bread of the harem"; cheese and cream dessert
falafel	mashed chickpeas, deep fried
Gandhi cap	a beret-like white cloth cap popularized by Gandhi
goonda	thug or hoodlum
harisa	a porridge-like dish of cracked wheat and chicken
Hayer	(or Hayastants) Persons of Armenian origin

hummus	a paste made from chickpeas, olive oil, tahni, lemon
idli	fluffy, steamed rice-cakes of South India
imam bayaldi	fried eggplant stuffed with onion, garlic, and tomato
kameez	long-sleeved, long upper garment worn with a salwar
kappa	cassava (called tapioca in Kerala)
Kerala coffee	made by boiling ground coffee, sugar, and milk
khachapuri	pies made of phyllo pastry with cheese or beef filling
kharcho	Georgian lamb/beef soup with herbs
khash	a dish of boiled cows' feet cooked all night long
khatchkar	an upright slab of stone with intricately carved cross
khateeb	the person who delivers the sermon at a mosque
khorovats	barbecued meat or vegetables (Armenia)
kurta	a collarless, long-sleeved upper garment worn by men
lahmajun	thin crust dough topped with seasoned ground beef
lakh	an Indian counting unit 1 lakh = 100,000
lavash	the thin, flat bread of Armenia cooked in a pit oven
loofah	vegetable sponge; dishcloth gourd
lungi	a casual colored/plaid sarong worn by men
madamma	a white woman
madras	cotton fabric patterned with checks
Malayalam	the native language of the south Indian state of Kerala
Malayali	native of Kerala who speaks the Malayalam language

masala	a mixture of ground spices
matchbous	a Middle-Eastern dish of lamb, tomatoes, and rice
moilee	fish curry of made with coconut milk (Kerala)
moru	a thin, yellow broth made from buttermilk
mundu	men's white sarong of cotton or linen
namaste	welcome greeting in several Indian languages
NPR	National Public Radio in the USA
NRI	Non-Resident Indian; an expat Indian citizen
otar	(pl. otarner) Armenian term for non-Armenians
paisa	the smallest unit of Indian currency
palappam	a South Indian breakfast food
pappadam	a deep-fried thin, crispy cracker eaten with meals
parinjil appam	fish roe omelet with grated coconut
parippu curry	a South Indian dish of lentils
paratha	thick multilayered flat bread
pastirma	beef seasoned, air-dried, and cured
pita	flat bread, often split open for filling
salwar	loose pants worn by women of the subcontinent
sambar	a spicy vegetable curry with lentils
sapota	the sapodilla fruit (Manilkara zapota)
sayip	a white man
shawarma	a dish of sliced lamb with vegetables and *pita* bread
tzhvzhik	a dish of liver, kidneys and gizzards
verandah	covered area outside a house at ground floor level
zaptieh	Turkish gendarme or policeman

Acknowledgements

I am deeply indebted to my friend **Anna Ayvazyan** for never tiring to enquire about *'the next book'* and for agreeing to translate this work into Armenian and Russian even before seeing a word of it.

I owe much to the following books and their authors for invaluable information on the history of Armenia and the Genocide.

Armenia and the Armenians	Yakobos Isavertens
Armenia and the Armenians From the Earliest Times until the Great War	Kevork Aslan
A Ride through Asia Minor and Armenia	Henry C. Barkley
History of the Armenians in India From the Earliest Times to the Present Day	Mesrovb J. Seth
Illustrated Armenia and the Armenians	Ohan Gaidzakian
Armenian Poems	Alice Stone Blackwell
Ambassador Morgenthau's Story	Henry Morgenthau
Armenia and the War	Avetoon Pesak Hacobian
Martyred Armenia	Fa'iz El-Ghusein
Ravished Armenia: The Story of Aurora Mardiganian	Aurora Mardiganian
The Blackest Page of Modern History	Herbert Adams Gibbons
The Tragedy of Armenia	Bertha S. Papazian

The author welcomes comments on this or other books at:
aa-books@outlook.com

For more information about the author's books, please visit:
www.abiealexander.com